Silence
of the
Lamps

Karen Rose
Smith

KENSINGTON PUBLISHING CORP.
http://www.kensingtonbooks.com

KENSINGTON BOOKS are published by

Kensington Publishing Corp.
119 West 40th Street
New York, NY 10018

Copyright © 2016 by Karen Rose Smith

All Kensington Titles, Imprints, and Distributed Lines are available at special quantity discounts for bulk purchases for sales promotions, premiums, fund-raising, and educational or institutional use. Special book excerpts or customized printings can also be created to fit specific needs. For details, write or phone the office of the Kensington special sales manager: Kensington Publishing Corp., 119 West 40th Street, New York, NY 10018, attn: Special Sales Department, Phone: 1-800-221-2647.

Kensington and the K logo Reg. U.S. Pat & TM Off.

ISBN-13: 978-1-61773-772-5
ISBN-10: 1-61773-772-0
First Kensington Mass Market Edition: May 2016

eISBN-13: 978-1-61773-773-2
eISBN-10: 1-61773-773-9
First Kensington Electronic Edition: May 2016

10 9 8 7 6 5 4 3 2 1

Printed in the United States of America

MESSAGE FROM A KILLER

Sitting on the glider on the porch, Caprice turned to the letters in her hand. There were bills, of course. A letter-sized envelope caught her eye. It was one of those envelopes with the blue stripes so that you couldn't see what was inside. No one wrote letters these days. They sent e-mails. So she couldn't imagine whom it was from. There was no return address.

That should have been her first warning.

But she was watching Lady and appreciating the day and thinking about meeting Roz and Vince at Cherry on the Top for ice cream.

She didn't expect the plain white piece of paper she pulled out of the envelope. It was folded in thirds, and when she opened it, the printing alerted her she might not like what it was going to say.

She didn't.

In printed letters it read, *If you value that pretty dog and your life, stop asking questions . . .*

Books by Karen Rose Smith

STAGED TO DEATH

DEADLY DÉCOR

GILT BY ASSOCIATION

DRAPE EXPECTATIONS

SILENCE OF THE LAMPS

Published by Kensington Publishing Corporation

To my grandmother, Rosalie Arcuri.

When I was a little girl, she fashioned and sewed pinafores and velvet jumpers for me. She also taught me many basics of cooking and how to make a Shirley Temple! Everyone needs a Nana and memories that live forever in the heart.

Acknowledgements

I would like to thank Officer Greg Berry, my law enforcement consultant, who so patiently answers all my questions.

Chapter One

Caprice De Luca caught sight of the guest who stepped over the threshold. She braced for trouble on this balmy June Saturday afternoon.

Spinning on her kitten heels, her long, straight brown hair flowing over her shoulder, she rushed to the living room of the 4,000-square-foot house. She'd staged the stone and stucco home with the theme of French Country Flair. Bringing the rustic country flavor from the outside in, she'd used the colors of lavender and green, rust and yellow, mixing them for inviting warmth. Carved curved legs on the furniture, upholstered in toile with its pastoral scenes, mixed with the gray distressed wood side tables.

Prospective buyers who entered should have been screened by real estate agents. So how had Drew Pierson ended up standing in the foyer of today's open house?

The chef was her sister Nikki's archenemy. Ever since he'd opened Portable Edibles, a catering company that competed with Nikki's Catered Capers, the two of them had been in a battle to make their businesses succeed.

Just why was he here?

Caprice hurried to the dining room with its wall-length, whitewashed wood hutch, rushed past the table with its pale blue tablecloth and white, gently scalloped stoneware dinnerware, and headed for the scents emanating from the grand kitchen. She hardly noticed the still lifes of flowers that she'd arranged on the walls.

The floor of the kitchen mimicked rustic brick, reflecting the colors in the floor-to-ceiling fireplace. Blue-and-rust plaid cushions graced the chairs in the bay-windowed breakfast nook. Two-toned cupboards—white on top, dark cherry on the bottom—along with copper pots hanging over the granite island made the space inviting for cooking or family-centered activities.

Nikki and her servers had almost finished readying the chafing dishes and serving platters in the state-of-the-art kitchen. The combination of Nikki's culinary skills and Caprice's staging talent would pull in prospective buyers. More often than not, houses sold quickly because of their efforts, and the real estate agent on board made a hefty profit. The luxury broker today was Denise Langford, and Caprice wondered if Drew Pierson knew her and that's how he'd added his name to her list.

While one server poured vin d'orange into crystal glasses, another took a cheese soufflé from the double oven. Nikki's assistant was stirring soupe au pistou—a thick vegetable soup with vermicelli—while a platter of pan bagnat hors d'oeuvres, which were basically tuna, tomato, green pepper, olive, and sliced hard-boiled egg sandwiches, rested beside her.

Since Caprice had gone over the menu carefully with Nikki, she knew other chafing dishes held blanquette de veau—veal in white sauce with carrots, leeks, onions, and cloves—and poulet basquaise, which was pan-fried chicken dipped in pepper sauce. Nikki was stirring the boeuf bourguignon. The braised beef cooked in wine with carrots and potatoes and garnished with bacon smelled wonderful.

Nikki was so intent on stirring the dish in front of her that she didn't see Caprice approach. Caprice was about to warn her that Drew Pierson had arrived when he appeared beside Caprice, looking over the food to be offered to interested house buyers.

"I thought I'd stop by and see what my competition was offering today," he said smoothly.

At the sound of Drew's voice, Nikki's head snapped up, her eyes widened, and she frowned.

"You're thinking of buying a French country bungalow?" Caprice asked, giving her sister time to compose herself.

"I told Denise Langford I wouldn't mind having a look at this place," he answered.

This "place" was definitely out of Drew's budget, since he was a fledgling business owner. Portable Edibles couldn't be making *that* much money yet.

Drew ignored Caprice and stared down at the boeuf bourguignon, sniffed it, then smiled at Nikki.

"Anyone can make boeuf bourguignon, but I see you added bacon. Nice touch."

"Don't think I'm going to serve *you* any of my food," Nikki responded, her tone kept in tight restraint. "If it were up to me, I'd have you removed from the property."

Drew, his handsome face producing a fake smile, clicked his tongue against his teeth. "Your envy is showing. I guess you heard I'll be catering the exclusive fund-raising dinner at the Country Squire Golf and Recreation Club. My bid came in lower than yours."

Caprice had to wonder about that conclusion. Nikki's bids were more than competitive. It was quite possible that someone on the selection committee for the dinner had favored Drew. She could read her sister well, and she saw that Nikki was thinking the same thing.

"Just because you won that job doesn't mean your food will win the taste test," Nikki offered. "I have a growing client base. Do you? I have repeat customers. Do you?"

"Your social media following is pitiful," he responded with bitterness, and Caprice wondered where that bitterness was coming from. What had Nikki ever done to Drew? They'd actually worked well together when she'd first hired him to assist her on a few catering jobs. It was after she'd turned him down as a partner that their relationship had fallen apart.

"I believe in growing my business one happy customer at a time," Nikki returned. "My followings will grow. The way ten thousand followers suddenly flowed into your Twitter stream, I suspect you bought them. How loyal do you think they're going to be?"

Everyone in the vicinity was listening and watching now, and Caprice knew the sparring match between Nikki and Drew would only escalate.

Caprice leaned a little closer to him. "We'll serve you if you want so you can sample Nikki's food to see exactly how delicious it is. But I don't think you want a scene here any more than she does. That could be bad for business, and business is what you're all about, isn't it?"

She didn't know what had made her throw that question in. But when she saw the look on Drew's face, she understood this wasn't just about business. There was something personal underlying his rancor for Nikki. Still, she must have gotten through to him.

He took a step back from the food and her sister. "Good luck, Nikki. You're going to need it, because I'm going to cut your business off at the knees."

After that shot, he turned and headed for the front door.

Everyone around Nikki went back to what they'd been doing and pretended they hadn't heard anything. But Nikki knew better and she looked upset.

"I knew you two were competing, but I didn't realize he nursed a vendetta against you. What gives?" Caprice asked.

Nikki lowered her voice. "It's more than professional. You're right. He made a pass at me before I turned him down as a partner. I had already turned him down as a love interest. I think that rejection really bothered him. Rejected by me both ways, he decided to try to wipe out my business. But he can't. My food's better than his. He's an efficient cook and he'll do fine at catering, but I don't think he has the creative spark to make his dishes really special. I'm determined to show him up next Sunday."

"What's next Sunday?" Caprice asked, thinking about her schedule.

"It's the wedding expo. Area bakeries, caterers, photographers, dress shops, and flower stores are going to be showing their wares. I'll have sample menus for couples planning their wedding and food they can taste. Drew will too. But mine's going to be better."

Of course it was. Nicoletta De Luca could rise to any challenge. Couldn't she?

Caprice sat with her sister Bella on a bench in the front yard of their childhood home the following evening, eating a slice of cake. The weather couldn't have been more perfect as dusk shadowed the lawn.

"You outdid yourself with the coconut cake this time, and the fluffy icing is wonderful. I don't think I have your recipe. You're going to have to e-mail it to me."

"I know coconut cake is Mom's favorite and she doesn't make it much for herself because Dad would rather have chocolate. Just like Joe and the kids. No palate at all."

Caprice laughed. Her sister Bella was nothing but blunt. With her curly black hair, sparkling brown eyes, and heart-shaped face, she'd always been a beauty. She was two years younger than Caprice but usually felt she knew best and never hesitated to give advice. She was the married sibling, and with a husband, three kids, a part-time job, and a burgeoning online business making costumes and christening outfits for kids, she was one busy lady.

"We have a house showing tomorrow night. Keep your fingers crossed," Bella pleaded.

When Bella and Joe had decided to sell their home and look for something to fit their growing family, Caprice had staged the home for them.

"I'll do better than crossing my fingers. I'll visualize the right couple finding your house."

After a few moments of comfortable sister silence, Bella nudged Caprice's arm. "Look at Mom with Benny."

Their mom sat on a lawn chair under a red maple, holding Bella's five-month-old son. Caprice could see he was almost asleep.

"Since Megan and Timmy are out of school," Bella explained, "I'm working only evenings at All About You. That way Joe can stay with the kids on those nights. Mom said she'd come over a few mornings and babysit Benny to give me time to sew costumes and christening outfits. I'm keeping up with the orders as long as I have blocks of time at the machine."

Bella's costume business was taking off. At some point, she might stop working at All About You, a dress shop that Caprice's best friend, Roz Winslow, owned. With her degree in fashion design, Bella worked there part-time, and it was a good fit for now. Roz was dating Caprice's brother, Vince, and Caprice didn't see either of them in the front yard. That didn't surprise her. They might have snuck around back to make out. Never too old to steal a few kisses.

Her gaze targeted Grant Weatherford, who was tossing a soccer ball to five-year-old Megan and nine-year-old Timmy, Bella's older children. Her heart did a little flip-flop when he caught her eye and smiled in that way he had of making her feel special. They'd been dating for about two months and, in spite of herself, she was dreaming about a future with him.

Suddenly Caprice's cocker spaniel, Lady, came running up to her, wound around her leg, and then settled on her foot. Patches was Grant's cocker, not golden like Lady but with patches of brown and white in a curlier coat. He scampered over too, followed by Caprice's uncle Dom. Her uncle had experienced a divorce and a financial downturn and was living with her parents temporarily until he got back on his feet. He and her family had had their differences, but he seemed to be at peace with them now, especially with Nana, her paternal grandmother, who was sitting on the porch in the shade talking to Nikki and watching them all.

Her uncle Dom, her dad's younger brother, grinned down at her. "A man doesn't need to go to a gym when he has dogs to chase."

Patches sniffed at Bella's white sneaker. She moved her foot and then got to her feet. "I'll let you enjoy your hairy companions."

Bella tolerated animals, but she wasn't a lover of them like Caprice, Grant, and her uncle.

Uncle Dom pushed his tortoiseshell-framed oval glasses higher on his nose and lowered himself onto the bench, stooping down to rub Patches's ear. She knew the dog liked to be scratched there, and apparently her uncle had discovered that too.

"How's the job hunt?" she asked him.

He grimaced. "I have two interviews lined up, one with a bank and another with an insurance agency. I never thought I'd be an insurance salesman, but it's something people need."

Her uncle had worked for a large financial agency that had collapsed with the economic downturn. He was having trouble finding a job in that sector. Even if he could, she wasn't sure he was enthusiastic about it. He definitely wasn't enthusiastic about becoming an insurance salesman.

"Tell me something, Uncle Dom. What do you love to do? What have you always wanted to do?" She was a big believer in putting your heart in your work for your life path to be a success. Bella was doing that with her online costume-making business, and orders were pouring in. Caprice had done that when she'd turned from interior decorating to house staging for high-end clients. She'd needed to turn something she loved into a business that would work in the present economy. Nikki invested her heart in her cooking. Her mom threw her heart into her teaching. Her dad, a mason, had put his life into building structures he could be proud of. She knew Vince and Grant cared about their clients in their law partnership. Yep, to be a success, you had to do what you loved to do.

Her uncle thought about her question for a moment, then motioned to Patches and Lady. "I've always wanted to tend to animals. Being around Lady and your cats has brought that home again. But I'm a little old to be a veterinarian."

"You're never too old if that's what you want to do. But you could tend to animals in another way."

"And that is?" he asked with a raised brow.

"Have you ever thought about being a pet sitter? I use one at times, and I have clients who would like to have their pets taken care of in their homes. They can't find someone to do it. To really make it a business, you'd have to be bonded and insured. But that's possible, isn't it?"

Her uncle studied the dogs again, patted Patches at his feet, and then nodded. "I never thought about pet sitting. But, you know, I think I'd like it."

"I can give you the name of the pet sitter I use who lives in York, if you'd like to interview her. That might give you an idea of whether you want to do it or not. Do you have your phone on you? I can give you her number."

After her uncle took out his phone and entered the number, Grant approached them. He nodded to her uncle. "Thanks for giving the dogs a run."

"Anytime," her uncle responded, rising to his feet. He gave Caprice's arm a squeeze. "Thanks for your idea. I'll let you know what I decide."

Once her uncle had moved off and joined her dad and Bella's husband, Joe, in conversation, Grant asked, "Are you ready to leave? We could go back to your place for a while."

There was a look in his eyes that told her he wanted to be someplace private with her. Maybe they'd have a make-out session of their own.

An hour later, Caprice brought tall glasses of iced tea into her living room. Grant stood at the floor-to-ceiling, turquoise-carpeted cat tree. As he petted her white Persian named Mirabelle, who was on a lower shelf, he studied Sophia, her long-haired calico, who was on the top shelf.

He said to Sophia, "I'm glad to see you two are getting along now." He glanced at Caprice. "Do they still squabble?"

"Now and then. Mostly if Mirabelle wants to be friendly and Sophia doesn't want to be bothered. But considering Mirabelle's been here only two and a half months, they're doing well."

She nodded to Lady and Patches, who were gnawing on toys near the sofa. "Mirabelle still stays out of Lady's way, but she doesn't seem scared of her anymore. And look at her. She doesn't even mind Patches being here."

Grant came to join Caprice on the sofa. It was striped in purple and lime and fuchsia to complement the sixties decor, including a lava lamp.

As he sat beside her—very close beside her—she took a sip of tea and then placed the sweating glass on the mosaic-topped coffee table. She hadn't turned the air on because the night breeze floated in the open windows.

"Dinner at your mom and dad's is always like a family reunion," he mused.

"That's why we do it once a month, whether there's a special occasion or not. Everybody enjoys going all-out—Nikki's antipasto, Nana's ravioli, Bella's lima bean casserole and cake, my bread, Vince's choice of wine."

"The weather was perfect for the kids to play outside afterward."

Kids were sometimes a sore subject with Grant,

though he tried not to let it show. He'd experienced a tragedy in his past. His daughter had drowned, and his marriage had broken up because of it. When he'd moved to Kismet to join her brother's law practice—she and her family had gotten to know him when he'd been her brother's college roommate—he'd started a new life. Yet he really hadn't been ready to move on. It had been only in the past few months that Caprice had felt he was putting the past behind him . . . or not regretting it as much.

"Megan and Timmy can be a handful," she agreed. "It's great when they can be outdoors to release some of that energy. Just wait until Benny joins in the fray."

Apparently wanting to leave the subject of children, Grant changed the direction of their conversation. "Last night at Grocery Fresh, I ran into a client who'd stopped in at your open house."

"Really? What did she think?"

"She liked the way the house was staged. I think she picked up one of your cards. She liked the food too, but—"

"But?" Caprice was surprised there was any question about Nikki's food.

"Apparently she overheard an argument between Nikki and some guy."

Caprice groaned. "That wasn't some guy. That was Drew Pierson. I think he came by just to goad Nikki . . . and maybe intimidate her. Thank goodness she didn't take him on as a partner. That could have been disastrous."

"This was a heated argument?"

"Heated enough. He threatened to destroy her business. Fortunately not too many guests were there yet. Nikki told me yesterday that Drew made a pass at her when they were working together. I have a feeling it was more than just a pass. She didn't confide the details to me, but I think whatever happened shook her up and that's why she didn't consider taking him on as a partner."

"Why would he do that if he wanted to work with her?"

"Maybe he thought their working relationship could have benefits. Maybe it was his way of thinking he could solidify the deal."

Grant set down his glass of iced tea next to hers. Then he curved his arm around her shoulders. "A kiss or a relationship should have nothing to do with a deal."

Caprice gazed up at him, totally lost in his gray eyes, and he seemed lost in her dark brown ones. "I absolutely agree."

For an instant she thought he was going to kiss her, but instead he asked, "How would you like to go with me to a concert in the park on Wednesday night? We could spread out a blanket, take some snacks . . . and the dogs."

"Who might want to eat the snacks," she joked.

Grant smiled. "We'll take a few treats for them too. What do you say?"

"I say it's a terrific idea."

The words were no sooner out of her mouth than Grant bent his head and kissed her. The living room became a psychedelic swirl, and she knew she felt something good and true and lasting for him. She just hoped he felt the same.

Caprice's childhood home was a haven for her. That's why she visited it often. As she strolled up the walk on Monday morning, Lady padding beside her, she realized once again how the house's Mediterranean-style exterior didn't fit its Pennsylvania surroundings. When her parents had purchased it, it had been a real fixer-upper. They'd been "fixing up" for years because there was always something to repair. Yet with her dad's masonry and carpentry talents and his coworker friends helping him, he'd kept up improvements year by year. A few years back when Nana had sold her house, Caprice's parents had built an addition so she could live with them but still be independent.

With Lady sniffing the grass edging the sidewalk, Caprice went around to her Nana's side of the house, mounted the steps, and knocked. Nana was an early riser and she might have turned on her morning TV programs. Caprice hoped she could hear the knock.

However, Nana immediately came to the door in yellow knit sportswear pants and a matching top. Her gray hair was fixed in the usual bun at her nape, and her golden brown eyes were alight with morning energy.

"Did I know you were coming?" Nana asked with a fond smile and a pat for Lady.

Caprice gave Nana a hug, then unhooked Lady's leash. "No, you didn't. But we didn't have much of a chance to talk yesterday and I wanted to catch up."

Nana motioned her inside. "I'm just having my morning cup of tea. You can join me."

As soon as they stepped inside Nana's small living room, Valentine came scampering from the bedroom. Caprice had found the gray tabby kitten in her yard one cold February night. Nana had decided she needed a pet, and bonds had formed quickly. Now, at five months, Valentine was becoming lankier and longer. She danced up to Lady, who took a sniff, then they both made a beeline for the kitchen.

"They want a midmorning snack too," Caprice translated with a laugh.

"I have fresh-made biscotti for us, Greenie treats for Valentine, and a Perky Paws peanut butter cookie for Lady."

Fifteen minutes later as the animals chased and played in the living room, Nana served Caprice tea at her small kitchen table, the TV sounding in the background.

"What are you watching?" Caprice asked, unfamiliar with morning TV. Morning was her best work time—meeting clients, making phone calls, or running errands to find furniture for her next house staging.

"*Mornings With Mavis*," Nana responded. "It's that new, local morning talk show. I learn about all kinds of businesses in the area, local charities, events that are coming up. It's very informative."

Caprice glanced at the TV as she pulled one of Nana's biscotti from the canister that her grandmother had brought to the table. Then she took a second look at the TV, realizing what she'd seen. "That's Drew Pierson!"

"Drew who?" Nana asked.

"Drew Pierson, the caterer who's competing against Nikki. Can we turn it up?"

They both moved into the living room and Nana picked up the remote, increasing the volume. Drew was sitting in one of the interview chairs, looking all dapper and casual, his hair perfectly gelled in that new mussed way, while another gentleman in a suit and tie sat next to him. Mavis—at least Caprice guessed it was Mavis—with her flaming red hair and broad lipstick smile sat across from them.

She said, "Your chain of restaurants, Rack O' Ribs, is well known up and down the East Coast, Mr. Cranshaw. And we're so glad you opened a restaurant in Kismet not so long ago. Tell me how you came to decide that Chef Drew's blackberry barbeque sauce would be used in your chain."

"You're kidding!" Caprice exclaimed. "He sold barbeque sauce?"

"Maybe he'll be rich now and stop competing with Nikki," Nana observed.

"I don't know about rich. But if he sold the recipe, that could be quite profitable."

"I tasted it," Mr. Cranshaw said. "As soon as I did, I knew I wanted it."

"The barbeque sauce is only the beginning," Drew informed Mavis. "My catering service, Portable Edibles, is going to specialize in original recipes—main dishes, pies, and cakes. If you want a sampling, come out to the Kismet wedding expo on Sunday. I'll be introducing a chocolate walnut groom's cake. I've been told the recipe is to get married for!" He laughed as if he'd made an exceptional joke.

As the camera zoomed in on Mavis, Caprice realized the show must consist of short interviews. Mavis said, "We'll post information about the wedding expo on our Web site. Viewers, make sure you check it out. If you're in the area, stop by the wedding expo on Sunday."

The segment over, the program went to commercial and Nana turned down the sound. "Do you need to tell Nikki about this?" Nana asked.

"I certainly do." Caprice was already reaching for her phone in the pocket of her yellow bell-bottomed slacks—a staple in her vintage wardrobe.

"You know," Nana said softly, "Drew's grandmother, Rowena Pierson, makes a wonderful chocolate walnut cake . . . with maple icing, if I remember correctly."

Caprice forgot the call to Nikki for the moment. "Do you know his grandmother?"

Nana frowned. "She attends St. Francis of Assisi church. Has for years. She has a reputation for being a wonderful cook. But she does have arthritis and some sight problems. She doesn't cook as much as she used to. The thing is, I can't imagine her giving anyone her recipes. She insists they're unique and she doesn't want everybody copying them. She once told me that she keeps them hidden."

Either Drew's grandmother had become generous with her recipes and given them to Drew, or else . . .

Could Drew have found those recipes and stolen them?

Chapter Two

Caprice had already been seated at Rack O' Ribs on Tuesday when Bella entered the restaurant. Caprice spotted her sister over the line of people waiting to be seated and waved.

Bella waved back and said something to the hostess, a redhead dressed in a white blouse, red tie, and very short black skirt. Then her sister wound her way around the rustic wooden tables, bumped into one of the black iron chairs, and met Caprice at her back booth. The vinyl on the booth's wooden bench sported a cowhide pattern.

Bella slipped into the booth across from Caprice with a resigned sigh. "And just why did you want me to meet you at this busy place? It's new and everybody's still trying it. We'll hardly be able to hear ourselves over the chatter."

"Good afternoon to you too," Caprice said cheerily.

Bella wrinkled her nose at her and asked, "Well? When Mom came over, I told her I'd be away for an hour. You could have just gone through the drive-thru and brought lunch to my house."

Yes, Caprice could have ordered the ribs, picked them up at the drive-thru, and taken them to Bella's, but she wanted to be in the midst of the action and actually experience the restaurant.

"You can take Mom some ribs after we finish lunch. I told you this is about Drew Pierson. I want us to taste his recipe for blackberry barbeque sauce. They just started serving it yesterday."

Bella looked around. "Rack O' Ribs is a nice all-around restaurant for families, teens, and couples." She turned her attention back to Caprice. "Why isn't Nikki tasting the sauce with us?"

"Oh, I'm sure she'll taste it. But she's too upset about the whole thing right now to think clearly, or to taste well. We need to be objective. She couldn't believe Drew had devised some secret recipe that was good enough to sell. She said he can cook well enough, he just can't create from scratch. He insists his catering business is going to be known for its original recipes, and Nikki's just shaking her head over the whole thing. He'll be at the wedding expo this weekend with a supposedly divine chocolate walnut groom's cake. Nana believes it's his grand-mother's recipe."

"Maybe it is," Bella responded. "You know how recipes are handed down."

"Maybe. But then he shouldn't say it's *his* recipe. I'm hoping this sauce isn't anything special. Then we can tell Nikki that."

"Does she know you're here?" Bella asked.

Caprice shook her head. "No, I want to get the verdict first. I ordered half a rack for both of us, sweet potato fries, and steamed broccoli."

"No carbs there. The broccoli will save us," Bella decided with a grimace.

"Tell me about your house showing last night." Caprice raised her voice a little so Bella could hear her over a sudden burst of loud chatter.

Bella squeezed the thin slice of lemon hanging on her tumbler into the water and dropped it in with the ice cubes. "The prospective buyers were a young couple, maybe in their midtwenties. They have one little girl who's two. The real estate agent said they seemed to be interested. It is a perfect starter home. She said they liked the way you had it staged with the sectional sofa, the colorful throw pillows, and the bright stoneware on the kitchen table. Apparently that attracts family buyers."

"That's what I was hoping. Your house is terrific for a family just starting out. Have you and Joe found anything you really like?"

"We have our eye on a couple of places online, but we don't want to go look at them and then get disappointed if it takes a long while for our house to sell."

"It won't," Caprice assured her. "The market's picking up, and you're right in the perfect price range."

"I wish I had your confidence. Joe insists we shouldn't seriously look until we sell."

"That's one way to do it, but then everything could happen really fast. You might have to move out of your sold house and move in with Mom and Dad."

Bella groaned. "Oh, right, with Uncle Dom there too. Wouldn't that be a hoot?"

"I don't think he'll be there that much longer,"

Caprice confided. "He's seriously considering setting up a pet-sitting business."

Bella shook her head. "I couldn't even imagine pet-sitting—walking dogs, cleaning up after cats, all day long and into the evening."

"If you love animals, it's not a chore, and I think Uncle Dom really does like caring for animals. Mix in house-sitting, and he could have a good business. It's hard to find qualified, trusted people who will pet sit or house sit and take care of everything.

"I think our food's here," Caprice noted, catching sight of a waitress who was winding her way toward them with a tray. The brunette with the jaunty ponytail and sunny smile set one dish in front of Caprice and the other in front of Bella.

She said, "The plate is hot, so be careful." She took foil packets from her pocket and set three in front of each plate. "These are to wipe sticky fingers. We know our customers like to eat their ribs with their fingers. Enjoy."

Once she'd left the table, Caprice glanced down at the ribs. They were heavily glazed and glossy, and did look delicious.

Bella was shaking her head. "There goes my diet."

"You can try just one or two," Caprice offered. "Isn't diet all about balance?"

Bella rolled her eyes. "Let's see how good these are."

Whereas Caprice was pulling the ribs apart with her fingers and then licking them, Bella used a knife and fork. Her sister was particular and wouldn't get her fingers dirty with something like sticky rib sauce if she could help it.

Bella stabbed a nice chunk of meat with her fork, smelled it, put it to her lips, and then ate it. Her eyes widened and she smiled. "I don't think one rib will be enough. Oh my gosh, Caprice, this is really good. If these are the kind of recipes Drew Pierson devises, Nikki's going to have a battle on her hands."

Caprice picked up a rib and, as delicately as she could, ate the meat from it. The taste on her tongue was fruity and sweet, yet with a bit of heat. Bella was right. This sauce was good. Maybe even genius.

"They're selling bottles of it up at the cash register," Bella informed her. "You can bet Drew Pierson will get his cut of each one."

Caprice suddenly realized what a lucrative deal this had been for Drew. He was definitely on his way. On his way to destroying Nikki's business?

Or on his way to something else?

Caprice sat at her computer working on Wednesday before she changed for her date with Grant. At least she was supposed to be working. But she was thinking about how good those ribs had tasted yesterday and whether she should tell Nikki. Mirabelle sat on the cushy lime-green chair beside Caprice's computer worktable. Every once in a while, she looked up and meowed and Caprice would pet her. Mirabelle was vocal, as lots of Persians were.

Suddenly her long-haired calico, with her strikingly beautiful white ruff, sauntered into the room and saw Lady sitting by Caprice's foot and Mirabelle on the chair. Usually laid back, Sophia hadn't been particularly happy about this recent addition to their family. The cats were adjusting to each other. Without hesitating, Sophia stood up on her hind legs and pawed at Mirabelle. It wasn't a nasty pawing, more like an I-just-want-to-bother-you pawing. Mirabelle meowed, hopped down, jumped over Lady, and dashed for Caprice's office closet.

Caprice always left the door open in case one of the cats wanted to take a nap in there. She knew the animals had to find their own relationships, and they were . . . slowly.

Caprice's doorbell rang, and she checked the small portable monitor on her desk. Since her last brush with a murderer, she'd had an alarm system put in her house. Now she saw her sister waving at her, and she smiled. After hurrying to the front door, she unlocked it and Nikki stepped inside.

"I didn't expect to see you today," she said.

"I came from Rack O' Ribs. I tried Drew's sauce and it's really good. I'm so disappointed." Nikki sounded dejected, and that wasn't like her.

"You wouldn't be able to create a sauce that's just as good?"

"I don't know. I don't know anything anymore, Caprice. Maybe I should just get a job as a chef somewhere."

"Don't talk nonsense. Your Catered Capers is doing well, isn't it?"

"I'm meeting my bills and paying my help. But I want more than that."

"Then we have to get your name out there, like Drew has gotten his out there."

"He's done more than that. If he sold the rights

to his recipe to the Rack O' Ribs chain, he's making major bucks."

Caprice led her sister into her living room. "You can't let him take jobs from you. What do you have planned for the expo on Sunday?" she inquired.

"You mean what food do I intend to serve?"

"Yes. How is it special or different from anyone else's?"

Nikki thought about it. "I'm cooking my roast beef with the white horseradish glaze, bite-sized duck l'orange samples, salmon with a bourbon sauce, and then assorted cookies and desserts."

"What's your pièce de résistance?" Caprice pushed.

"I don't know what you mean."

"Well . . ." Caprice drawled. "Drew is advertising this groom's chocolate walnut cake as his specialty item. What are you going to advertise as the epitome of wedding cakes?"

"Oh, I see what you mean. I'll have to think about that. Maybe I can coax Serena, who helps me sometimes, to decorate a mini–wedding cake."

"Think about the topper too. Something different and really classy, like Waterford crystal."

"You do have ideas."

"I've always told you that. Bring plenty of those new pamphlets you had printed up, and run over to the Quick Print shop and have a poster with Catered Capers and your name and your specialties printed so we can put it on an easel. It's time to go big, Nikki."

"Or go home," Nikki muttered, again with that note of dejection.

"This isn't like you. You're usually filled with confidence. What's going on?"

Nikki sighed. "I'm tired of working and feeling like a hamster on a wheel. Maybe if I had a social life and somebody to care about, all of it would seem more worthwhile."

"Or more frustrating," Caprice offered. "But I know what you mean. Dating Grant . . . It's become part of the focus of my life. We're going to the park tonight for the concert. Why don't you come along?"

"I'm not barging in on your date."

"We're bringing both dogs, and they'll be chaperones. There will be a hundred other people there. Come. I know Grant won't mind."

"You know him so well?" Nikki asked with a wink.

"We're becoming very well acquainted," Caprice assured her with a sly smile.

Suddenly Mirabelle dashed out of Caprice's office into the living room and jumped up to the back of the sofa. Sophia wasn't far behind, chasing after her and then settling on the arm of the couch. Lady ran to Nikki, sniffed her pants legs, then rolled over and lay down at her feet for a tummy rub.

"I was just going to change," Caprice said. "Why don't you help me choose what to wear? You're better at this dating thing than I am."

"Are you trying to distract me?"

"Am I succeeding?"

"You have to promise to wear whatever I pull from your closet."

If this were Bella making that offer, Caprice would probably refuse. But she trusted Nikki's taste, even if it wasn't vintage. That was the fashion she most enjoyed wearing.

"You've got a deal," Caprice decided, knowing Nikki's choice would be something Grant would appreciate.

Seated on a blanket next to Grant two hours later, his arm wrapped around her shoulders, Caprice was absolutely happy. The band on the temporary park stage was playing oldies but goodies, her favorites. She couldn't think of any place she'd rather bc, as Lady and Patches romped around the blanket on their leashes and then settled down with chew toys. Folks on folding patio chairs, from teenagers looking for something to do to seniors letting the music bring back memories from the past, were seated across the grass lawn. Her parents might be somewhere in the crowd. She wasn't sure yet.

Grant leaned close and kissed her on the cheek. "What are you thinking about?" he murmured at her ear.

"I'm thinking about how much I enjoy our dates," she said truthfully.

He squeezed her a little tighter.

"You two look too comfortable," a voice behind Caprice said. "I have a feeling you're slipping into the older crowd instead of going out and raising Cain on a Wednesday night."

Caprice glanced over her shoulder and spied her brother, Vince. With his dark good looks, wearing a tan Polo shirt and navy board shorts, he looked younger than he did in his business suit. Beside him, Roz looked her beautiful self in a violet blouse and matching shorts. Caprice imagined her friend's leather sandals came straight from Italy. Roz always wore jewelry. Her amethyst earrings and ring sparkled even though the sun had begun to dip below the horizon. She was holding a leash with her dog Dylan who excitedly greeted Patches and Lady and sat on the blanket with them. Dylan was a Pomeranian-Shih Tzu mix and his fluffy tail swept back and forth over the blanket.

"Can we join you?" Roz asked. "We forgot our blanket."

"The more the merrier," Caprice said.

After Vince and Roz settled themselves on the blanket, Roz took imported chocolate bars from her purse, passing them around. "This is the fun part of a lawn concert. Better than those greasy fries in that service cart over there."

The white Chuck's Snacks truck contracted with the Chamber of Commerce to do business at these concerts. But its offerings were limited to sodden fries, greasy burgers, and ice-cream sandwiches.

Roz took a bite from her chocolate bar, then winked at Caprice. "Are you ready for the reunion?"

Their high school reunion was only five weeks away. She and Roz were members of the planning committee. "I'm ready, but I don't know if the committee is. Did Alicia look into decorations yet?"

"Are we going to talk flowers?" Vince muttered.

Roz jabbed him in the ribs. "Do you have a better idea than flowers in vases on the tables?"

"Let's see. Fifteen years ago. Why don't you do movie themes from that year? Incorporate that into centerpieces."

"It's a little late for an all-new concept," Caprice said. "Though that would have been a good one.

We'll probably just stick to our class's colors with the flowers."

"You *are* bringing a date?" Roz asked Caprice, with a sly look at Grant.

"I might ask a certain lawyer I know," Caprice teased back.

"And maybe this time I'll ask you to dance," Grant assured her.

Grant was referring to the Valentine's Day Dance when he hadn't asked her and she'd been terribly disappointed. From the affectionate pressure of his hand on her arm right now, she knew that wouldn't happen this time.

Suddenly Nikki was beside Caprice, unfurling her own blanket beside them.

"This will give you all a little more room," she said.

Nevertheless, there was something in her tone that alerted Caprice that something could be wrong . . . something *new* could be wrong.

While Vince spread his long legs over onto Nikki's blanket, Caprice waved her hand over her outfit. "See, I wore what you suggested."

Her blouse, reminiscent of Stevie Nicks, was gauzy, though not Nicks's representative black. It was turquoise with embroidery and flowed over her white culottes. Her white sandals with jewels of fuchsia, lime, and turquoise completed the ensemble. Nikki knew her well and wouldn't have suggested anything Caprice didn't want to wear.

"Perfect," Nikki said with a glance, though she looked distracted.

Grant raised a brow at Caprice. He was coming to know her sister too. Usually energetic and effervescent, this was a different Nikki.

"Are you nervous about the expo, Nik?" Caprice asked her, leaning closer.

Vince overheard. "What do you have to be nervous about? You've done expos before."

"None of those was this important," Nikki maintained. "I've come up with my pièce de résistance," she told Caprice. "Carrot cake with cream cheese icing. I'm going to bake it tomorrow and freeze it. Serena is going to frost and decorate it for me early Sunday morning."

"Then you'll be all set."

"I just hope my presence there will make a difference and stop Drew from stealing my clients. I lost another to him—Warren Shaeffer, who's president of Kismet's Chamber of Commerce. He lives in Reservoir Heights, and I catered a cocktail party for him last year."

"He belongs to the Country Squire Golf and Recreation Club," Roz said. "I can ask around and find out how Drew stole Warren away from you. For all we know, he could be giving a discount that you could never give, just to take clients away from you."

"And what good would that do?" Vince asked.

"That discounted event might help him to capture further events by spreading his name around. I don't know, but I'll find out for you, Nik."

"Your carrot wedding cake is going to beat Drew's groom's cake. I'd bet my life on it," Caprice assured her sister. "Let Drew Pierson be the king of barbeque sauce. You can be the queen of catering."

Although Nikki tried to smile, Caprice could see that her words weren't assuring her sister. Nikki was worried she'd lose her business . . . and Caprice couldn't blame her.

Chapter Three

The building where the wedding expo was held on Sunday was huge, probably the largest public building in the town of Kismet. So many of the edifices in the town, especially downtown, were old and refurbished. This expo center, however, on a plot of ground where old houses had been demolished to make room, was shiny, bright, and about eight months old. The town council and mayor, after doing some research, had decided Kismet could bring in revenue by having a facility where wedding receptions could be held, or businesses could show their wares, where craft shows could flourish, where gun shows could have their day. A building like this could draw crowds, not just from York, Harrisburg, and Lancaster, but maybe from farther away—from Philadelphia and Baltimore. Who knew what people might come to see?

Caprice was meeting several people here. Nikki, of course, would be inside serving. Juan Hildago, Caprice's assistant in her house stagings, would be sampling food and thinking up ideas for future open houses. Yes, it was a wedding expo, but ideas could be gathered anywhere. Roz and Vince might be here too, if matrimony was anywhere in their heads . . . or if they weren't too hesitant to admit it. Since Uncle Dom was trying out his pet-sitting skills, Caprice had left her furry crew with him. She'd seen him interact with Lady and her cats since he'd been living with her parents, and she trusted him. A pet-sitting career could be just what he needed. A pet sitter was just what *she* needed when she didn't want to impose on family or friends.

The expo center was spacious and divided into several groupings. Bridal gowns and bridesmaids dresses, mothers of the bride dresses, and elegant shoes were displayed against the eastern wall, each vendor having something different to offer. Deejays were set up showing off their sound systems and computer-generated music, trying to lure in customers with particular playlists. Jewelry vendors took an aisle down the center. Every bride needed jewelry, not only for herself, but for gifts. There were leather makers who provided suggestions for male groomsmen, and china dealers with everything from Spode to Fiesta dinnerware. Flower shops showed off representative floral bouquets for the church and for the bride to carry, as well as potted palms and hibiscus to dress up reception areas.

As Caprice navigated the aisles and checked out the wares, a little thrill of excitement jumped up her spine. If she and Grant were really serious, if they really meant what she thought they did to each other, they could be walking around here together, not only dreaming but planning. Maybe next year if the wedding expo was here again.

The bakers' aisle garnered her attention as she strolled down the row where bakers were presenting their specialty wedding cakes. Caprice passed one ten tiers tall with beautiful pale pink flowers, silver balls, and white pillars. It was a little much for Caprice's taste, but some brides would love it.

The food sampling stands were all located against the west wall. Nikki had called Caprice when she was setting up so Caprice knew where she was located. She headed that way, easily spotting the top of Nikki's head. She'd had her dark brown hair highlighted with golden lights again. Since she was serving food today, she had it pulled back in a bun. But her beautiful oval, Madonna-like face only looked prettier with the severe hairstyle.

Nikki was busy testing food in the food warmers. Caprice knew her routine. She didn't let anything go by untasted. But before she could reach Nikki's table, she spotted Drew . . . and he wasn't behind a table of his own. He approached Nikki's table and took one of the business cards from a cut-glass stand right next to the pamphlets about her catering business. He pocketed it with a little show and grinned at Nikki. Then he went around the corner of the table where Nikki was holding a spoon in one hand and a fork in the other. With her hands busy, with customers stopping and looking and sometimes asking questions, she was at an obvious disadvantage with her enemy so close. And close he was. He leaned in to her, his lips almost brushing her cheek, and he whispered something in her ear. Caprice rushed forward when she saw Nikki blush. Her sister didn't only blush, she elbowed him away. He, however, just laughed, gave her a wave, and returned to his own station, two tables up from hers.

Caprice hurried over and scurried around the back of the table. "What was that about?"

Nikki laid down the fork and the spoon, got hold of the chafing dish's lid, and plopped it on top with a clang. "Nothing."

"Your face is still flaming, so it wasn't just nothing. What did he say?"

"It was a lewd remark, and I'm just going to ignore him. I don't have any other choice."

"He's behaving like an adolescent who wants a pretty girl's attention. You turned him down, and now it's like he's going to do anything possible to make you notice him again."

"Even if that means putting me out of business?"

"That's not going to happen. That's why you're here. Just look at that carrot cake."

Instead of the traditional round shape, Nikki had created a square wedding cake. Her friend Serena had made classical swirls and twists with the icing. The three layers looked professionally done yet practical too. The topper on the cake was a beautiful cut-crystal heart.

"Who wouldn't want this cake?" Caprice asked, then took one of the small dishes with samples—Nikki had baked sheet cakes with the same icing—used the plastic fork, and transferred the bite into her mouth. She sighed with gastronomical pleasure. "The carrot cake is moist and rich, and that cream cheese icing . . . You've got a winner with this one."

A couple who had been standing about a foot

away closed in on Nikki now. They held a copy of one of her sample menus in their hands, looking quite interested in it.

The man spoke first. "I'm John Laughton, and this is my fiancée, Danica. We tasted your wedding cake, and we've checked out your menus. We're quite interested in hiring you. We like the variety of food you have to offer. Is it possible to change up these menus, or are they set? We have food restrictions in our family."

As Nikki explained they could come up with a custom-made menu, Juan Hildago appeared by Caprice's side. In addition to helping with all of her house stagings, Juan sometimes assisted Nikki in planning the menus in order to fit the theme. He was as familiar with Nikki's food as Caprice was. Right now he looked seriously disturbed.

"What's the matter?" Caprice asked before he said a word.

Juan lowered his voice as he explained, "You know that horseradish-glazed beef dish Nikki is giving samples of?"

Caprice nodded.

"Pierson is serving the same dish."

"You aren't serious."

"More serious than the price on that designer wedding dress over there. Do you think we should tell Nikki?"

Caprice considered what she should do. She and Nikki didn't keep secrets from each other. The young couple who had approached her sister seemed to be finishing up their conversation with her. She noticed Nikki pick up her phone and enter the woman's number. The man took a business card and one of the pamphlets. After smiles all around, the couple moved away.

"I'm going to get a sample of Pierson's beef," Juan said. "Be right back."

Nikki's questioning gaze followed him as he got lost in the crowd. "Where's he going in such a hurry?"

"You'll find out in a minute. I'm not sure you're going to be happy when you do. But knowing your competition is ninety percent of the battle. Juan said that Drew is serving horseradish-glazed beef. He's gone to get us a sample."

Nikki's expression was that worried look Caprice had seen so often on her face lately. "We made it together when he worked for me."

Juan was back, saying, "Pierson didn't see me. One of his assistants handed off the sample. Taste it and see what you think."

Both Caprice and Nikki picked up forks. They each took bites. Nikki looked as if she was going to blow a gasket.

"That is *my* recipe. I can taste every spice I put in it. I taught Drew how to make it when he was cooking with me. He'd never heard of horseradish-glazed beef, let alone known there was a white horseradish. I'm going to tell him he's not going to get away with this."

Caprice caught her sister's arm. "Wait, Nik. Think about this." She was usually the impulsive one, not her sister. But when Nikki was angry—

"He can't think it's right to do this," Nikki protested.

"No, he can't," Caprice agreed. "But making a scene here is just going to reflect badly on you.

Maybe that's what he expects you to do, because you face issues head on. Let me go sneak a sample of his groom's cake, the one Nana thinks is his grandmother's recipe. We can taste it together. Besides . . ." Caprice waved to a line of people coming their way. "You have customers and you need to drum up business. Put a smile on that pretty face and do it. I'll be back."

She noticed her sister make an effort at that smile when prospective clients approached.

Caprice flitted from table to table at first, then honed in on Drew's table. He had three assistants working with him, and it was very easy to just slip a plate with the groom's cake from the table and carry it along with her. When she reached Nikki's stand again, Nikki stepped away from the servers, letting her assistants take over. Then she and Caprice and Juan put their heads together in a quiet corner as they each took a bite of the chocolate walnut groom's cake.

"I hate to say it," Juan said, watching Nikki carefully, "but he's nailed this. Every groom in town will probably want it."

Caprice threw her assistant a warning look.

"Sorry," Juan mumbled.

Nikki sighed. "You're right. It's delicious. But I just can't believe he came up with it himself. If it's his grandmother's recipe, does she know he used it?"

There were lots of possibilities, Caprice supposed, giving Drew the benefit of the doubt. He might have heard about his grandmother's cake and decided to try to replicate it. But if he wasn't good at creating recipes, that would be darn hard to do. Maybe Drew's grandmother had just handed over the recipe. After all, giving it to her grandson was much different than giving it to an acquaintance, right?

Nikki's table was becoming deluged with customers wanting to sample her food, as well as examine the menus. This was her sister's chance to grow her business, to spread the word about her services, to let new customers realize how good a cook she was.

Suddenly Bella appeared at the table and checked out the line of people taste-testing Nikki's food. "She's doing great."

"What are you doing here?" Caprice asked.

"Joe took the kids to the park so I could stop in. I knew Nikki needed some support. But she looks like she's doing fine."

"For now," Caprice said, with some doubt in her voice. "Did you stop at Drew Pierson's table?"

Bella lowered her voice. "I didn't want to tell Nikki, but his food is good. I wasn't going to mention it."

"She already knows. He stole her recipe for the horseradish-glazed beef. She's wondering whose recipe he stole for the cake."

Seeing that Nikki was too busy for conversation, Bella nodded to the runway show across the room. "Let's take a walk over to those bridal dresses."

Bella had an opinion about everything, and never hesitated to express it. Passing a table filled with decorations for wedding centerpieces, she said, "They look cheap. I'd never put them on my table at a reception."

Caprice smiled. No, Bella would want quality all

the way, even if she had to cut corners somewhere else to pay for it.

A dais and stairs had been set up near the bridal dress vendors. Now a crowd was gathering around that area, and Caprice suspected why. Models would be showing off some of those wedding dresses.

Bella grabbed Caprice's arm and pulled her along, snaking around women until they both had a good vantage point about five feet from those stairs.

"We don't need to be so close," Caprice murmured.

"Yes, we do. You're interested, aren't you? I mean, you and Grant are dating, and he's what you want, isn't he? You sent Seth packing so Grant could be your exclusive."

Her exclusive. Just what did *that* mean?

"But we're not . . ." Caprice waved her hand at the model climbing the steps who stopped on the high dais and smiled at everyone around. "We're not *this* serious."

Bella faced Caprice squarely, staring straight into her eyes. "When you close your eyes at night, do you see Grant's face? When you wake up in the morning, do you think of him? Aren't you weaving dreams about kids and dogs and a minivan?"

Caprice was always straight with her sisters. "Just because I'm thinking of Grant that way doesn't mean he's thinking of *me* that way. And I already have a van."

"You're in denial," Bella warned her. "If you don't accept what you're feeling, Grant won't either. You have trust issues, Caprice. I know that. You've been hurt before. But you have to forget about Craig going to California to college and sending you a Dear Caprice e-mail. You have to move on, past Travis going back to his ex-wife. You're the one with that antique silent butler full of affirmations. You've got to look ahead, not back, and embrace it. That's what Father Gregory told me and Joe—embrace our future. That's what you need to do too."

That was sage advice coming from Bella. Apparently she and Joe had been listening carefully to Father Gregory when they'd had counseling sessions with him, and they'd taken everything he had said to heart.

She hesitated a moment and leaned close to Bella. "Grant has a past too."

"I know that," Bella commiserated. "And losing a child isn't something he's going to ever forget. That tragedy ruined his life for a while. But now you can help him really make a fresh start, can't you?"

Caprice had been telling herself that Grant had to be ready. Maybe she was the one who had to embrace the future first.

She studied the model at the top of the stairs. Her dress was a strapless concoction of tulle, froth, and glass beads that made the whole gown shimmer. It was beautiful. Still— "That's not me," Caprice said with certainty.

Bella cut her a sideways glance. "It's gorgeous."

"Maybe, but I don't want Cinderella. I want retro-elegance."

Bella rolled her eyes, something she did quite often. "Are you going to search for a vintage wedding gown?"

"When the time comes, I might."

"The time is now, dear sister, especially if you're going to hunt down one of those."

It could be fun checking online websites for vintage wedding gowns. Not that she had a lot of spare time to do it. Nevertheless . . . Searching for a vintage wedding gown might help embrace the future.

Wasn't she ready to dream again?

Carrying bags from her stop at Grocery Fresh after she'd left the expo, Caprice let herself into her house and was immediately struck by the silence. Quite a difference from the music and constant background hum of voices at the expo or the Sunday shoppers at the grocery store. Silence could be good or it could be bad. Where were Uncle Dom and the fur babies?

Hanging her purse on the antique oak mirrored stand in her foyer, she looked for signs of the cats and Lady in the living room and the dining room. Had something gone terribly wrong and Dom had to cage everyone and take them to the vet?

In the kitchen, she set her bags on the counter and spied Mirabelle and Sophia in one of their rare moments of close proximity. Mirabelle sat on the counter at one corner of the window over the sink while Sophia sat at the other. They were both staring outside.

Caprice suspected they were watching more than a stray ladybug. They didn't seem mindful of her at all as she came up behind them. She touched them both at the same time, not wanting to play favorites. Mirabelle meowed loudly and then directed her focus back out the window. Sophia butted her head against Caprice's hand but didn't move away from whatever was out there.

"I guess I'd better look too," Caprice capitulated. She laughed when she saw Uncle Dom rolling around on the ground with Lady. They seemed to be tussling over a toy that Lady used to play fetch.

"I'll be back in," she told her two felines. "As soon as I round up Uncle Dom and Lady."

She opened the back door and the screen and stepped out onto the porch. One side led into her garage. Another side was decorated with wrought-iron railing. The third side led down two steps into her backyard. She hopped down the steps and went to stand by her uncle.

He looked up, his face wreathed in a grin. "Lady's giving me a workout."

"Or you're giving her one."

Uncle Dom got to his feet and tossed the toy about ten feet away. Lady scampered to it, picked it up in her mouth, and shook it back and forth several times.

Dom waved his hand at her. "You can play with it. Bring it in when you're ready."

He walked to the porch with Caprice. Instead of going up the steps and sitting on the fifties-style, robin-egg-blue glider, he sank down onto one of the steps. "I think I'm going to like this."

"*This*, meaning pet sitting? You've made a decision?"

"I have. One of your mom's friends, another teacher, hired me to pet-sit her Lab and two cats for a week starting tonight. I'm going to house-sit too.

That way I'll be out of your parents' hair. I know living there is a real imposition. My background check is being completed to become bonded, and I'm making inquiries into the insurance. If this pet-sitting experience goes well and she gives me recommendations, I'll be able to move into my own place. We're heading into vacation time, so more work will be coming. I've been doing bookwork on the side for a couple of small businesses, and I've stowed that money away. I'm sure your mom and dad will be happy about it."

"But they'll miss you too. I know they will. You're going to stay in Kismet?"

"Yes, I think I'd like to. When I was a kid, I used to complain like everyone else that there was nothing to do here. But now that I'm an adult, I can see the possibilities. There are plays at Hershey Theater, at the Fulton in Lancaster too. Baltimore and D.C. aren't that far away for concerts."

"Don't forget the Giant Center in Hershey. Ace Richland's going to play there soon." Caprice had staged a house that Ace, a rock star legend, had purchased. Since then, they'd become friends.

Like a whirlwind, Lady came bounding over to Uncle Dom, dropping the toy at his feet. Then she turned to Caprice, circling her legs, pushing against her, wagging her tail.

"She certainly seems happy enough. And I can't believe the cats are sitting together at the window."

"I brought a secret along. A woman at the farmers market in York makes catnip pouches. I brought one for each of them. They played with them for about a half hour, and they weren't that far apart then. So maybe catnip promotes peace."

Caprice laughed out loud at that thought. She was about to ask her Uncle Dom if he'd like a glass of iced tea when the phone in her pocket played "Let It Be." She was surprised to see the caller was Nikki.

Uncle Dom said, "Go ahead and take it. I made a pot of coffee. I'll have another cup."

Caprice answered her phone. "Hey, Nik. Did something happen while you were wrapping up?"

"No, I just had more time to think. The hairs on the back of my neck are tingling, and I think my blood pressure's up. I want to confront Drew."

"About the white horseradish beef?"

"About everything. He's not going to get away with this, Caprice. Using my recipe, stealing my clients. He needs to know I won't put up with it."

"When are you going to do it?"

"Well, that's the thing. I want to be reasonable and civil. Will you go with me?"

"When?"

"Now. I want to get this over with. Can you meet me at Drew's grandmother's house?"

"How do you know he's there?"

"When I was closing down my stand and carrying things to my van, I overheard him say he was meeting someone."

"And you want to just barge right in?"

"Yes, I do. I want to take him by surprise. I want to catch him off guard."

"I need some time to thank Uncle Dom properly, put groceries away, and make sure Lady and

Mirabelle and Sophia are happy to curl up for the evening. If I feed them before I leave, they should be ready to do that."

"Maybe Uncle Dom can stay."

"He's starting to pet-sit tonight for a friend of Mom's. I think he's really going to like the pet-sitting profession."

"So how long do you need?" Nikki asked.

"An hour and a half should do it. I'll meet you at Rowena Pierson's house at seven-thirty."

Caprice disconnected and went inside. There she thanked her uncle. When he wouldn't accept payment for his stay with her pets, she insisted he take along slices of the chocolate-coffee loaf that she'd baked that morning.

After he left, she stowed away her groceries, played with Lady for a while, and made sure the cats got affection too. Then she went to change clothes. If she was going to help Nikki confront Drew, she wanted to be comfortable doing it. She changed into shorts and a tie-dyed T-shirt. Her platform sandals were retro all the way. After she fed her furry crew and cleaned up a bit, her watch said seven-fifteen. Time to hit the road.

She left Lady with a ball that dispensed kibble for treats, picked up her fringed purse, and headed for her yellow Camaro. The car had been in an accident recently, but thanks to Don Rodriguez's body shop, it was as good as new. It varoomed nicely as she started it up, backed out of her driveway, and headed for an older section of town.

On her way, she drove through downtown Kismet with its sand-blasted brick buildings with white window frames and black shutters, heading for a neighborhood on the south side of town. She drove up the tree-lined street, knowing she liked the older neighborhoods better with their maples and elms, poplars and birches, myrtle and ivy. She spotted Nikki's blue car parked in front of a two-story brick home set back from the street about twenty feet. She pulled up behind Nikki's car and exited her Camero, meeting her sister at the curb.

"There's Drew's van," she said, nodding to the driveway. It was large and white with Drew's Portable Edibles logo painted on the side.

"Do you know why Drew lives with his grandmother?" she asked Nikki.

"When we were on talking terms, he told me he moved in with her because she was having more trouble getting around and seeing properly."

"That was nice of him."

"*If* that was the real reason he wanted to live here," Nikki added. "From what he said, I think he spent some of his childhood here."

As they walked up the cement block path, Caprice said, "So you two really got to know each other."

Nikki hesitated. "Some, before I realized—"

Caprice stopped her sister by grabbing her arm. "Did he only make a pass?"

Nikki hesitated, then sighed. "Let's just say it was a very strong pass, and I had to knee him where it hurt to get him to back off."

"Nikki! Why didn't you tell me?"

"Because I took care of it. At least I thought I did. But I think this rivalry between us is all about that."

They walked up the rest of the path in silence and mounted the three porch steps sandwiched between mature arborvitae. On the porch, they stared at each other. The screen door was a wooden one. The door inside was open.

They both stepped up to the door rang. It was shadowy inside.

Nikki called, "Drew? Mrs. Pierson?"

There wasn't an answer.

"Is his grandmother hard of hearing?" Caprice inquired.

"I don't know."

"The door is open. Just step over the threshold and call inside."

Since Nikki wanted to get this over with as much as Caprice, she opened the screen door and did what Caprice suggested. But a moment later, she gasped, let out a yelp, and backed out quickly.

"What?"

"Drew's on the floor. There's blood all around his head."

Caprice didn't hesitate. She stepped inside and saw for herself what Nikki had seen.

"Call nine-one-one," she told Nikki. "I'll see if he has a pulse."

But from the blood pooling on the floor around his head and the flat look in his wide-open eyes, Caprice was fairly sure that Drew Pierson was dead.

Chapter Four

Caprice wrapped her arm around Nikki and felt her sister tremble. A patrol car had arrived, and so had the paramedics.

"What happened in there?" Nikki asked Caprice, not for the first time.

"I don't know, Nik," Caprice answered honestly. She tried to remember the details she'd absorbed by standing in the room for a few minutes.

A Tiffany-style lampshade sat on a side table with the base nowhere in sight. A tall Tiffany-style floor lamp had obviously been knocked over and lay on the carpet near the sofa. Miraculously it hadn't broken. Whether they were true Tiffany lamps only an expert could determine. But if they were . . . Caprice remembered some auction figures on Tiffany lamps from her design courses. Besides the possible worth of the lamps, she had noticed another thing. There had been a slip of paper sticking out from the base of the floor lamp. She knew better than to handle anything that could be considered evidence, or else she would have examined it. As it was, that piece of paper was part of the crime scene and she knew she shouldn't touch it.

There had been one other important detail. The outside back door in the kitchen had stood open. She wished she could record all of this on her electronic tablet, but she'd left that at home. If she concentrated on those details, maybe she could forget about seeing Drew's body. Maybe she could forget about the blood.

Yet she knew that might be impossible, because she'd witnessed crime scenes before.

"When I called Vince, he said he'd be here right away," Nikki murmured.

Caprice patted her back. "That was only a few minutes ago. Grant said the same thing." Caprice knew what was going to happen next, and they both would want a lawyer by their sides.

Ten minutes later, she was proven right. Detectives Carstead and Jones drove up in the same sedan, an unmarked vehicle.

"The patrol officer should have separated you," Jones snapped as he passed them and nodded to one of the officers to do just that.

Caprice watched Carstead and Jones as they pulled on booties, filled in the police log, and went inside. Five minutes later, they were back out.

Caprice was at the curb with a patrol officer at one end of the property, and Nikki was with another officer at the other end . . . outside the crime scene tape.

Detective Carstead approached Caprice, and Jones went toward Nikki. Caprice wished it was the other way around. Nikki was shaky, and Caprice didn't want her to say something to the hard-core detective that could be misinterpreted.

Carstead just arched his brow at Caprice as if asking why she was at another crime scene. But he didn't vocalize the question, at least not that one. Rather he inquired, "Are you ready to tell me what you saw?"

"I'll tell you whatever I can," she assured him.

"Did you touch anything inside?"

"No. Just the door when I went in after Nikki."

"So she went in first?"

"She did."

Just then a gray SUV pulled up in back of the patrol car and parked. Caprice told the detective, "I called Grant Weatherford."

Again Carstead arched a brow. "Well, of course you did. You're getting to be an expert at this, aren't you?"

She didn't answer. She knew better than to say too much. That had been drummed into her by her brother *and* Grant time and time again. Being helpful was one thing. Being too chatty was another.

Grant made a beeline for Caprice, took her hand, and squeezed it.

Carstead gave Grant a nod, noticing. "Can we go on?" he asked Caprice.

"Sure. Ask away."

"How did you know Drew Pierson?"

"He was a chef and worked with Nikki for a while."

Carstead made notes in his pocket-sized spiral-bound book. "For a while? Were they working together now?"

"No."

"Just no? Was there a reason?"

Caprice thought carefully about what she wanted to say, and then decided to give him a little bit of information. After all, Nikki did have a connection to Drew.

"For a while Nikki thought she and Drew might go into a partnership with her catering business. But then Drew decided to go out on his own, and Nikki decided she might want to partner with someone else."

The detective made notes. "Were you friends with Pierson?"

"No."

He eyed her carefully. "When did you last see him?"

"I saw him this afternoon."

The detective said, "I thought you said you weren't friends."

"We aren't . . . weren't. There was a wedding expo in Kismet, and he had a booth. So did Nikki."

"And why did you come here tonight?"

"I came along with Nikki to discuss business."

"Your sister's business?"

"Yes."

"And you just came along for support?"

This detective seemed to know her a little too well, but maybe that was because he'd done background checks on her, including looking into her family. After all, Bella and Joe had been involved in a murder investigation. So had Caprice's friend Roz. And then there had been Ace's situation . . .

"I did come along to support her."

Grant gave her arm a little squeeze, maybe because he didn't want her to say more.

Carstead saw the signal and sighed. "You can go

for now, but you're going to have to come down to the station tomorrow for more questions and to give your statement."

Caprice noticed that Vince had arrived and was standing beside Nikki. She was glad he was there . . . glad he could protect her.

"I want to stay and wait until Detective Jones is finished questioning Nikki."

"I know if I tell you you can't, you're just going to give me an argument, and then your lawyer friend here is going to weigh in on it too. As long as you stay on the public side of the tape, you can wait."

As Carstead moved away, a snazzy red sedan zoomed down the street, pulled up at the driveway, and parked right across it.

Vince and Nikki came over to join Caprice and Grant.

"How did it go?" Vince asked Caprice.

"All right. I have to go down to the station tomorrow and give my statement."

"So does Nikki. But I have a feeling Jones is going to put the screws to her. He's got a chip on his shoulder that I'd like to knock off. But I know better."

Caprice could see that Grant was ready to take her home and get her away from yet another crime scene when two women emerged from the sporty red sedan and Detectives Carstead and Jones immediately went to them.

"The woman with the cane is Drew's grandmother," Nikki told Caprice. "He had her photo on his phone. I saw it when she called him. I've seen her at church too."

"And I know Kiki Hasselhoff, the woman with her," Caprice said. "I often stop in at her bookstore for the latest crime novel." She also knew Kiki from Chamber of Commerce meetings.

Caprice could see Rowena Pierson was in tears now. She'd taken a handkerchief from her purse and was dabbing her eyes. Kiki had her arm around her friend's shoulders.

"Detective Jones isn't going to let them inside," Grant said.

"Maybe we should stay until after the detectives talk to them," Nikki offered. "Drew's grandmother might need something."

"But you shouldn't be the person who offers to give it," Vince warned her.

"Don't be silly, Vince," Nikki scolded. "Nana and Mom know Mrs. Pierson from church. Both would want us to help her if we can. Imagine how devastated she is."

They all thought about that.

"Wait until Carstead and Jones are finished talking to them," Grant counseled. "If Drew's grandmother and her friend don't leave, you can approach them then."

Fifteen minutes later, Rowena Pierson looked wrung out and shaky as Detectives Carstead and Jones went inside the house to the crime scene once more.

Nikki nudged Caprice. "Let's talk to her."

Vince advised, "Maybe you shouldn't, Nikki. Just let Caprice go."

Nikki looked defiant. "I didn't do anything wrong. I'm going to tell this woman that I'm sorry her grandson is dead. If the police don't like it, they can arrest me for being compassionate."

With that, she started toward the two women. Caprice just gave her brother an I'll-watch-over-her-look and followed her.

Nikki approached Kiki and Rowena slowly. Caprice could see that Kiki recognized them both.

When they stopped beside the two women, Kiki said to Caprice, "You must be the person who found Drew."

"My sister did," Caprice responded.

Nikki introduced herself to Rowena. "Mrs. Pierson, I'm Nikki De Luca. Drew and I worked together at one time. I'm so sorry for what's happened here."

"You found him?" Rowena asked. "They won't let me see him. That detective asked if I had a photo, and I did in my wallet. But they won't let me go in."

Caprice gently touched the older woman's arm. "You don't want to see Drew like that. You don't want to remember him that way."

"He was like a son to me." Tears dripped from Rowena's eyes. "I raised both Drew and his sister, Jeanie, you know." Rowena went on, "Drew and Jeanie came to me when they were just little ones after their parents died in a small plane crash. Drew was ten and Jeanie was eight. Oh my gosh—Jeanie. I need to call her."

Kiki stayed Rowena's hand as the woman rummaged in her purse. "Give yourself a little time to absorb what's happened. The detective said he'd notify Jeanie."

"Did he?" Rowena asked, looking a little lost. "I don't remember that."

Caprice knew that devastating news was enough of a shock to make a person forget her name. She said, "We don't want to keep you. We just wanted to give you our condolences. Do you have someplace you can stay? I imagine the forensics unit will have the house tied up at least through tomorrow."

After studying Caprice, Kiki remembered, "You've been through this before." Apparently Kiki remembered the articles about Caprice in the *Kismet Crier* when a reporter had interviewed her in conjunction with murders she'd solved.

"A few times," Caprice responded.

"Rowena's going to stay with me," Kiki revealed. "For as long as she needs to." She shook her head. "I just can't believe that two hours ago we were sitting at the American Music Theater enjoying a production."

Rowena said, "I can't see too well. I have to have that cataract surgery I've been putting off. But I can hear just fine. The music was lovely. I expected to come home and hear how Drew's day had gone—"

Kiki opened the passenger side of the vehicle. "The detective said we can go. Let me take you to my place. Then you can call Jeanie and maybe she'll come over for a while."

After Caprice and Nikki gave their condolences again and said their good-byes, they returned to Grant's SUV. There was more hubbub around the house than before because the crime scene unit had arrived. Now the evidence gathering would begin in earnest.

Vince was still standing at Grant's vehicle too. He asked, "How is she?"

"She's devastated," Caprice answered. "It seems she was more like a mom to Drew than a grandmother."

Vince nodded toward the house. "Carstead was on the porch watching you two. If your conversation had gone on too long, he might have broken it up. As it was, I think he realized you were just giving your condolences. I want to talk to you and Nikki about what you saw and heard. Let's go back to your place," he said to Caprice.

"Since your car and Nikki's will be impounded, why don't you go with Vince and Nikki," Grant suggested. "I'll pick up Patches and meet you back at your house."

They heard the front door of Rowena's house open and shut as techs went inside. Carstead was still on the front porch watching them.

"I think he likes you," Grant muttered to Caprice.

She was totally surprised by that remark. "Why do you think that?"

"I've seen him question witnesses before. He's always respectful, not like Jones who can be sharp. But Brett was almost kind with you."

"We've crossed paths several times before. He knows I wouldn't kill anyone."

"Maybe," Grant said thoughtfully.

In spite of the situation, Caprice's heart turned just a little bit lighter. She asked, "Do you mind if Detective Carstead likes me?"

Grant took a long moment to answer, and then he said, "Yeah, I mind."

Caprice liked the idea that Grant could be just a little bit jealous. But she didn't want him to worry that she had eyes for another man. So she rose on tiptoe and kissed him on the cheek. "I'll see you and Patches in a little while. I'll make lemonade."

After Grant gave her a hug, she joined Nikki and Vince. The four of them were going to have a lot to talk about.

By the time Grant and Patches arrived at Caprice's house, she had served Nikki and Vince tall glasses of lemonade and had set some out for herself and Grant. With golden eyes, Mirabelle watched them from her perch on the lowest shelf of the cat tree. Sophia was stretched out on the fireplace hearth, just looking pretty. Lady ran to the door to greet Patches when Grant came in. It wasn't long until they were all sitting around the coffee table, sipping lemonade, and eating slices of chocolate-coffee loaf.

Vince gobbled up half a slice and then shook his head. "I don't know how you always get involved."

"I'm not involved," Caprice protested. "Nikki is. She's the one who knew Drew."

"Not really," her sister disagreed with a little sigh. "I mean, I knew his work history. I knew where he'd studied and where he'd cooked before coming back home. But I never knew his grandmother raised him. I thought he just lived with her to help out. In fact, that was one of the things I admired about him."

"*Did* he live there to help out?" Grant asked. "Or had he moved in with his grandmother again because his finances were on the downturn? That wouldn't be unusual if he lost a job one place and came back here to find another."

"I wonder if he was going to stay there now that he was making it big," Vince offered.

"Selling the barbecue sauce might have gotten him a nice nest egg and a licensing royalty," Grant interjected. "But he'd have to sustain his business and his reputation." He studied Caprice. "Are you going to poke around in this?"

"Is Nikki the number one suspect?" she asked both her brother and Grant.

Vince shrugged. "The detectives always look at anyone who found the body. I'm not as concerned about that as about the fact that she told them she and Drew worked together. They're going to be looking at her closely because of her association with Drew, and because they parted ways."

"After that fight we had at the open house, they could also think I have a motive." Nikki sounded worried, and Caprice didn't blame her. "Drew as much as threatened me, and several people over-heard him."

"It all depends on what the York County Forensics Team finds," Vince reminded them. "Nikki, tell me exactly what you saw when you went inside."

"I don't remember a thing," Nikki admitted. "I saw the blood and everything in my mind went blank."

Vince turned to Caprice. "What do *you* remember?"

Unfortunately, Caprice had done this type of exercise before and hated doing it. But because she hadn't remembered the evidence correctly on one of the murder scenes, she'd almost missed something important. This time she wouldn't let that happen.

She took a sip of her lemonade, then a deep breath. Closing her eyes, she attempted to relive the moments when she'd walked inside behind Nikki.

"Drew was on the floor, and my guess is from his injury and the way he had fallen, he'd been hit from behind. There were two Tiffany-style lamps. Well, not exactly two. Just the shade for one was sitting on the library table beside the sofa. The base was missing. Based on the shade size, it wasn't a huge lamp, so someone could have carried that base out with them if they'd used it to hit Drew. There wasn't anything else lying around him that could have been the weapon. A floor lamp was lying on the floor. There seemed to be a piece of paper sticking out from its base."

"They aren't hollow, are they?" Vince asked.

"It would be easy to stick something up in there around the cord. If those are true Tiffany lamps, they were designed from the 1890s to the 1930s and they could be worth hundreds of thousands of dollars. A Magnolia lamp that was auctioned in the eighties sold for more than five hundred thousand."

Absorbing what Caprice had said, Grant decided, "I don't think the motive was robbery, or the lamps would have been gone."

Vince suggested, "Most people might not realize what they're worth . . . or think they're reproductions."

"Or," Nikki added, "maybe the killer knows their worth and was interrupted and will be back."

"A murder like this in the victim's home means

Drew knew whoever killed him," Grant deduced. "He let that person in. If he knew them, it had to be personal."

"Look how he treated Nikki," Caprice pointed out. "If he was that bitter about her, he could be bitter about lots of other people. We don't know anything about his friends. Do you know anything about his sister?" she asked Nikki.

"No, he never talked about her. Nana might know since she's acquainted with Rowena." Nikki took out her phone, jumped up from the sofa, and went into the kitchen.

"I've never seen her this fidgety," Vince said. "She's really shaken up."

"Finding a dead body will do that," Grant said wryly. "You two aren't going to stay out of this, are you?"

Caprice gave him a weak smile. "Are we going to have an argument about it?"

"There wouldn't be anything to argue about if you and Nikki just sit back and let the police do their job."

"How can we just sit back when Nikki could be a suspect?"

Grant held up both hands in surrender. "I give up. No argument. Just consider each step you take carefully, because Detective Jones will be watching *you*."

Grant's absolutely serious warning shook her this time, a way it hadn't in the past. Maybe because he was right. Detective Jones did not like her interference. Would he take that out on Nikki?

Vince leaned over to Caprice and asked in a low voice, "Did Nikki and Pierson really go at it at the open house, enough that more than a few people would notice?"

"They raised their voices," Caprice acknowledged. "Truth be told, I think Drew was angrier than Nikki. She really tried to restrain herself. But then she let loose with resonating barbs too. I'd say five to ten guests were around, along with Nikki's servers, so there were a lot of witnesses, if that's what you're asking."

"And each one will have a different take on the argument," Vince said.

He was probably right. Except one fact was obvious. Nikki and Drew were competing for business. That could be motive for murder. Caprice hated to admit it, but it was true. It all boiled down to the detectives' perspective on the evidence. If they decided Nikki was their main suspect, they'd go after her.

Grant tapped Caprice's hand. "Let's not worry before we have to."

She liked the way he used that word "we."

Nikki returned to the living room looking somber.

"What did you find out? Does Nana know anything?" Caprice asked before the others could.

"First of all, she told me to tell you to be careful."

"She knows I will be."

Both Grant and Vince arched their brows.

Caprice insisted, "I try to be." She swiveled her attention back to her sister. "So what did Nana say?"

"She admitted she doesn't know Rowena Pierson well. But she does know that Rowena's arthritis over the past few years has gotten worse. She doesn't climb steps if she can help it, and Drew helped her arrange her bedroom on the first floor in what was once a study."

Caprice hadn't seen much of the house, just the living room and a glance into the kitchen. And that open back door.

Nikki continued, "Nana said Rowena hasn't talked about Drew and Jeanie much, but here's something interesting. Jeanie was married when she was nineteen but divorced six months later. Her married name is Jeanie Boswell and she owns Posies."

"The flower shop?" Grant asked.

"She's the 'Jeanie' from Posies?" Caprice asked. "I know her. I've dealt with her now and then to get flowers for stagings."

"Uh-oh. You know her. That sounds like trouble. What are you thinking?" Grant asked, sounding worried.

"I don't actually *know* her. But I've spoken with her on the phone and purchased flowers from her. Because you and Vince and Nana want me to be careful, I'm not going to do anything, at least not yet. Nikki and I will see how it goes tomorrow morning when we give our statements."

"I'll be there with you," Grant assured Caprice, just as Vince said the same thing to Nikki.

"We really don't need both of you, do we?" Nikki asked.

"You do," Grant answered firmly. "They're going to separate you. They'll want to make sure every detail of your stories lines up. They'll ask you the same questions over and over again. I'll be with

Caprice, and Vince will be with you. We're going to make sure you stay calm and focused and don't blow your tops, even if they try to push your buttons. You can't just *be* innocent, you have to *look* innocent and *act* innocent."

"It's not an *act*," Caprice protested.

"I know it's not," Grant maintained. "But I also know that both you and Nikki have Italian tempers when riled. I don't want them popping out at the detectives. Just consider Vince and me your reasonable buddies to keep you on an even keel."

Gazing up at Grant, Caprice knew she wanted more than buddyship with him, but she also knew what he meant.

Tomorrow had to go smoothly for her sake, but especially for Nikki's sake. A public argument with threats and a rivalry were two good reasons to find evidence to pin this murder on her sister.

Chapter Five

Caprice sat across from Detective Jones in the interrogation room at the police station the next morning. No, she didn't expect a rubber hose and brass knuckles from the detective, but he was sharp, sometimes inconsiderate, and even harsh. She wondered where Detective Carstead had taken Nikki. His office, maybe?

Grant sat next to her, and she was glad of that. He was a tall, comforting presence beside her.

The police station had been refurbished several years ago. Workers gave it a face-lift by sandblasting the brick and repainting the cupola. But whoever had picked out the paint colors for the rooms had gone for drab. She would never have picked the interrogation room's ugly green shade for painting anything.

"Go over it for me again, Miss De Luca," Detective Jones ordered. "You touched the door handle when you went in even though your sister had gone in first?"

It would be so easy for Caprice to become impatient with Detective Jones. But Grant had warned her over and over again to keep her cool, to listen to Beatles music in her head if she had to in order to calm herself down.

"Nikki went in first," she explained. "I held the screen door as she went inside."

"I see. And your fingerprints won't be anywhere else in the room?"

She thought about that all over again. "If you could capture them from skin, you'd find them near Drew's carotid artery and on his wrist. I placed my hand in front of his mouth to see if I could feel breath. But I did *not* touch anything."

Detective Jones had a hard cleft jaw, a nose that looked as if it had been broken, and medium brown hair that appeared to have seen a breeze.

"All right," he said, pushing a legal pad over to her along with a pen. "Write it all down—from when you got there to when you left. I'll have it typed up and you can come in and sign it."

Wanting to leave as soon as she could, she took the pen and started writing. She'd been over it so many times she wrote quickly, remembering each detail, relating each fact of what she'd seen and what had happened.

When she was finished, she pushed the pad over to the detective and then stood. "You know, instead of treating me like a criminal, you ought to go after who did this."

"Caprice . . ." Grant laid a warning hand on her arm.

"If you and your sister didn't have anything to

hide, you wouldn't need lawyers here," Detective Jones snapped.

She slipped away from Grant's arm. The detective's reasoning was as fake as his sly smile, and she wasn't going to let him bully her.

"Your police department almost charged Roz Winslow, who was innocent, when her husband was murdered. Your department was also ready to charge my brother-in-law for a crime he didn't commit. Of *course* Nikki and I need lawyers here. Thank goodness we're fortunate to have a lawyer in the family and his partner as a close friend."

When she glanced at Grant, she could see he was worried for her, but he didn't stop her. She just hoped he'd bail her out if Jones arrested her for mouthing off.

"You De Lucas think just because you know Chief Powalski you can say and do anything," Jones returned stone-faced. "You can't. There are rules. There are regulations. And there is protocol."

Suspecting Jones was still miffed because she'd called on Chief Powalski, her dad's friend, to help with the first murder she'd solved, she was silent for a moment.

Grant stepped in. "The De Lucas have never received special treatment because of Chief Powalski. I suspect he'd be insulted if you imply otherwise."

Jones frowned and looked away as if maybe he'd gone a little too far. Just then, Detective Carstead appeared with Nikki outside the door with a glass window.

Jones opened the door and said to Caprice, "You can go. Someone will call you when your statement's ready for signing. But you'd better take my advice. Don't stick your nose into this."

If Caprice wanted to be childish, she would have tossed back, "Or what?" But she knew challenging the detective wasn't in her best interest or Nikki's. She didn't say anything. She just preceded Grant out the door.

Once they were all standing in the parking lot by Vince's car, Grant said to her, "You didn't assure him you'd stay out of it."

"That's because I'm not going to lie."

Vince took out his remote to open his car doors. "You'd better be careful. You've solved their crimes for them in the past, and none of them is happy about that."

"I called Detective Carstead the last time . . . *after* I figured out who the murderer was."

"I'm not worried so much about Carstead," Vince said. "He didn't hammer Nikki to death, just drew her story out of her. After all, what was there to hide? Practically everybody in town knows about the rivalry between Nikki and Pierson. But Jones— if he can nail you with anything, Caprice, he will, including obstruction of justice."

"Don't warn me again," she said with a sigh. "He can't arrest me for talking to friends, giving condolences, finding out more about Drew's barbecue sauce."

Vince just shook his head. "Are you riding with me, Nikki?"

Nikki gave Caprice a hug, and then climbed in the passenger side. "Call me," Nikki said to Caprice right before she shut her door.

"I will," Caprice assured her.

As they walked to Grant's SUV, he asked her, "Do you and Nikki talk every day?"

"That depends on what's going on. But I talk to somebody every day—Bella, Mom, Nana, Nikki. Then the news gets around. You know how that is."

Grant was silent. Finally he confessed, "No, actually I don't know how that is. I have one brother, Caprice, and we're not close. My parents aren't like yours. They're terrifically conservative, aren't prone to outbursts, and don't express emotion well."

This was the first Grant had talked about his parents and brother with her.

"You told me your parents live in Vermont."

"They do. Our family home is in a rural area, and they don't have particularly close friends. Mom plays bingo in town with the women from her sewing group, and my dad plays poker about once a month."

"My dad does too."

"Your dad plays poker with men he's known all his life. My dad . . . He grew up on a farm where daily life was about sunrise and chores and more chores and sunset. Out of high school, he got a job at a canned foods company in a nearby town bigger than where he was from. When he married Mom, they bought a house near the family farm. Dad commuted every day until he retired. He didn't make friends at work, maybe because the factory was in the next town over. I don't know. Maybe because he doesn't know how to make friends. My parents and my brother are just very different from your folks."

They were at Grant's SUV then, and he stopped talking. She wished he'd go on. They'd had conversations about lots of subjects, but nothing as personal as this.

After they were in the vehicle, Grant started the ignition and the air conditioning, but he didn't make a move to drive out of the parking lot. Instead he turned toward Caprice. He took her hand in his and asked, "Am I a close friend?"

She remembered that that's exactly what she had told Detective Jones—that Grant was her brother's partner and a close friend.

"What would you have preferred I say?" she asked him, hoping he'd say that she should have told Jones she was his girlfriend.

After a long pause, when Grant obviously thought about it, he gave her a half smile and a shrug. "Close friend will do it for now."

She was disappointed by that, but she also knew Grant had to be ready for whatever came next. However, the conversation they'd just had gave her hope that he'd be ready for a lot more than close friendship soon.

Caprice was deep into work later that afternoon when she received a text from Nikki. Let's go to Bella's. She's home sewing costumes today.

Caprice knew Nikki was agitated and restless, and when something was happening to one sister, all three sisters united. So she didn't question Nikki's text.

She texted back, I'll be there in fifteen minutes.

When Caprice arrived at Bella's, Lady by her side, there was frantic activity. Pots and pans were stacked in Bella's sink. Megan and Timmy were squabbling over toys that they were either taking out of a carton or putting back into it.

"What's going on?" Caprice asked after hugs for the kids. Lady stayed with Megan and Timmy, knowing they were more likely to play with her.

Bella threw up her hands. "We have a house showing in half an hour. I was working on costumes and I didn't expect that today. Megan and Timmy are supposed to be picking up toys. Thank goodness Benny is taking a nap."

Caprice glanced around the living room and kitchen. She'd encouraged Bella to remove some of the furniture, and she'd restyled other pieces with bright throw pillows and even a fresh coat of paint. She'd changed the drapes too. Before, everything had been drab in rust and green, mostly because of Joe's taste in colors and furniture. But now the house was colorful, letting light in. However, it was a mess.

"I'm not going to have time to run the sweeper," Bella wailed as she scrubbed the bottom of the stainless steel pot that she'd apparently made a batch of soup in.

"It's more important we clean up the kitchen and put the toys away," Caprice advised her. "Usually you know a day ahead about a house showing."

Caprice had hooked Bella and Joe up with a real estate agent who handled mostly midpriced dwellings, families searching for their first or second homes. Kayla Langtree was a top-notch agent and usually well organized.

"Kayla called and said she had a couple that just stopped into the office. They're moving to the area and they're in a hurry to buy. They wanted to see properties today. I couldn't say no."

As she set the pot on the drainer, Nikki took it and swiftly dried it.

Bella rinsed tomato residue from another pot. "So what are you going to do to make sure Nikki doesn't get charged with Drew's murder? She told me all about what's going on. You know Mom and Dad and Nana are worried sick. They remember what Joe and I went through."

Caprice and Nikki exchanged a glance, and Nikki explained, "Everyone is warning Caprice away from this one. Maybe we should just let the detectives take over."

Bella stopped washing, took a towel in her hands and dried them, and plopped her fists on her hips.

"Let the detectives take over? Since when? Come on, Caprice. You're not going to do that, are you?"

Caprice almost had to smile at Bella's vehemence. Almost. This really wasn't a smiling matter. She could stick her feet into some deep doo-doo if she wasn't careful.

"I'm thinking about our best strategy."

"Well, don't think too long," Bella warned her, "or Nikki could end up in jail. From what I understand, her car was already parked at Rowena Pierson's when you arrived. And she doesn't have an alibi from the time she left the expo until the time you found Drew."

Timmy ran into the kitchen, Lady right behind him. "Megan won't let me put her toys in the box. I can't do it if she keeps taking them out."

At nine years old, Timmy tried to lord it over his sister, but his sister wouldn't let him.

"How about if Caprice helps you and Megan put all the toys in the box? Would that help?" Bella asked.

Timmy grinned up at Caprice. "Sure would."

"Where are you going to go during the house showing?" Nikki asked.

"I called Mom. We're going over there."

"Do you want me to help you?" Caprice asked.

"If you help me load them in the car, I'll be fine." Bella studied Caprice again. "So what are you going to do?"

"I think Nikki and I are going to make a stop and see Drew's grandmother. She's probably still at Kiki's house and could use a care package and some comforting. What do you think, Nik?"

"I think Nana's biscotti, a tin of tea, maybe some nice hand lotion might be appreciated. But don't you have anything pressing you have to get done right now with work?"

"I'm caught up for the moment, though I've left Lady, Sophia, and Mirabelle alone a lot lately. I'll see if my neighbor Dulcina Mendcz can watch Lady so we can spend whatever time we need with Rowena. She never minds short notice."

Timmy pulled on Caprice's hand. "Come on, before Megan takes everything out of the box."

Lady barked as if she agreed with that assessment. Caprice laughed and followed Timmy and Lady to the living room. She wished cleaning up the mess of murder was as easy as cleaning up toys.

Caprice was thankful she and Nikki had a passing acquaintance with Kiki Hasselhoff, Rowena's friend. Caprice loved books and enjoyed just being around them. She often went into the store to browse, and so did Nikki.

Kiki lived in a two-story Colonial in an older section of Kismet. It was neat with its white siding, black shutters, and brick front facing on the first floor. The yard was pristinely landscaped with trimmed shrubs. Caprice would have added annuals to give the front dabs of color, but if you planted them they had to be tended and pulled out when fall came.

Caprice moved the basket she and Nikki had put together from one hand to the other. Nana had baked a fresh batch of biscotti and they'd included a canister of those. After taking Lady to Dulcina's house, they'd stopped at Country Fields Shopping Center where they'd visited the specialty tea shop Tea For You. While Caprice bought tea, Nikki had gone to a bath and body shop, purchasing cucumber and melon hand lotion and body wash. They'd put all of it into a basket, and Caprice hoped it would help Rowena feel just a little better. Her grandson murdered. How must she be feeling? If Rowena had raised Drew, he'd be like a son.

Kiki answered the door looking very solemn. "Thank you for coming," she said to Caprice and Nikki when she saw the basket of goodies. "Rowena hasn't received many condolences. With murder involved, even people she thought were her friends are staying away."

"I'm sorry to hear that," Caprice said. "She needs her friends now more than ever. It's nice of you to let her stay here."

Kiki waved her age-spotted hand. "Nonsense. That's what real friends do. I've offered her my downstairs bedroom. She's in my den right now watching an old movie, but I don't think she's paying much attention to it. Come on in."

Kiki's house was a mixture of comfortable and stylish. The multi-cushioned sofa wore a fabric of bright flowery blooms, most of them hydrangeas in pink and blue. An oversized chair with an ottoman accompanied it. Glass-topped tables were sparkling bright and streak-free. Kiki, in her late sixties, obviously took good care of herself and her surroundings.

She led them to a room adjacent to the living room. In this parlor, the color theme was sage green and gray. Two recliners in sage faced a flat-screen TV. The furniture was polished pine. Although the entertainment center housed the TV, all of its shelves were filled with books. Caprice caught sight of mysteries and romances, spy thrillers, and nonfiction titles too.

"You have visitors," Kiki announced to her guest.

Rowena began to lower her footrest, but Caprice stopped her.

"Don't get up. We brought you a basket of goodies we thought you might enjoy. Nana included some of her biscotti."

Rowena smiled. "Everyone loves Celia's biscotti. They're so different from those hard cookies you buy at the market."

Nana's biscotti were lemon-iced, soft cookies that went well with coffee or tea. Caprice tried to replicate them and did to a certain extent, but they never tasted just like Nana's.

Kiki said, "I'll let you talk. Just call me if you need anything."

After she left the room, Nikki sat in the other

recliner and Caprice sat cross-legged on the floor near Rowena.

"How are you doing?" she asked gently.

"Not so well, I'm afraid. I want to get back into my house. I don't even have clothes. Kiki let me borrow some of hers." She motioned to the black slacks that were a little too long, and the green striped blouse that was a bit too big.

"Jeanie was here for a while last night," she offered. "She's taking care of many of the arrangements. She's a go-getter, that one, though she and Drew were never really close."

"You said they came to live with you after their parents died?"

"They did," Rowena assured her. "There wasn't anyone else. My husband had passed away, and somehow we all muddled through. They were so lost for a while. And Drew?" Rowena shook her head. "I was really worried about him. As a teenager, he was a handful. Even when he received his inheritance—"

Rowena stopped as if remembering Drew and the years they'd spent together was a little much right now.

To keep the conversation going and to help Rowena, Nikki jumped in. "I suppose Drew used his inheritance to fund chef school."

Rowena seemed to rally. "I was the trustee for Jeanie and Drew's inheritance until they were twenty-one. Then the money was split and they received the balance. Jeanie used hers to go to business school and to buy her flower shop. She's done quite well— except for an impulsive marriage after she graduated high school that was practically over before it started. After she bought Posies, she seemed to find her footing. At first, I thought Drew was going to waste all of his inheritance and there wasn't a thing I could do about it. He went through most of it quickly, buying an expensive car, taking vacations. He used the last of it to go to cooking school and he seemed to settle down after that. When he came back here, he was really kind to me. I had had a fall and broken my arm, so he came here to live to help out, and he stayed. I was so proud when he sold that barbecue sauce recipe. He even told me the secret ingredient," she said with a shaky smile.

"Can you tell us?" Nikki asked kindly.

"Sure. I don't know all the ingredients, but the secret one was the habanero sea salt. Just a touch. It gave the sweetness a kick."

"Did you ever make barbecue sauce?" Caprice asked.

Rowena fluttered her hand. "Just the traditional kind, with vinegar, oil, and sugar . . . and a bit of tomato."

"Did Drew tell you about the expo he was cooking for?"

"I just knew he'd be gone all day Sunday."

"I was there too," Nikki said. "It was a wedding expo where prospective brides and grooms could study the kind of flowers they might want to use, or gowns, or food. Drew introduced a chocolate walnut cake. My nana said you used to make one of those. Did you give your recipe to Drew?"

Rowena slowly shook her head. "No, I didn't give him any recipes."

"Drew didn't have access to them?" Caprice asked, keeping her voice light.

"No, he didn't. Years ago, a member of my

canasta club tried to steal them. So I hid the more important ones where no one will find them. The chocolate walnut cake with the maple icing was one of those. Only Kiki knows where I've hidden them in case something happens to me."

Caprice wondered if the hollow tube around the cord of the lamp was one of those hiding places. That lamp could be heavy, but not so heavy that Rowena couldn't tilt it on the floor and stuff a few papers around the cord. But she could see Rowena was tiring, and she didn't want to upset her by going into more of it now.

Kiki must have overheard some of their conversation, because as she swept into the room with a tray holding a coffee carafe and mugs, she explained, "Eventually Drew would have inherited the recipes as well as Rowena's Tiffany lamps. They *are* Tiffany, by the way."

Rowena's hands fluttered in her lap. "Those lamps have been in my family since the early 1900s. We always knew they were Tiffany because of the special glass and the *Tiffany New York* stamp on them with a number."

"Now half of one of them is missing, according to what the police are telling Rowena," Kiki said. "We're hoping they can find it."

"If you don't mind my asking," Nikki said, "if Drew was inheriting the lamps and recipes, what would Jeanie inherit?"

"Jeanie was going to inherit my house, jewelry, and the rest of my belongings."

In other words, now Jeanie would inherit the house and everything else too, Caprice thought. Was that a motive enough for murder?

Chapter Six

Caprice knew that some of her clients owned valuables, but she never knew exactly how much they were worth.

She asked, "Most people don't understand the value of lamps like yours. Did you ever have them appraised?"

"They'd be worth stealing, maybe even killing over," Rowena said with a frown. "I told the police that. Isaac Hobbs from Older and Better consulted a New York City contact of his who's an expert authenticator. So I do know what they're worth," Rowena assured her. "It was after his appraisal that I set up a new will."

"Did Drew and Jeanie know about the new will? Did they know what the lamps are worth?"

"Yes, they knew about it. I'm not like some older folk who keep everything secret. They would inherit everything I have some day, so I wanted them to know what I was thinking. They didn't pressure me in the least. Drew always liked the lamps, and Jeanie, well, I guess I have to say, she's more interested in the bottom line."

"So she'd only be interested in what your house and belongings are worth? Not the sentimental value of keeping everything?"

"Exactly. And I understand that. Young folks are different these days. Neither she nor Drew had a happy time growing up here because of what happened to their parents. They had trouble bonding to me. Their school counselor told me they tried to stay detached because they didn't want to get hurt again if something happened to me. It made perfect sense. I had no illusions about either one of them. If I died, they'd sell off whatever I gave them and do whatever they wanted with the money. But I think Jeanie would do that quicker than Drew."

Kiki was nodding her head as if she absolutely agreed. These two women apparently had no secrets.

"I was around during those rough years," Kiki elaborated, pouring the coffee. "Their parents suddenly being taken from them was earth-shattering. Jeanie withdrew. Drew acted out. Sometimes I thought the only time he was really happy was when he was cooking with Rowena. Then he forgot about the fact that he hated the world, and he started getting closer to her in that way."

"Did you see that?" Nikki asked Rowena.

"Oh yes. He would always make such a mess in the kitchen. But I didn't scold him. Because when I watched him cook, I saw in his eyes a bit of that sparkle that he had when he was a boy."

Caprice decided to take the conversation down another path. "When kids can't bond with adults, sometimes they bond with their peers instead. Did

Jeanie and Drew have a group of friends? Anyone they could confide in?"

Rowena thought about it. "Jeanie pretty much kept to herself. She spent a lot of time in her room reading. When the weather was nice, she'd plant flowers in the yard or sit on the back porch swing reading."

"That one could get lost in books," Kiki agreed. "She devoured everything I brought her. Drew, on the other hand, couldn't be bothered with books. He wanted to be out and about doing something. And he had friends he'd do it with. I don't know if he confided in them, but he spent a lot of time with them."

"When he was in high school, I hardly ever saw him," Rowena explained. "He had two best buddies— Larry Penya and Bronson Chronister. The three of them seemed to be like brothers."

"It was odd, really," Kiki said. "The three of them were very different."

"How so?" Caprice asked.

"Are you familiar with Happy Camper Recreational Vehicle Center?"

Caprice noticed that when Rowena picked up her mug of coffee, her hand shook a little. All of this talk about Drew and his past could be having an adverse effect.

"I've heard of Happy Camper RV Center," Nikki responded. "Their sales center is on the east end of Kismet. Some of their campers look like mini houses. One of my servers has a pop-up tent camper she bought there."

"Bronson Chronister's dad built up that business," Rowena told them. "He once had a little store downtown where he sold camping equipment. That developed into the enterprise existing today. Bronson runs it now. When he lost his dad a few years ago, he took it over with nary a glitch. And he's rich enough to have bought one of those fancy one-of-a-kind houses in Reservoir Heights. Drew was using Bronson's kitchen for his catering business."

"Bronson isn't married?" Caprice asked.

"No. He's one of those bachelors like you see on TV. He has everything he wants. He travels a good bit. Just hasn't settled down, I guess."

"I thought maybe Drew was renting kitchen space somewhere," Nikki mused, looking thoughtful.

"Oh, no. He didn't have to. When Drew decided to open his own business, Bronson was right there for him. The three of them were always like the Three Musketeers."

"What does Larry Penya do?" Caprice asked.

"That's another story," Rowena acknowledged. "He came from the wrong side of the tracks. His father left when he was a boy, and his mom always struggled to make ends meet. In high school, Larry had a job bagging at the local grocery store so he could help her out. Unfortunately he's still struggling. He was an electrician and worked for one of the contractors in town for years. But then with the economic downturn, he was let go. He opened a handyman business that Drew said was taking off, but I'm not sure Larry has the business sense to make it work. He's married, with a little boy who's around four, I think. But Drew had mentioned that Larry and his wife, Linda, separated. Such a shame for their child."

When Rowena picked up her coffee mug again,

the trembling in her hand was evident, and she set it down quickly. Then she ran her hand across her brow as if she might have a headache.

Caprice caught Nikki's eye and nodded to the door. Rowena was still processing everything that had happened. She looked as if she hadn't had much sleep, and Caprice guessed that the insomnia might go on for a while. Murder and the grief and shock surrounding it could steal sleep as well as peace and happiness.

"We don't want to take up any more of your time. You really should rest," Caprice suggested.

"I don't think I got a wink of sleep last night," Rowena admitted. "Maybe a nap would help me cope with everything a little better. I have to speak with the funeral director tomorrow, but I don't know what I'm going to tell him. I don't know when the police are going to let me plan the funeral."

"The detectives will notify you as soon as they can," Caprice assured her.

"After an autopsy," Rowena murmured.

Yes, the body would be released after the autopsy, though the cause of death seemed pretty obvious. But there *was* evidence that could be gathered from the body.

Nikki rose now too and came to stand by Rowena. "We just wanted to tell you again how very sorry we are. Drew and I . . ." Nikki stumbled. "We weren't on the best of terms, but I just want you to know, I didn't wish him any harm."

Rowena patted Nikki's hand. "My dear, I never suspected that you did. A few months ago when Drew was working with you, he seemed happier than I've seen him for a long time. He was in a foul mood when you told him you didn't want him for a partner. In fact, he was all grouchy and grumpy until this barbecue sauce deal came through. I just wish . . ." She stopped and shook her head. "I wish a lot of things," she said with a sigh. "I just can't imagine why someone would have done this to him."

Caprice couldn't imagine why someone would do it either, but someone *did* have a motive. Could she figure out who that person was, and what kind of motive would drive them to murder?

Nikki had no sooner closed the door of Caprice's van when she asked, "Does anyone really know anyone else?"

Caprice glanced at her. Although her hand was on the ignition, she didn't turn the key. "Do you think everyone has a secret life?"

"No, but we skate on the surface of one another's lives. Do you know what I mean? I never suspected everything in Drew's background. Just imagine losing your parents at an early age and not being able to adjust."

"Are you thinking more kindly about him?"

"Not really. I just wonder if I'd known all this whether I would have treated him differently, maybe a little more gently."

After a few moments' hesitation, Caprice suggested, "You mean you wouldn't have kneed him where it hurt when he assaulted you?"

"He didn't—"

"Think about it, Nikki. Think about what he did and how you reacted. Would you have kneed him if it wasn't assault?"

"You want me to put it in plain terms and it's not that easy. I might have given him signals that I wanted him to come on to me."

"And he didn't know when to stop."

After a brief silence, Nikki admitted, "He didn't know when to stop."

"That has nothing to do with knowing him or not knowing him."

"Are you going to try to figure out who murdered him?"

"Yes."

"But we didn't even really like him," Nikki protested.

"Liking Drew or not isn't part of this, Nik. Drew nudged close to you at the expo. I saw you push him away. What if your DNA or hair or something transferred onto him? He was wearing the same clothes he had on at the expo when he was killed."

"Oh my gosh! I never thought of that. How could you notice something like that, with the blood and the smell—"

"Because I've witnessed murder scenes before. Taking in details wasn't even a conscious choice. You have to protect yourself. We have to protect you, and there's only one way to do that. Talk to Vince about how to do it, but you've got to tell Detective Carstead about that encounter at the expo. He might find your DNA. Be up front about it, and in the meantime I'll look for motives."

She just hoped she'd find that someone else had a motive other than Nikki.

After Nikki pulled away in her work van, Caprice crossed the street and climbed the steps to Dulcina's house. Lady barked before she even rang the bell, and she smiled. Lady had good intuition.

Dulcina opened the door with a wide smile. "She knew it was you. I think she knows the sound of your van. Her tail started wagging when she heard it. Can I interest you in some butter rum coffee? New flavor."

"You can always interest me in coffee."

Caprice followed Dulcina through her living room decorated in gray and blue to her pristine kitchen that was blue and white. Caprice liked the white counters, but if she was cooking on and around them, they probably wouldn't stay white. She'd admit she was a messy cook.

"You still didn't get one of these brewers?" Dulcina asked as she placed a pod in the coffeemaker.

"No, I didn't buy one yet, though I'm thinking about it. It would be nice to make one cup of coffee like that when I'm on the run. I could just keep the other coffeemaker in the closet for when family and friends come."

Dulcina quickly brewed two cups, set the mugs on the table, and pulled sugar from the cupboard and milk from the refrigerator. After they were seated, Lady by their chairs chomping on a treat Dulcina had given her, Caprice's neighbor said, "I need to ask you something."

"Sure. What is it?"

"Since I've been dating Rod the past six months, I feel as if my life is . . . more fulfilling."

"That's a good thing."

"Yes, I suppose so. But my problem is . . . his girls. The older one especially. Janet really did a number on him, and he hasn't dated much. So Leslie and

Vanna aren't used to having women in their dad's life. I felt their resentment from the first moment they met me, and I don't know what to do about it. Leslie is becoming almost belligerent, and I'm having a tough time getting to know her. I don't know what to do."

After Caprice thought about Dulcina's situation for a moment, she asked, "Are his daughters into music?"

"I see them wearing their earbuds a lot, so I suppose they might be."

"I have an idea. It concerns Ace Richland. Do you think his music would be appropriate for them?"

"I don't see why not. He does pop rock, right?"

"Yep, his new stuff's in line with his old hits."

Last fall, Caprice had staged an estate to sell in a Wild Kingdom theme. Ace Richland, an eighties pop star legend, had decided he needed a haven on the East Coast, not so far from his daughter. He'd bought the estate Caprice had staged and they'd become friends. They'd become even closer friends in March when his girlfriend had been murdered. Caprice had helped find the killer and gotten Ace off the hook.

"He's doing his comeback tour. He started on the West Coast, but he's returning east in a couple of weeks for a concert at the Giant Center in Hershey. What if I can get you, Rod, and the girls tickets and VIP passes? Do you think they'd be impressed meeting somebody like Ace?"

"That's a wonderful idea." Her neighbor rose from her chair and came over to hug her. "I'll be forever grateful. When do you think we'll know if you can get tickets?"

Caprice took out her phone. "Let's see if I can find out. Ace might still be at his hotel."

She pressed speed dial for the rock star's number. Ace, who was once Al Rizzo from Scranton, Pennsylvania, had a family background similar to hers, and they'd connected for that reason. He could have a short fuse sometimes, but he was a great guy.

He answered on the second ring. "Hey, there," he said. "Do you need my help staging a house?"

She laughed. "Only if you have some nautical ideas up your sleeve." Nautical Interlude was the theme on a new house-staging contract.

He chuckled. "Fresh out. Though I should have you stop by my place to see if the landscaper is doing a good job on the fire pit I'm having built out back."

"I might have to enjoy s'mores at your fire pit sometime."

"Any time. What can I do for you?"

"Do you remember my talking about my neighbor Dulcina who pet-sits for Lady sometimes?"

"Sure."

"She'd like to impress the daughters of a man she's dating. They're having a little problem . . . communicating, finding common ground."

"I certainly understand that."

Ace and his daughter, Trista, had experienced problems after his divorce. But since he'd moved to Pennsylvania, they were bonding once again now that they were seeing each other more often.

"Do you think I could get them tickets for the concert and maybe VIP passes at Hershey?"

"After the way you helped me dodge a very big bullet, I'll do anything for you. This favor is easy. How many tickets do you need?"

"Four for Dulcina."

"How about front-row seats for your friend and your family too. Tell Vince to bring Roz and you can bring Grant. How does that sound?"

"That sounds stupendous. Are you sure you can get that many?"

"I'm Ace Richland. I'll make sure the promoter puts them aside. Marsha and Trista will be there too. You can all visit me before the concert. I'll make sure everybody has VIP passes."

"Ace, you're wonderful!"

"My mom tells me that a lot."

She laughed. "Believe her."

"I'll have my agent overnight all of it to you so you'll have it in plenty of time. Sound good?"

"Sounds perfect. Do you have a show tonight?"

"I'm headed over to the theater now for a sound check."

"You'll do great."

Ace had been nervous about going out on tour again, afraid he still didn't have "it." But the first few venues had proven he certainly did.

"From your mouth to the audience's ears. Give Lady an ear rub for me."

"I will. Thank you."

"Front-row seats and VIP passes. Rod and his daughters will get first-class treatment," Caprice told Dulcina after she ended the call.

Dulcina gave Caprice another hug. "If that doesn't work, I don't know what will."

Caprice knew teens and preteens weren't always

easy to impress. But kids liked excitement. Caprice hoped that they'd have a great evening and see Dulcina in a different light. They might respect her for knowing Ace and sharing his spotlight. Or maybe they'd finally see her as a kind woman who wanted to get to know them better.

The following morning, Caprice needed to visit Isaac Hobbs's shop, Older and Better, to select rustic pieces to make her Nautical Interlude theme work. The house was a bit unusual. She wouldn't be planning a catered open house right away for this one. The owners decided to forgo that expense and just let the uniqueness of the property stand on its own.

Older and Better was located on the outskirts of Kismet. When Caprice entered the store, she felt as if she were in a time capsule, stepping back decades earlier.

. . . Until she heard static and chatter from a police scanner that Isaac kept under the counter. As she approached him, she saw him stoop to turn down the sound.

Lady was always good in the shop, and she made a beeline for Isaac. A fast-food biscuit concoction layered with eggs, bacon, and cheese sat on the counter in front of him. Even though Lady had just eaten her own breakfast, the aroma drew her.

"Uh-oh," Isaac said. "I'm going to have to share my biscuit."

"Lady just had breakfast. Don't give her more than a bite."

Isaac leaned down to Lady. "I'll give you two bites."

"While you two are conspiring, I'm going to look around."

"What house this time?"

"It's near Reservoir Heights but not in it. It's the house that looks as if it has a lighthouse on one side. Nautical Interlude is the theme."

"How far into it are you?"

"The owners moved back to Maine last month. The husband descends from a family of lobstermen and wanted to settle back there. So I have an empty house and rental furniture to work with. I need primitive pieces."

She gravitated toward a highboy with distressed wood, probably walnut or chestnut. "I'd like to use this, but I don't want to buy it."

"It's probably cheaper to buy it than rent it for a couple of months or longer. Then you'll have it."

"My storage sheds are full. I was thinking about renting another one."

"You have back-to-back clients, and you signed a contract to decorate those model homes again. Go for it. You can always empty out the storage units and drop them."

"You just want me to buy more stuff here and put it there."

Isaac laughed and wiped biscuit crumbs from the corner of his lip with a napkin. "You know me too well." He waved at the side of the shop by a window. "Check out those lamps and shelves."

Caprice went to the wall in question and spotted a primitive shelf where three old hurricane lamps sat. They would be perfect.

"Okay, sold on the shelf and the hurricane lamps."

As she wandered about, Isaac said, "I heard about the Pierson murder. The scanner was all abuzz that night. He was the one who tried out for Nikki's partner, wasn't he?"

"Yes, he was. And Nikki and I found the body."

Isaac just stared at her. Finally, he shook his head. "Caprice, I don't want to say you have a black cloud hanging over your head, but bodies seem to crop up wherever you go."

"Don't exaggerate. At least this didn't concern one of my house stagings." That had happened four times before!

"So are you trying to solve this one too?"

"I am, for Nikki's sake. She and Drew were at odds, and the police could think she has a motive . . . and no alibi."

"Would they be right?"

"Nikki didn't do it, if that's what you mean."

"I know she wouldn't do it. She's your sister. All of you De Lucas have honesty and integrity in your blood. But can the police pin a motive on her?"

"Yes, they can. Drew was taking clients away from her, and her business was suffering. He even threatened in public to kill her business."

Isaac shook his head again. "How can I help?"

"Tiffany lamps are involved. To be specific, Rowena Pierson's Tiffany lamps. She said you appraised them. Do you remember what they're worth?"

Isaac finished his biscuit, crumpled up the paper, tossed it into the fast-food bag, and stashed it in a trash can under the counter. "A friend from New York who's been in the auction business over forty years actually came down here to appraise them. The floral lamps bring the highest prices, and that's what Rowena has. My memory isn't what it used to be, but I do recall the two lamps together were worth well over a half-million dollars. I probably still have the info on them. That appraisal's probably in a box in the storage shed. I can get back to you after I go through the papers."

Caprice walked up to Isaac's counter and gave him a wide smile. "I'll take the highboy."

"Tit for tat?" he asked.

"Not exactly, but we'll be doing each other a favor."

"That's what friends are for."

Caprice thought about friendships, hers and Roz's, hers and her sisters', Kiki and Rowena's, Drew's and Larry Penya's and Bronson Chronister's. Friends helped make the world go round. Who knew anyone better than longtime friends? Maybe it was time to find out if Drew's friends knew how much those Tiffany lamps were worth. She'd think about that as she swam laps at Shape Up. Maybe a little exercise would clear her thinking and help her solve a murder.

Chapter Seven

If Caprice could take Lady with her, she would.
But of course, she couldn't. Not to Shape Up,
Kismet's popular gym. Caprice didn't like exercise.
Oh, she walked Lady. But as far as machines and
jogging, she didn't particularly like to sweat. That's
why swimming suited her. She knew the best time
to hit the pool was when the fitness center wasn't
too busy. There always seemed to be a lull between
eleven and noon. Today, as soon as she walked in
the locker room, she ran into Marianne Brisbane,
who probably had the same idea she did. Marianne
was a reporter for the *Kismet Crier* and had helped
Caprice on a couple of cases.

Now Marianne greeted her with, "I like getting
wet better in the summer than in the winter, don't
you?"

Caprice laughed. "At least I don't have to dry my
hair in the summer. Are we going to race?"

"Maybe for the first five laps, but then I just need
to work out all the muscles that cramped up sitting

at my desk. Actually, I was going to give you a call today."

"You were?" She wasn't exactly sure what was on Marianne's mind, but she could guess. Marianne had sources and contacts who kept her up-to-date on the most recent developments in Kismet. Murder was a recent development.

"Video footage crossed my desk yesterday," Marianne said.

"What video footage?"

"I have a contact at the police station who phoned me that someone had put video on their social media page about Drew Pierson's murder."

"Witnesses?" Caprice's heart started thumping.

"No, not in the way you mean. You and your sister Nikki were on the video."

"You're kidding."

"Nope. It was cell phone footage captured by a bystander. When Detective Jones found out about it, he made the guy take it down. But you and Nikki were standing outside the house. The footage showed a patrolman leading you one way and Nikki another. Split up for questioning, I would guess. Did you find the body?"

"Nikki did, but I was right behind her. I went in to see if there was anything we could do, and she called nine-one-one. So, this video is no longer spreading around the fact that we were there?"

"Nope. The police handled it. I went over it with a fine-toothed comb but couldn't find anything important. It didn't start until the police were already on the scene. Are you going to try to investigate this one?"

"I might have to. The detectives will be looking at Nikki, and I want her in the clear."

"If I had a sister, I'd want her in the clear too. If there's anything I can do, let me know."

Taking a stab in the dark, Caprice asked, "Do you know Jeanie Boswell, Drew's sister?"

"Can't say I do."

"How about Larry Penya or Bronson Chronister? They were friends of Drew's."

"Bronson Chronister. I've been hearing that name batted about lately. He's become influential in Kismet. He's good-looking, has family money and business sense. I think he'll be the next Chamber of Commerce president."

Caprice turned to the lockers, opened one with a key she'd picked up at the desk, and plopped her duffel bag on the bench. "Drew's grandmother is the only one who's given me any information. I don't want to push and prod her right now. She has enough to deal with. But I need to learn more about Drew's background, even his younger years."

"I graduated a year before your sister Nikki. I think Drew graduated the year after you did, didn't he?"

"I really hadn't thought much about that," Caprice answered. "But that would be easy to find out. The library has old yearbooks."

Marianne closed her locker door. "There's somebody working out in the gym you might want to talk to if you want to know about Drew's teenage years."

"Who?" Caprice really hadn't paid any attention to the members who were working out when she'd entered Shape Up.

"Louis Fairchild was on the treadmill when I

came in. He was the shop teacher when we were in high school, wasn't he?"

Caprice thought about it. She remembered the shop teacher with his red hair, freckles, and friendly green eyes. He'd been well liked. She hadn't crossed his path in years.

"He left teaching, didn't he?" she asked Marianne.

"He did. Rumor had it he wanted to make more money doing something else. He crafted the most beautiful furniture. I think he opened a store for a while. But he ended up as an insurance salesman. I don't know if learning what Drew was like in his classes would help, but he might be a good source."

Caprice glanced toward the door that led to the pool entrance, then back to the door that led out to the gym. "I'll catch up with you in a few minutes. I'm going to see if I can talk to him, if he's still here."

Louis Fairchild was in the gym area. His red hair was almost all gray now, but he still had freckles. He'd beefed up a bit since she'd known him. That's what working out would do. He was wearing black sweatpants and a white T-shirt. His jowls were a bit more saggy than she remembered, and he didn't seem quite as tall. But she knew that was an illusion. She'd been a kid when she'd walked the halls of the high school. Back then, adults had just seemed taller, she supposed.

When she approached him, he held up a finger. "One more minute, then you can have it." Sweat beaded his brow, and he had a towel slung around his neck.

She didn't try to explain she didn't want the machine. She just waited.

When he completed his time, he turned down the treadmill, took a few deep breaths as it slowed, then stepped off the machine. "It's all yours."

"Do you remember me?" she asked, knowing he probably wouldn't. Fifteen years was a long time. He studied her for a few moments, from her straight brown hair to her jeweled flip-flops.

"Your picture was in the paper." Then recognition dawned on his face and he snapped his fingers. "Caprice De Luca, isn't it?"

"Right. I went to Kismet High when you taught there."

He smiled at her. "That was a lifetime ago."

"I was wondering if I could talk to you for a few minutes about Drew Pierson."

A somber look stole over his face. "Drew. I can't believe what happened to him."

"I know. He wasn't in my class, but my sister knew him."

"Then or now?" Louis Fairchild asked, curious.

"Now." Caprice motioned to a quiet corner of the gym. "Can we go over there?"

"Sure, but I don't quite understand why you want to talk to me."

"Nikki and I found Drew."

He frowned. "I'm so sorry. That must have been a terrible experience."

"It was. And what makes it worse is that the police are questioning my sister. She and Drew had rival businesses."

"What kind of businesses?" Fairchild asked.

"They're both chefs. Drew opened a catering

company in competition with Nikki's. So I'm guessing she's on the detectives' persons-of-interest list."

"I'm sorry to hear that."

"I'm looking into Drew's background. I know he was still friends with his high school buddies, Larry Penya and Bronson Chronister."

"Those three were fast friends, and they could be hellions."

"Drew's grandmother hinted at as much. Can you tell me about them?"

"There's not much to say, really. They were your typical guys who didn't want to be in school. Anything and everything was more interesting. Shop interested them somewhat because I kept them busy, working with their hands."

"Did they get into trouble at school?"

"They were ordered to detention now and then, never suspension or expelled. They got caught drag racing a couple of times, but they weren't charged."

"Why not?"

Fairchild looked as if he shouldn't say, but then he shrugged. "It's really no secret. Bronson's dad knew the police chief back then. That's the way it was before Chief Powalski took over as chief of police. Money talked. One of the other teachers claimed they cheated on tests, helped each other out somehow, but no one could ever prove it. They weren't just drinking buddies. You know, beer out on top of Lookout Point on weekends. They were as thick as thieves."

She realized that was just a saying, but she knew it was true. Until thieves turned on each other.

Were Bronson and Larry really Drew's good friends

now? Or had one of them turned on him for some reason?

Fairchild glanced at the weight stations, and she knew he wanted to continue with his workout. She should get to hers. Marianne would be about ten laps ahead of her by now.

"Thank you for talking to me."

"No problem," he said with a wry smile. "That article I read about you—it said you rescue stray animals."

"They seem to find me."

"It's good work. My dog Nanook is a constant companion, a best buddy."

"What kind is he?"

"Shepherd-husky mix. I rescued him from a shelter. Good luck with looking into Drew's background. I hope you and the police can figure it out."

She hoped they could too. Wouldn't it be great if they could work together for a change? But she knew that wouldn't happen. She was a civilian. Carstead and Jones wouldn't let her near the info they collected. But if Grant kept his ear to the ground, maybe he could find out what was going on. At least, whether there was a hint that Nikki could be charged.

Caprice said good-bye to Louis Fairchild and headed for the pool. Twenty laps would clear her head enough so she'd know what step to take next.

After an early supper, Caprice was enjoying a cup of coffee and checking her list for the Nautical Interlude house staging with her pets nearby when Bella called her.

"I know Jeanie Boswell."

"What do you mean, *you know* Jeanie?"

"She prepared the flower arrangements for the school's Christmas pageant last year. I worked with her, positioning them on the stage, and hanging garlands, setting up fake candles. I think we should stop in her flower shop and have a chat with her. Posies is open until eight, and Joe said he'll watch the kids for an hour."

It was unusual for Bella to get involved in one of Caprice's murder investigations, but they were all involved now because of Nikki.

"I want to go see her. But she might not even be at the shop," Caprice mused aloud, thinking about the grief a sister would feel. "Unless she's working at Posies to keep busy. I was just trying to figure out an angle for stopping in, and I didn't want to tell Nikki, because I didn't want her to go along."

"Exactly," Bella agreed. "Nikki needs to stay out of this. The police will just look on whatever she does as suspect. I know because of what Joe went through."

When Joe was suspected of murder, his family and his life were in turmoil. Thank goodness he and Bella had gotten back on track. It had taken a lot of hard work and counseling with Father Gregory, but they were doing it.

"Does Joe want you involved in this?"

"Joe understands. We can stop in at Posies and tell Jeanie we need a bouquet of flowers for Nana. It's true. Nana would like a bouquet of flowers."

"Do you want me to pick you up?" Caprice asked her. "I have the Camaro back." The police had released it.

"You know I think riding in that is as rad as Timmy does. Sure, I'll save on gas. When can you be here?"

"I'll let Lady out and be there in twenty."

Lady wanted to go along, of course, but tonight Caprice thought it was better if she stayed home. She patted her on the head and ruffled her ears. "I'll leave treats in your kibble ball. You can entertain Mirabelle and Sophia."

Lady cocked her head and stared at Caprice with those huge brown eyes. Then she gave a little resigned "ruff" and went off to find Sophia and Mirabelle, who were taking their evening nap and were about to be bothered.

Caprice's retro fashion sense seemed to irk Bella, but she didn't let that bother her. Tonight she chose a sixties-style shift with vertical stripes in lime and fuchsia. She added white ballet flats, a white vinyl retro purse and was ready to go.

After Bella slid into the passenger side of the Camaro, she gave Caprice's outfit a once-over and shook her head. "You're an escapee from the past. Someday you'll learn how to dress up-to-date."

"I don't want to learn. I have a whole history of fashion to choose from. Isn't that more fun?"

Bella rolled her eyes. "I hate to think what you're going to wear to Ace's concert. Leather and rivets?"

"Maybe," Caprice said with a laugh. "Grant might like that. I haven't talked to him about it yet. I left a message, but we've been playing phone tag."

Bella couldn't help but break into a smile. "Yeah, he might like leather and rivets. My next-door neighbor's going to babysit, so Joe and I are all set."

"I'll have to use a pet sitter to check on Lady and the felines."

"Have you heard whether Uncle Dom has started pet sitting yet?"

"I don't know if his whole bonding and insurance process has gone through, but he started Sunday night for a friend of Mom's. He'll be at the concert too, or I'd ask him. I hope pet sitting works for him."

"I'm sure Mom and Dad hope that too," Bella said wryly. "Any guest who stays as long as he has must cramp their style."

"Their style?"

"You know, running around the house in a nightie, she and Dad going on a date night once a week and coming home to just watch a movie together. That kind of thing."

Caprice remembered when her friend Roz had stayed with her during her husband's murder investigation. Caprice had enjoyed having her there. But that was different.

In the summer, Kismet drew tourists from Gettysburg, Harrisburg, and Lancaster. They wandered in and out of the shops and helped the local economy. In spite of the increased traffic, however, Caprice found a parking space directly in front of Posies.

Twinkle lights surrounded the windows on both sides of the flower shop's door. A summery display of silk flowers was arranged attractively in one window, and hanging baskets were displayed in the other. Inside the store, refrigerated cases held fresh arrangements and vases of roses, tulips, and lilies. The rest of the store was dotted with glass shelves displaying gifts and silk flower arrangements.

Posies sold everything to do with flowers, as well as the trinkets and baubles to decorate them. One corner housed the balloon station, and several Mylar samples with printed sayings from *Get Well* to *Congratulations* to *Happy Birthday* bobbed near the ceiling.

"There she is," Bella said, elbowing Caprice.

A woman around their age sat at the counter, studying the computer monitor before her. Caprice could see photos of flowers, and she guessed the page pointed to a website for ordering.

When they'd opened the door, a buzzer had sounded. At their footsteps, Jeanie Boswell looked up. She wore her brown hair pulled back into a low ponytail. She had a round face and wide-set eyes and didn't resemble Drew at all. When she stood, she pursed her thin lips. She was wearing blue jeans and a T-shirt emblazoned with POSIES.

Her scowl almost made her look ferocious. "Your sister did it, didn't she?"

Caprice was totally taken aback. Glancing at Bella, she saw her sister's face was reddening, and Caprice knew that happened when Bella got angry.

"Why would you say such a thing?" Bella shot at Jeanie. Bella was always one to give as good as she got. She wasn't particularly a peacemaker.

Caprice, on the other hand, tried to throw a wet blanket over conflict. Now she jumped in. "Jeanie, we're sorry about Drew. So sorry. I can't imagine what it would be like to lose a brother."

At that Jeanie backed up a step, but her face didn't show any other expression. She was silent as she crossed her arms over her chest. Ignoring Caprice's condolences, she said, "I call it as I see it.

Your sister had the most to gain from Drew being taken out of the picture. With him gone, she doesn't have any competition."

After another quick look at Bella, who appeared ready to pick up one of the flower bouquets and toss it at Jeanie, Caprice decided a little bit of fire of her own might not hurt. "Don't *you* have something to gain with Drew dead? You'll be your grandmother's only heir."

Now Jeanie's face pinkened. She blurted out, "I would never—"

Caprice held up her hand as if to try to stop the whole interchange. "Let's start over," she suggested. "We didn't come here to accuse you of anything. I'm trying to figure out what happened to Drew."

"Someone bashed his skull in," Jeanie muttered.

"Nikki and I saw that firsthand. We're trying to figure out who might have had a grudge against him, or something worse. Can you tell us who he hung out with the most?"

Standing and pushing her stool under the counter, Jeanie thought about it. "Drew knew a lot of people, but his best buddies were Larry Penya and Bronson Chronister. Bronson owns that Happy Camper Recreational Vehicle Center."

It seemed everyone close to Drew knew about Larry and Bronson. "Your grandmother told us Drew was cooking and catering out of Bronson's kitchen. Do you know anything about that?"

"You should see Bronson's house," Jeanie said as if she envied the man. "Drew took me over there once. Bronson's got a state-of-the-art refrigerator. You know. The walk-in kind?"

Caprice did know, because Nikki had one.

Jeanie went on, "His kitchen is all that stainless steel and black granite, three ovens, with an island in the middle. It was perfect for Drew to work out of. And Bronson isn't there all that much. He's either working or traveling."

"That sounds like a friend helping out a friend. He didn't charge Drew rent?" Caprice asked.

Jeanie shook her head. "No, those guys are tight . . . or *were* tight. They helped each other whenever they needed it."

Again Jeanie sounded wistful, as if she wished she had friends like that.

"Did he hang out with anyone else?" Bella asked.

"There was another chef he once worked with and toured restaurants with. You know, if a new place opened up, they'd go and try it. His name is Mario Ruiz."

The name sounded familiar to Caprice, but she wasn't sure where she'd heard it.

"They worked together at a high-class hotel in D.C.," Jeanie continued. "But when the hotel cut staff, both Drew and Mario came back to Kismet. Mario works at a downtown York restaurant now, a little expensive bistro that I can't afford. He and Drew catch up when they can."

"I heard a rumor that Drew got into trouble in his teens," Caprice prompted.

"So you know about the drag racing," Jeanie commented.

Playing along, Bella said, "Just a little. Drag racing is serious trouble. You know I have a son. If he even thought about doing that, I'd lock him in his room."

Jeanie gave a wry laugh. "There was no locking Drew up anywhere. He was stubborn and wild. Just ask any of his teachers. But then he seemed to get some sense when he went to chef school. He was different when he came back. I couldn't believe it when he moved in with Gram after he left D.C."

"You couldn't believe Drew would do that, or you couldn't believe your grandmother would want him to do that?"

"I'd never seen that side of Drew before," Jeanie confessed. "Gram had broken her arm, was starting to have trouble seeing and getting around. So he said he'd help her out instead of getting a place of his own. He cooked her meals, bought groceries, drove her to doctors' appointments when he could. I think he was trying hard to do what was right because it didn't come naturally. Maybe he felt he wasn't grateful enough for all those years she took care of us. On the other hand, he didn't have to pay room and board, and he could save whatever he made. I think in the back of his mind, he nursed the idea that he wanted to open up a restaurant someday."

That was new information. Had Drew changed his mind about that? Maybe he decided to go in a different direction after the barbecue sauce recipe sale?

"You've told us about Drew's friends. Do you know if he had any enemies?" That was an important question in any investigation, Caprice knew.

Jeanie had to think about that. "I don't know of anybody specifically. But Drew could rub people the wrong way without half trying. I don't know anything about the staff he hired to help him cater."

The buzzer on the door sounded, and a couple walked inside. They migrated to the refrigerated cases.

"Be with you in a minute," Jeanie called to them. Then she asked Caprice, "Are we done?"

"For now," Caprice said gently. "We really are sorry about Drew."

"Thank you," Jeanie mumbled.

"We'd like to buy one of those bouquets of sweetheart roses in the case," Bella told her. "It's for Nana. I think the yellow one would be great."

Jeanie said, "I'll wrap it up for you."

Caprice was done asking questions for now. She really had no other choice. Jeanie had given her information to explore, even if she didn't know about specific enemies Drew might have had. Caprice remembered how nasty he'd been with Nikki. Anyone who could be that nasty had to have enemies.

She just needed to find out who they were.

Chapter Eight

"Your uncle Dom isn't here," Nana announced, as she arranged the sweetheart roses in a crystal vase.

Caprice exchanged a look with Bella and her mom. Their mom had joined them at Nana's for a glass of iced tea and girl talk.

"That's just an opening gambit so you ask where he is." Fran's smile for Nana was affectionate. Caprice knew her mom had come to look on Nana as the mother she'd lost.

Valentine jumped up on the counter to explore the flowers.

"Oh, no, you don't," Caprice said, scooping her up and setting her back on the floor. "I have a feeling you're going to have to put that arrangement someplace she can't get to it."

"That will probably be in the pantry closet," Nana teased.

"I didn't think of that when we bought them," Bella said.

"I can keep them in our living room," Fran

suggested. "You can still enjoy them there, but Valentine won't be tempted."

Nana nodded. "Good idea."

Caprice said, "I don't want to steal your thunder, but I know Uncle Dom is pet sitting. I think it's terrific."

Her mother added, "Roberta and her husband had vacation plans and airline tickets when their pet sitter cancelled. When she mentioned it to me, I told her about your uncle."

Caprice was about to say more, how her uncle was suited for the profession, when her phone played "Let It Be." Automatically, she took it from her pocket and glanced at the screen.

"It's Grant. We've been playing phone tag. Mind if I take this?"

Nana gave her a sly look. "It doesn't matter if we mind, does it?" She waved toward her small bedroom. "Why don't you go in there for some privacy."

"I won't be long," she assured them. To Bella she said, "I know you have to get back home."

"When Joe takes care of all three at once, he appreciates me more when I get home."

Caprice had to smile as she headed for Nana's bedroom, suspecting Bella was right. At one time, Joe had been a very macho and almost removed husband. He'd thought his job was to earn money and Bella's was to take care of the kids and cook. But Bella's third pregnancy had caused a crisis in their marriage. Now they were more appreciative of each other and worked as partners. It was good to see.

Valentine scampered after Caprice as she headed toward the bedroom. When Caprice sat on the mauve-and-lilac quilted spread, the kitten jumped up beside her and rubbed against her arm. She petted her soft fur as she answered Grant's call.

"Hi, there. I got your message that you were tied up in court all day."

"I'm sorry we couldn't connect last night either. My client meetings went late."

That's what one of Grant's messages had told her. She'd wondered about it, though, because late didn't seem to matter with them. They'd talked at midnight some nights. She just wanted to share her excitement about Ace's concert tickets and VIP passes that would be coming by overnight courier tomorrow.

"You sound tired," she noted.

There was a long pause, and Caprice didn't like the vibrations she was getting. She scooped Valentine onto her lap and rubbed the kitten under the chin. Valentine purred.

"About the concert, Caprice," Grant said. "I can't go. I have an appointment that day . . . that night."

That was a funny way to put it. "Can't your appointment be changed?"

"No, it can't. I was going to tell you about it as soon as we had a few quiet minutes."

She kept petting Valentine as wariness stole over her. "Why do we need a few quiet minutes?"

Again he paused as if this was something he didn't want to tell her. Her heart skipped a beat, and anxiety stole into her stomach.

"Naomi is coming to town. She'll be here for about a week to ten days, staying at the Purple Iris. I'm going to have dinner with her that night."

Rarely was Caprice speechless, but she was now.

Grant's ex-wife had moved to Oklahoma after their divorce. Why was she coming here?

"I didn't really want to talk to you about this over the phone. How about we get together tomorrow evening?"

Caprice heard Grant's dog, Patches, barking in the background.

Grant said, "Just a minute, boy, and I'll get you something to eat. He's been with my neighbor all day," Grant explained. "Simon does a great job with him, but he missed me. I need to feed him and settle him for the night."

Was that really what Grant needed to do? Or was he avoiding the conversation they were going to have. And just what would that conversation result in? Their splitting up?

As if Grant could almost read her mind, he said kindly, "Caprice, don't jump to any conclusions. Please. We'll talk about this tomorrow night."

From past experience, Caprice knew Grant compartmentalized. That's the way he'd handled losing his daughter and losing his marriage. Now she wished they'd talked about all of this over the weeks they'd been dating. Now she wished she knew exactly how he felt. But this was Grant, and she didn't want to wish him away. Maybe she didn't have anything to worry about. But that conclusion didn't ring true.

"I can cook tomorrow night," she offered. "I modified Nikki's recipe for beef bourguignon for the Crock-Pot."

"You're inventive."

Small talk wasn't either of their fortes. "When I have to be," she joked. "Is around six all right?"

"Around six is fine. I'll see you then."

After Caprice murmured "I'll see you then" and ended the call, she sat and studied her phone for a couple of seconds. She had a knot in her chest that wasn't going to go away until she and Grant talked.

And maybe not even then.

"I need your help."

Caprice had been playing fetch with Lady out in the backyard the following morning when her phone played from her pocket. She'd taken it from her jeans and heard her uncle's voice. If he needed her help—

"Is it Nana? Mom or Dad?"

"No, no, everyone's fine. But I'm still house and pet sitting. I have been for the past few days."

"How's it going?"

"It's going fine. It's like being on vacation, really. I'm calling because you've had more experience with animals than I have."

"I've had some. What's the problem?" She wondered if he was encountering a behavioral issue with the animals he was pet sitting. That wasn't uncommon when their owners were away.

"There's a stray cat that's been coming around every day. She's a tortoiseshell."

"Silver or dark?"

"Lots of silver, but gold and white and stripes too. My clients told me about her—that they'd fed her now and then. She's thin and she looks like she really needs some care. This house is out in the country and there aren't any close neighbors. So it's not like I can go checking door-to-door to see if anybody lost her. If I had a place of my own, I'd keep her."

"Have you talked to your clients about this since you've been there?"

"I called them last night. They already have two inside cats and a dog, and they don't want to take on another animal. But I told them about you, that you've taken in strays and found them homes. They said it was okay if I consulted you. What do you think?"

"Can you tell if she's feral? Does she want any human contact?"

"They haven't had contact with her. She stays at least twenty feet away until they put the food down and go inside. Then she eats. With me, it's been a little different. The first evening I saw her in the yard, I put the food down and waited. I just sat on the patio and kept really still. It took her a while, but eventually she came up and ate. I did the same thing each day. Yesterday, she came closer, maybe about three feet away. She looks like she wants contact, but she's afraid."

Caprice needed something to keep her from thinking about Grant's visit tonight. She feared he was going to tell her that they were over before they started. Instead of worrying about that all day, she might as well help her uncle.

"What time did she come around before?"

"She was here around ten yesterday morning, and then again around seven in the evening."

Caprice checked her watch. It was eight o'clock.

"I'll come out and we'll see what we can tell about her from a distance if she won't get close. Then we can talk about our options. I can be there in about half an hour. Give me the address."

A half hour later, she drove toward York, taking side roads according to her uncle's directions. She ended up on a beautiful bucolic property. Alaskan cedars that had to be at least thirty years old flanked one side of the two-story house. The rest of the property was dotted with decades-old silver maples. Pink and white petunias bordered the front gardens while a hanging basket with impatiens in a beautiful fuchsia color dangled from the front porch ceiling.

After Caprice parked, she went up to the porch and her uncle Dom was there, ready to let her inside. A chocolate Lab greeted her too.

"He's friendly," her uncle said with a hug for her. "His name's Loafer because he likes to loaf by the sofa."

"How old is he?" Caprice asked.

"About eight. They rescued him from a shelter, so they're not sure. Come on in and I'll introduce you to Mitzi and Tux. They were rescue kittens too and are brother and sister."

"I think I like your clients and I haven't even met them."

Dom laughed. "They're good people. I could tell right away. I'll give Loafer a toy with some treats in it, and we can go out on the patio and sit. How about iced coffee?"

"That sounds great." She wiggled a Ziploc bag she'd brought with her. "I brought you some of my choco chunks and chips cookies."

"Now that's a breakfast my doctor wouldn't approve of, but I'll run it off with Loafer later."

"You're going to make me feel guilty enough to go for a swim, aren't you?"

Her uncle laughed. "Come on. If we sit out here long enough, maybe our visitor will arrive."

On the patio her uncle asked, "Have you made any headway in the Drew Pierson case?"

"You make me sound like a private investigator."

"Ever think of getting a license?"

"Like I don't have enough to do. No, if I give up home staging for anything, it will be to run an animal rescue shelter. But that's not on the horizon right now."

He pulled two patio chairs close together. "So, any progress on the case? Do you have any suspects?"

Caprice sat, and waited for him to do the same. "Not yet. I do have people I want to question, though. I just have to figure out the best way to do it. Bella and I talked with Drew's sister. She told us about some of his friends, and I want to talk to them."

"Did he have many friends?" her uncle asked.

As she related what she had learned about Drew's friendships, her uncle held up his hand to stop her.

"Over there," he said. "Under the gnarled redbud. I've seen her there before. She uses it like a tent. I think that's where she takes her naps in the afternoon. She's completely shaded and surrounded by the leaves and branches that reach to the ground. She must feel safe there."

Caprice watched as the silver-haired tortie snuck under one side of the bush and the leaves jiggled. The branches swished a little, and then she came out on the other side where she could see them.

"Do you mind if I talk to her?" Caprice asked.

"Go ahead. I've mostly been just sitting here like a statue, afraid I'd scare her away."

"I might scare her, but let's see." She lowered her voice. "Hey, pretty girl. Are you hungry? We have some food for you."

Caprice had made up a dish of cat food, and now she stood and took it over to the edge of the patio. The tortie retreated under the redbud bush but didn't run off.

Caprice kept talking. "We just want to see how you are, and if you need somebody to take care of you. Do you think you'd like that?"

"Somebody else who talks to animals as if they're human. At least I don't feel so crazy," her uncle muttered.

"I'm going to let you eat, and I'm going to go back over to that chair and sit. Okay? You can come over. It will be all right."

Caprice went back over to the chair and sat down beside her uncle. She kept talking. "It's okay, baby. Come on. Get some breakfast."

After a few minutes, when the cat saw that the coast was clear around the dish, she came out from under the bush and unevenly walked toward the food. She kept her eyes on Caprice and Dom, though.

Caprice murmured to her uncle, "I think she's limping a little.

"Back right leg. I've noticed it too. It's one of the reasons I called you."

As the feline ate, Caprice took her camera from her pocket and zoomed in to examine her. The cat was thin, yet rounded a little at the belly. Bloating, or something more? Her green eyes looked clear, not at all weepy.

The tortie suddenly stopped eating, sat back, and scratched at her neck.

Caprice suspected she had fleas. She needed good nutrition and maybe a flea treatment to get healthy again.

After the cat finished eating, she sat on the corner of the patio in the sun, washing herself. She cast wary glances at Caprice and her uncle Dominic every once in a while, but seemed more relaxed than afraid.

"I'm going to try to approach her," Caprice said. "I really don't want to use a trap cage unless we have to."

Caprice approached the cat until she was about three feet away. She sat down on the patio on the same level. The tortie eyed her but didn't run. She lowered herself, facing Caprice, her paws tucked under her.

"You're not afraid of people, are you? What happened? Did you get lost?"

And so it went. Caprice spent about half an hour just sitting there, talking to the cat, letting the tortie eye her and get used to her. She knew she'd be taking a risk if she tried to pick up the animal. Cat scratches and bites were nothing to fool around with.

Suddenly the cat stood, looked around, finished a few scraps on the dish, and then went to the bush and hid underneath.

Caprice picked up the dish, stood, and turned toward her uncle. "If you lived here and we had all the time in the world, I think we could gain her trust."

"I only have two days left here," her uncle said.

"All right. Then we'll use the Havahart trap. I'll bring it out here tomorrow and put tuna inside. Once she walks in, she'll trip a mechanism and the door will shut. I'll call Marcus and see if I can get an appointment. He'll understand if this doesn't work out and we have to cancel."

"Then what will you do with her? Not take her to some shelter—"

"Of course not. I'll try to find her a home. I *will* find her a home. It might take a little time, but she can stay in my garage until I find someone who will take her."

"I'm glad I called you," Uncle Dom said with a grin.

"I'm glad you did too. I'll come back tomorrow around the same time and we'll see what we can do."

After her visit with her uncle and his new feline friend, Caprice drove to the storage locker center. She punched in her passcode, and the gate slid open. She drove to the row where her units were located.

As she usually did, she parked to the side so another car could pass. After she climbed out of her van, she found her key ring and chose the small key for her padlock. She unlocked the first of her three storage units.

Grasping the door handle, she lifted the door and it rumbled up.

Her compartments were ten feet deep and fifteen feet wide. Although they were stacked with staging items—rolled rugs, lamps, and tables—she could reach everything. Labeled boxes lined the sides of the units, and she kept a path open to walk through.

As she sorted through items, she tried to keep her mind distracted from thoughts about seeing Grant later. Not that she didn't want to see him. She just wasn't sure she wanted to hear what he had to say.

Taking a clipboard from a side table, she checked her inventory list for the unit. Crossing to the rear, she pulled a box of old bottles from the top of the stack. She remembered there were several cobalt blue ones in there. They'd look perfect on the primitive shelf she'd purchased from Isaac.

She found another carton she was looking for in the second storage shed. It was tucked along the side on the bottom of a stack. She lifted off the top two cartons and then opened the flaps on the bottom one. There was a fishing net. She'd picked that up at Colonial Days in East Berlin, she remembered. It would be perfect draped on a wall in the octagonal room of the house.

She was checking her list again for other possibilities when her cell phone played. She thought about letting it go to voice mail, but her curiosity usually won out. Vince's face stared up at her and she answered.

"Hi. What's up?" she asked. It was unusual for him to call her during the day.

"I wanted to let you know that the police cleared the crime scene, so Rowena should be back in her house. Not that you should go talk to her or anything."

"Did you let Nikki know?"

"No, I did not. She needs to stay away from this, Caprice. Don't argue with me on that point."

She wouldn't, because she knew Vince was right. "Rowena won't want to go back there if the place needs to be cleaned up."

"From what I understand, that was supposed to happen yesterday. Rowena asked the detectives for a recommendation for a cleaning service that specializes in this kind of cleanup. They gave her one."

"How do you know all this? I'm sure Detective Jones didn't tell you."

"I have my sources."

"Like someone you used to date who still works at the police department?"

"Maybe," he drawled. "At least my romantic past is good for something."

"You mean other than experience?"

He chuckled. "What are your plans for today?"

"I'm at my storage units collecting a few items, but then I'm going home and taking Lady to visit Dulcina while I work at the house I'm staging. I just came from the house where Uncle Dom is pet sitting. Tomorrow we're going to catch a stray cat."

"What are you going to do with another cat?"

"Take her to Marcus. But then I'll help find her a good home."

"Pretty soon you're going to run out of people in Kismet who want animals," Vince said wryly.

"Then I guess I'll have to expand my reach, won't I."

"I'd expect nothing less from you."

Of course, Grant was still on Caprice's mind, and since Vince worked with him . . . "Has Grant talked to you about anything unusual happening?"

"You're going to have to give me a more specific hint than that. He still works mainly from home. You know that. He drops in here only when he needs something, or meets a client here instead of there."

"You do talk, though, right?"

"Guy talk and girl talk are two different entities. What do you want to know?"

"Did you know his ex-wife is coming to town?"

Her question was met with silence. Then Vince whistled low. "No, I didn't know that."

"He hasn't said anything to you about it?"

"Caprice, this is *Grant* we're talking about. He doesn't talk about his personal life, not even with me. He told you about it?"

She explained about Ace's concert and how that was the night that Grant was having dinner with Naomi.

"So he won't be coming along to the concert, huh?"

"I'm not as upset about that as I am about the whole idea of his seeing her again. What if—"

"Caprice, just stop. You said you're seeing him tonight?"

"Yes, he thinks we should talk about it in person. I'm afraid he's going to say we should stop dating."

"It's not like you to be a doomsday proponent. Talk to Grant. Then worry if you have to."

Her brother's advice was good. She just didn't know if she could take it.

A half hour later, she was back at home rounding up Lady and then taking her to Dulcina's.

"Thanks so much for watching her for me today," she told Dulcina as Lady ran inside her neighbor's house. "After leaving her alone earlier, I didn't want her to be alone the rest of the day. I was at the property where my uncle is pet sitting. A stray has been visiting, and we're going to try to catch her tomorrow."

Dulcina was already kneeling on the floor, rubbing Lady's belly. "You know I've thought about adopting a pet."

"I know you have."

"I just wasn't sure about the timing, with dating Rod and all."

"Were his girls excited about the concert tickets?"

"Not as excited as I'd like them to be. They didn't even know who Ace was. Rod and I showed them photos on the computer and told them about his tour. His younger daughter seems more excited than his older daughter. I don't know, Caprice, I'm not sure this is going to work out."

"But you don't know that it isn't either," Caprice interjected hopefully.

"No, I don't know that it isn't. But I do know one thing for certain. I can't live my life waiting around. I can't live my life for him and his daughters when I'm not even really included in his life yet. Do you know what I mean?"

Caprice knew exactly what she meant. "You have to live your life just in case Rod isn't the one for you."

"Exactly. And you know, I think I'd like a cat. It just seems like serendipity that you're going to catch one."

"Maybe. Sometimes they can outsmart the cage."

"How old do you think the cat is?"

"I'd say between two and five. It's hard to tell. She's a tortoiseshell."

"I don't care what color or breed," Dulcina responded.

"This cat could need a lot of care and attention,"

Caprice warned. "She's malnourished. I can tell that just from looking at her. She doesn't seem frightened of us, but I'm not sure she wants close contact with us either. Would you be ready to take on a pet like that?"

"Dating Rod and being around his daughters, I realize I need to nurture. I'm a patient person. I think I could help an animal like you're talking about."

"She could be out on her own for a reason."

"You mean FIV?"

"So you know about that?"

"I do. And I say let's cross one hurdle at a time. You said you have a vet appointment for her?" Dulcina asked.

"I do. That's if all goes well."

"If she has FIV, I could still take care of her, right? Especially if she's not showing symptoms."

"It would be best for you to talk to Marcus about that if it happens."

"Text me if you capture her. Text me from Dr. Reed's, then I'll decide what to do. Fair enough?"

"Very fair."

Just what were the chances that everything would go as planned? What were the chances that she could capture a cat? What were the chances the cat would be healthy?

What were the chances that she and Grant would still be dating when the night was over?

Chapter Nine

That evening Caprice was out back playing with Lady when Grant and Patches arrived. She'd needed to do something to burn off excess energy and excess worry.

He came into the yard from the back gate, and he'd never looked so good. He was wearing blue jeans that fit just right and a chambray shirt with the sleeves rolled up. His black hair was a bit mussed from the breeze.

Grant bent and unleashed Patches. The dog ran to Lady and they began rooting through the shrubs together. As Grant approached her, he gave her an unsure smile. She couldn't quite find a smile to give him back.

He asked, "Do you want to toss balls for them, or do you want to go up to the porch and talk?"

"Is this going to be a long conversation or a short one?" she returned, in a way just wanting to get the conversation over with. Would Grant even stay for dinner?

"It's whatever we decide it's going to be." He simply motioned to the glider on her back porch.

Lady and Patches came running when they moved to the porch. Both dogs followed them, took a few slurps from the water bowl there, then settled at their feet as they sat together on the glider, though not quite close enough to touch.

"How was your day?" he asked. It seemed he wasn't eager to jump into their conversation.

"Dulcina might take in a stray I'm going to help Uncle Dom catch."

"Your uncle Dom likes pet sitting?"

"He seems to."

Caprice had already had enough of this surface chitchat. She slanted toward him, bringing her leg up onto the glider. "Talk to me about what you're going to do."

He looked nonplused for a few seconds. "I'm not going to *do* anything. You have to trust me, Caprice."

Her dad was the only man she truly trusted. Well, okay, maybe she trusted Vince too. But as far as her romantic life? She'd trusted men and they'd hurt her. Her first love had been in high school. Craig had gone to California after graduation and had eventually sent her a "Dear Caprice" letter, breaking off their relationship once he was established in college. Okay, so long distance didn't work. If she had truly learned that lesson, she and Seth Randolph would have gone their separate ways when he'd taken the fellowship in Baltimore to pursue a career in trauma medicine. But she'd been infatuated with the handsome doctor and had let that linger a little too long. A few years ago, she'd fallen in love with a man with a daughter. Travis had seemed ready to move on, but then he and his ex-wife had reunited. That reunion made her doubly wary of Grant's situation.

He took her hand as if he could read the thoughts running through her head. "I know you've been hurt before. I don't intend to hurt you. But this is something I have to do. Naomi and I have never had closure. She's coming to town the weekend of Ace's concert. We're going to have dinner and talk. Maybe more than once. She's going to sightsee while she's here, driving down to the Inner Harbor, possibly the Smithsonian and the art gallery in D.C., touring Gettysburg for sure."

"Are you going to sightsee with her?"

"I can't tell you what I'm going to do because I'm not sure yet. I'm leaving my schedule open for the week, and Simon assures me he'll watch Patches if I'm away for an afternoon or an evening."

"You've covered the bases."

"You're upset."

Truthfully, she said, "I think you're putting our relationship in jeopardy. I thought you'd moved beyond the shadows in your past."

"That's what I'm trying to do, Caprice. Honestly I am."

Patches's nose went into the air. He rose to his paws and Lady did the same. Patches jumped down the steps and Lady gave Caprice a look that asked, *Can I go too?*

Caprice nodded and waved her hand for Lady to follow her friend. The two dogs romping across the yard now, headed toward a flower bed. Maybe they'd seen a squirrel. She watched them instead of looking at Grant. She couldn't gaze at him without her heart breaking. She didn't have a good feeling about this, whether it was gut instinct or only her own anxieties and insecurities. The thought of him seeing Naomi again just didn't feel right.

Grant gently nudged her chin around until she faced him. "Are you telling me you can't trust me?"

"I don't know," she confessed. "It's hard. I feel like it's déjà vu. I've been in this situation before. I know how it ends up."

He shook his head. "You're putting a wall up between us."

Maybe she was, but it was in self-defense. "If anything happens, will you tell me right away?"

He scowled and looked almost angry now. "*Nothing* is going to happen."

She wasn't thinking about sex as much as Naomi and Grant resurrecting the bond they once had. "Just promise me you'll tell me right away if your feelings toward me change."

The truth was, he'd never declared his feelings toward her, but she'd felt them whenever they were together and whenever they kissed.

"I'm not going to give you a blow-by-blow, hour-by-hour. Sometimes trust isn't a feeling, it's a decision you have to make."

Was he right?

"Do you want me to stay or go?" he asked.

"If you stay, we won't resolve anything, not until after this is all over."

He studied her for a long few moments, then he rose to his feet and picked up Patches's leash that he'd laid over the side of the glider.

"Don't be incommunicado," he told her. "I know you're going to be involved in Drew Pierson's murder investigation. If something happens, if you're in danger, if you're unsure, call me."

She couldn't promise that she would. Grant had saved her life once and she was indebted to him for that. But he wasn't a knight on a white charger. He was a real man and she was a real woman—a strong woman. She could take care of herself and solve her own problems.

When she didn't tell him she'd call, he accused, "You're stubborn."

"No more stubborn than you," she responded.

After a long, last look straight into her eyes, he called to Patches. His cocker came running to him and they left the way they'd come in, the gate closing behind them.

Caprice sank down onto the glider and Lady came running to her and looked up at her as if sensing something was wrong.

Something was wrong, all right. As far as Grant was concerned, she didn't know exactly how strong she was. But she was going to find out.

The late-June day was rife with sunshine as Caprice and her uncle set up the Havahart trap the next morning. Instead of putting it out on the patio, they decided to place it near the redbud where the tortoiseshell usually took haven. The leaves from the bush partially covered it there, so it would be some camouflage. Caprice hoped the cat would be hungry enough not to notice what she was walking into. Uncle Dom had already exercised his client's dog until they were both tired out. The animals inside would not be a problem if she and her uncle were occupied outside.

Caprice forked tuna onto a dish inside the carrier. Then she and her uncle crossed to the other side of the patio to wait. They sat, not knowing how long this would take.

"With the warmer temperature, we can't leave the tuna inside the cage too long. If she doesn't come within a half hour or so, I'll have to change it and put a new dish in."

Food spoilage could always be a problem with outside cats. People thought they could just put the food out and let it sit forever. But it broke down, grew bacteria, and could make an animal sick.

As she and her uncle sat there in the almost eighty-degree heat, Uncle Dom took a sheet of paper from his pocket and unfolded it.

"This is a form I made up to keep notes for my clients. What do you think?"

Caprice took the page and studied it. Her uncle had drawn blocks on the left for each visit—the time he came and left—and then another space blocked off to the right of that, where he could make notes. He'd documented what he'd done this morning and had details about yesterday. He mentioned how much the dog and cats had eaten, how far he and Loafer had gone for their walk, and how eagerly the cats had played with their toy mice.

"While I'm house sitting like this, I'll write in notes every few hours. For other clients, I'll just fill in a block for each visit."

"Other clients?" Caprice asked.

"I'm going to be walking two dogs next week and

one day checking in on a cat when her owner has a medical procedure. Your mom has been great about spreading the word. And since the pet sitter I interviewed already has too many clients, she recommended me to someone who called her. Most people are just so grateful to have someone take care of their pet, they don't care if I'm bonded and insured. I'm still going to go through with all that. It's safer for me and for them. It will definitely be necessary if I want to take on anyone to help me with this."

"You're thinking about expanding?" Caprice asked with a grin.

Her uncle looked a bit sheepish. "I know it's early days yet, but I can dream, can't I?"

"Of course you can. I'm sure you can turn this into a thriving business. What are you calling yourself? I mean, the name of your business."

"I'm going to keep it simple and just call it Pampered Pets. After I'm finished here, day after tomorrow, I have a few apartments to check out. I just need a one bedroom. I don't want anything fancy. Even a studio apartment would do. The first place is going to be low budget and temporary. Once I'm on my feet, I'll find someplace a little nicer, someplace with a yard so if I want a dog, it would be a good location."

"I'll be on the lookout for you. Are you still going to be doing bookwork for small businesses?"

"Oh yes. That will fill in the rest of my time, at least until the pet sitting really takes off."

"You know this is going to be seven days a week, holidays too."

He raised his hands in surrender. "What else do

I have, Caprice? Really. This will keep me busy so I stay out of trouble."

They had kept their voices low, and both scanned the area across the yard and anywhere around the redbud. Her uncle nudged her elbow. "There she is, over by the pampas grass. She takes cover there too. Do you think we made a mistake not putting the food on the patio?"

"Too late now. If we go rustling around we'll scare her off. Let's see what happens."

The cat slowly walked down the grassy incline and canvassed the area outside the patio doors. When she walked, Caprice detected that limp again—her back right leg. The stray stopped a few feet from the pampas grass, washed her front paw, and then continued on, maybe looking for a shady spot. She headed for the redbud and raised her nose into the air as if she was sensing something good. Then she saw the dish of tuna.

"In the sun, she looks as if she has a halo on her head," Caprice whispered. This tortoiseshell had a lot of gold in her, and there seemed to be a circle of it on the top of her head. "Halo could be the perfect name for her."

The straw Caprice had laid in the forefront of the cage hid the metal. The cat must have been hungry, because she walked straight in, and when she did the door came down.

Caprice moved immediately and her uncle followed her. The cat was already meowing and circling inside the cage, looking for the way out.

"Do you have the burlap?" Caprice asked her uncle.

He went to the patio, picked it up from a spare lawn chair, and brought it over. With the cat meowing loudly, they laid it over the top of the cage, hoping that would help calm her.

"I wish I could go with you," he said. "Are you sure you can handle this?"

"Sure I can. I've done this before. It's not a pleasant ride over to Furry Friends, but we'll survive."

"I'll carry her to the van for you."

As Caprice suspected, the trip to the vet wasn't pleasant. In fact, it was even more unpleasant than she expected. Apparently this cat got car sick. Caprice heard the sounds, she smelled the result, but there was nothing she could do about it while she was driving. She just kept talking to Halo, assuring her everything would be all right. But just as when you assured a sick child, the patient didn't believe her.

The receptionist at Furry Friends knew Caprice. The vet tech, Jenny, came out to the front when the receptionist buzzed her, and she and Caprice took the cat to an examination room.

"It's a mess," Caprice said. "I'll help you clean up."

Jenny disappeared for a moment into the back, returning with a second roll of paper towels. They removed the burlap, and Halo looked up at them, meowing pitifully.

Caprice said, "I don't think she sat in it, and I don't think she has any on her. She's small so there was plenty of room in the cage."

Jenny opened the cage. "Come on, pretty girl. Come on out."

Halo cowered in the cage.

"Let me try something," Jenny said. "I don't want to scare her further."

She went to the cupboard, took out a little bag,

and pulled a few treats from it. Then she laid them on the counter and stepped back.

Halo looked from one of them to the other and meowed again. But then she sniffed and she saw the treats. After another moment of hesitation, she emerged from the cage.

Jenny said, "I'll take this to the back and wash it up. It will be easier that way. Are you okay in here with her?"

"Yes, we're fine. But I hate to put her back in that to take her along with me. Do you have one of those cardboard carriers?"

"Sure. Let's see what Marcus says first."

Caprice knew what Jenny meant. If the cat was sick . . . She wasn't going to think about that right now. She took out her phone and texted Dulcina, telling her she was at the vet. Then she stood by Halo and talked to her.

"We have to get you checked out. It's not healthy or safe for you to be out there, especially since you're limping a little. We need to see what that's all about."

Halo finished the last treat and looked up at her warily. Caprice took another step closer so she was against the table. Halo came over to her and sat in front of her.

A few minutes later Marcus came in.

"I hope I didn't mess up your schedule," Caprice apologized.

"I was running a little late, but my next appointment cancelled so we're good. Let's take a look at her."

Marcus was African American, big and burly. His buzz cut was just part of his character, and he usually had a smile on his face. He was running his big hands over Halo, and she was letting him.

"She seems to be a sweetie," he said.

"Either that or resigned. She limps a little, back right leg."

After a few more minutes examining her, Marcus said, "I think the limp was caused by an injury that healed." Then he looked directly into Caprice's eyes. "You probably don't want to hear this."

"You didn't even take any tests yet."

"I will. But she's about a month pregnant."

"You can tell that just by running your hands over her?"

"And palpitating a little. In another month, somebody's going to have kittens."

This had happened to Caprice before, only it had been a dog she'd taken in, not a cat. How would Dulcina feel about taking care of a pregnant stray?

"What does that mean for her health?"

"I'll test her for FIV and feline leukemia. I can give her a flea treatment and a wormer that's safe for a pregnant cat. But I can't give her any shots until she's finished nursing. She should be separated from other cats for a couple of weeks just to make sure nothing else develops."

"I might have someone who's willing to take her."

"Of course you do. If all my clients did what you do, I wouldn't have any strays to worry about."

"How old is she?"

"She's older than she looks. She has a couple of teeth missing, and some decay. I'd say she's between three and five. I also think her back leg might have been broken, but it's healed now. This little gal could have gotten hit by a car or was in some kind of accident."

Caprice's heart went out to the cat as she patted her. "Let's do the testing," she said, trying to detach a little.

A half hour later, she breathed a huge sigh of relief. Halo's FIV and feline leukemia tests were clear. Now Caprice called Dulcina.

"How is she?" Dulcina asked, already concerned.

Caprice told her everything Marcus had found, including the pregnancy.

"I don't know anything about taking care of a pregnant cat, let alone helping one deliver."

"I helped deliver puppies," Caprice offered. "I'm sure Marcus will advise you. I found a lot of things online, especially on YouTube. I watched actual deliveries that made me feel a little more confident. Letting nature take its course is usually the best rule. But this is up to you, Dulcina. I'll keep her until I can find her another home if you don't want her."

This time Dulcina didn't hesitate. "I want her. I'll take care of her and her babies. I need to feel I'm doing something good."

"Do you have any supplies? A litter box, litter, dishes, food?"

"I bought a litter box and litter. No food because I wanted to see what you would suggest."

"I can pick up some food for you here."

"That works. Do you want me to take Lady over to your place?" Dulcina had been keeping Lady at her house while Caprice helped her uncle.

"That would be great. Marcus gave Halo a flea

treatment. Do you have someplace washable you can keep her? A bathroom, maybe?"

"I'll do better than that. I'll let her stay in my sunroom. It's air conditioned like the rest of the house, so if it gets too warm she'll still be okay. Do you think that would be a good place?"

"I think that would be great. I'm going to be running an errand later this afternoon." Caprice had already made up her mind that she was going to check on Rowena and the house and see what else she could find out. "So I can stop at Perky Paws," she went on, "and get you whatever you need."

"Do you think she'll like me?" Dulcina asked Caprice.

"She'll learn to like you," Caprice assured her. "What she's going to love most is your kindness."

Caprice smiled as she headed for Rowena's house later that day. Dulcina and Halo were settling in together. Dulcina had laid old washable rugs on the ceramic-tiled floor of the sunroom and dimmed the shades a bit on one side. Caprice had taken her a bag of catnip she'd purchased at the clinic and sprinkled a little on the rugs. After eating and drinking, Halo had settled on one of them and fallen asleep. All was well there for now.

As far as Rowena went, however . . .

As Caprice approached Rowena's house, she hoped the woman had friends other than Kiki who could help her. Would she be able to stay in that house by herself? Would Jeanie consider moving in with her? How spooky would it be to know someone was murdered in your house and you were still going to live there?

Parking in front of Rowena's home, Caprice noted that all looked quiet. But that didn't mean anything. Of course, Rowena could have returned to Kiki's.

Once at the porch, however, Caprice saw the main door was open. She stood at the screen and rang the bell.

She heard Rowena call, "Be right there."

From what Caprice could see in the living room, everything looked to be in order. The Oriental rug that had covered the floor was gone. But other than that, there didn't seem to be any sign of what had happened here.

Caprice could just glimpse the shade of the Tiffany lamp sitting on the side table. Still no base. Had the murderer taken it? Or had the police found it and collected it as evidence?

When Rowena came to the door, she peered at Caprice a few moments as if she had trouble seeing her. So Caprice said, "It's Caprice, Rowena."

"I thought it was you," she said. "No one but Kiki wants to talk to me since my grandson was murdered."

Caprice suspected that Rowena wasn't just being paranoid. A murder in a family wasn't the same thing as a death. Friends shied away from getting too close to it. She'd seen that happen with her friend Roz.

"I'm glad you have Kiki."

"So am I. Come on in. Everything's been cleaned up, at least that's what Kiki tells me. She went out to buy groceries for dinner. She's staying with me a few nights."

"That's kind of her. I'm glad you have a good friend you can count on."

"It's not like I can count on Jeanie. Sometimes I don't think that girl has any sense of family at all."

"Maybe she just doesn't know how to express what she's feeling."

Rowena nodded. "That's always been the case. Would you like to sit in the living room . . . or in the kitchen?"

Caprice couldn't help but remember Drew's body lying in the living room right next to the sofa. She took another quick look around but didn't think she'd learn anything from sitting in there.

"The kitchen would be great. My family did their best talking in the kitchen."

"Preparing meals?" Rowena asked.

"Exactly. When we were chopping or dicing or mixing, we'd reveal things we wouldn't share otherwise. Maybe that's why Mom liked to see us cook."

When Caprice stepped into the kitchen, she realized it looked like a throwback to the fifties. The maple cupboards were worn from years of being open and shut. The floor had been tiled in beige and white, and the counters were covered with green Formica. She did notice that an old stove and refrigerator must have been replaced with stainless steel ones. Had that been Drew's doing? A red teapot sat on one of the stove's burners.

Caprice offered, "Would you like me to make us cups of tea?"

Rowena sank into one of the kitchen chairs and pulled herself in at the round oak table. "That would be lovely. I miss Drew not being around here and doing . . ." Her voice broke. She composed herself. "Things like that."

Caprice patted Rowena's arm. "I'll make us that tea." After she filled the kettle with water, she said, "I guess Drew cooked for you."

"Yes, he did. He found his vocation with cooking. In recent years I didn't worry about him as much as I did before."

"Did he come up with lots of original recipes?"

"No, not really. He was always finding recipes on his computer. When he started out with something new, especially for his business, he didn't usually test the recipe here, but rather over at his friend's house."

"Bronson's."

"Yes, Bronson's. Drew described that kitchen of his to me. It didn't surprise me. Bronson's family has always been wealthy. Now he's rich too, and he enjoys nice things. It was so nice of him to let Drew use his kitchen for his business. Drew told me he couldn't have rented a place any better."

"You know, I was at the expo on Sunday. Nikki and Drew were trying to convince the wedding crowd to hire them for their receptions."

"Drew cooked for me, but he didn't tell me much about his business. But that sounds like a good place to drum it up."

"He called his chocolate walnut cake a groom's cake. At a wedding, there's often a traditional cake, considered the bride's cake that is served to the guests. But often now, a couple chooses a cake called the groom's cake."

"Really? How odd. No more just white cake. I

guess that's supposed to give everybody a choice." She was quiet a few moments, then asked, "Did Drew's cake have maple-flavored frosting?"

"Yes, it did."

Rowena looked away from Caprice into the living room toward the tall Tiffany floor lamp by the armchair. Caprice remembered the piece of paper she'd seen peeking out from its base. Had Rowena hidden her recipes in there and Drew had known that? Could someone have murdered him for the recipes?

"That certainly does sound like my cake," Rowena said in a soft voice. "I've been making chocolate walnut cake with maple icing since I was about ten. It was my father's favorite recipe, and my mom made it often. Drew enjoyed eating it. I don't remember him ever asking me about it, like what spices I put in it, what kind of maple syrup I might use for the icing."

"It's possible that Drew's palate was so well honed he could replicate your recipe just by tasting it."

Rowena shook her head. "I don't think so. He was never good at that kind of thing. I used to make these glazed carrots and he couldn't even tell I had ginger in them. No, either that recipe wasn't mine or . . ." Rowena just trailed off.

Or Drew had somehow stolen the recipe and not given his grandmother credit for it.

"In which cupboard might I find the teabags?" Caprice asked.

"Top cupboard, on the right, next to the sink. Take your pick. There's some of that herbal stuff that Drew liked."

"What would you prefer?"

"I like the plain green tea with just a little bit of sugar."

Caprice chose the green tea too, found two cups and saucers in the cupboard, and brought them over to the table. "Your china is beautiful." The teacups were painted with tiny roses, as were the saucers. The cream china looked like fine porcelain.

"They were my mother's too," Rowena explained. "Using them brings back so many memories. Drew had his morning coffee mugs, but I always prefer to use these."

"My Nana has a collection of teacups we use whenever we have tea together."

"Your Nana and I came from a time when there was pride in everything that was made, from china to the towels we used, to the beautiful linens for the table. Wash-and-wear is important now. People toss away anything damaged and buy new. Not the way I was taught, and probably not you either."

"No, that wasn't the way I was taught." She took a seat across from Rowena. "Maybe that's why I enjoy vintage clothing and antique jewelry and antiques themselves." She looked toward the living room. "Your Tiffany lamp is absolutely beautiful. And those colors in the table lampshade—Is there any word on the base?"

"No one knows what happened to it. It was here that day before I left for the performance. The police think the murderer used it to hit Drew and then ran off with it."

Because it was valuable? Or because he knew he had to get rid of it? And exactly how much value would it have without the shade?

Caprice added sugar to her tea and stirred. Rowena did the same. They both took tentative sips.

"There's something about a cup of tea that's comforting, don't you think?" Rowena asked.

"I agree."

"Kiki and I finished Celia's biscotti. They were delicious."

"I try to bake them too, but mine aren't as good as hers. Next time I visit, I'll bring you some of mine and you can compare."

"I'd like that," Rowena assured her. "I have a feeling I'm going to be lonely here all by myself. A visit now and then would be nice."

"I could bring Nana too, and we could have a real tea party."

A smile played on Rowena's lips. "That would be wonderful." She sighed. "I should probably pack everything up and move to a retirement center. But I like having memories around me. I want to stay here as long as I can."

"Nana felt the same way for a long time, but then she realized she could be happy living near my mom and dad as long as she had some of her memories around her."

"I have to have cataract surgery soon or I won't be able to see what's around me. I've been putting it off and putting it off. Jeanie says she'll take me and bring me home, and I suppose I'll have to depend on her."

"Maybe if you depend on Jeanie, she'll open up to you more."

"I can always hope." Rowena reached out and patted Caprice's hand. "You're a nice young woman. I've heard about you, you know. At church. At the beauty parlor. You've helped the police solve a few murders."

"I never intended to do that," Caprice admitted. "It just sort of happened."

"Are you going to try to figure out who killed Drew?"

"How would you feel about that?"

"Those detectives were awfully grumpy and gruff. If they're like that with everyone, they won't learn anything. Now *you*, on the other hand . . . You can get people to talk to you. I imagine that's what solves a murder."

There was merit in what Rowena said. Maybe that's why she had solved four murders.

"Can you try to find Drew's murderer?" Rowena asked.

It wasn't just for Nikki's sake anymore. It was for Rowena's too. Caprice didn't hesitate to say, "Yes, I can."

Chapter Ten

Caprice didn't think she'd slept much the past two nights. The conversation she'd had with Grant weighed heavily on her since he'd left her yard. Both of her cats had stayed close again through the night as if they'd known she needed some kind of furry comfort. While Lady snored beside her in her bed on the floor, Caprice thought of all the things she should have said to Grant. But she didn't know if any of them would have made a difference, because his mind had been made up.

The phone on her bedside table rang at seven a.m. and she was grateful for the noise. When she picked it up, she saw her mom was calling.

"Is everything okay?" Caprice asked automatically. Ever since the scare with Nana not so long ago, she worried.

"That depends," her mom answered. "Can you help out at the soup kitchen today? Nana and I are signed up, but two of the volunteers have come down with something and we're shorthanded for a Friday."

"How long do you need me?"

"We're almost through with breakfast, so we'd need your help preparing for lunch and then through service."

"Okay. I'll call Nikki. If she's planning menus or just making calls today, maybe she can watch Lady. I'll text you back in a minute."

A little over an hour later, Caprice entered Everybody's Kitchen, a community effort staffed by several different churches that provided volunteers. Caprice had helped out here on occasion but wasn't a regular like Nana and her mom—when her mom wasn't teaching . . . or babysitting Benny. The directorship of this facility was a paid position. The kitchen manager received a monthly stipend. She didn't know who was filling that spot now. It seemed to change every few months.

The soup kitchen was located in a renovated older building that had once housed a chain grocery store. Part of the edifice was dedicated to the Kismet Food Pantry, which took any and all donations, as long as the foodstuffs weren't expired. The pantry doled out food to needy families on a weekly basis, rationing according to donations.

Caprice almost never wore her hair in a ponytail. However, she did so today so she could confine it in a hairnet while she helped make and serve lunch. She detected the scent of broiling meat as she approached the kitchen. Today was burger and red-skinned potato day. It was a popular lunch, and Caprice knew the dining area would be full. After the burgers were broiled, they were kept warm in a spicy sauce. No chafing dishes here, just steam trays, and they hoped enough food to last through the luncheon line.

She spotted her mom. She was scraping carrots while Nana halved potatoes.

"What can I do to help?" Caprice asked.

A volunteer was setting up trays that would be placed at the head of the cafeteria line. Another pulled dishes from the dishwasher. A third wrapped silverware in napkins.

With a knife in one hand and a potato in the other, Nana came over to Caprice and gave her a hug. "Good to see you, honey."

"Do you want me to help you with the potatoes?"

"I think it will take your mom longer to scrape the carrots. Better help her."

"Who's in charge of the kitchen?" Caprice asked, looking around, seeing that everyone was doing their job and doing it effectively.

"Mario Ruiz is here this month. He made up the menus and is overseeing the cooking."

Caprice watched a woman take a tray of burgers from the broiler. "No one's overseeing now."

"He went into the pantry. There was some confusion about a delivery."

Caprice realized where she'd heard Mario's name. When Jeanie had mentioned him, Caprice couldn't quite remember where she'd come across his name before. But now she knew. She'd heard it in conjunction with the soup kitchen. Her mom or Nana had probably told her he was involved, but she hadn't paid much attention.

Fifteen minutes later, Mario appeared. He seemed to be everywhere at once. He was short and thin with black curly hair, a long nose, and a wide smile as he supervised everyone. Caprice wanted to talk to him, but that would have to wait until after lunch was served. In the meantime, she finished helping her mom with the carrots and then found Nana wasn't finished slicing the potatoes.

Caprice slipped over beside her.

"My hands aren't as agile as they once were," Nana complained.

"I'll help."

"I noticed you working with your mom," Nana said. "You weren't as talkative as usual."

No, she was too busy thinking about Grant. "I have a lot on my mind."

"Anything you want to unload?"

Caprice shook her head. "This isn't the place."

"Any place is the place. What's going on, *tesorina mia?*"

My little treasure. Her Nana called her that when she felt deeply about something. So Caprice had to tell her what was wrong.

"It's Grant. He's going to be talking to his ex-wife."

Nana gave her a long look. "And you don't think he should."

"I'm not sure what he should or shouldn't do. I just know that marriage creates deep bonds. They had a child together. And whether they know it or not, the trauma of that child dying brings them together in a way that will always connect them. What if they decide they should try to get back together?"

"Then you need to know it now," Nana said practically.

That shocked Caprice. She hadn't really thought about the situation like that, but it certainly was true.

"How do you feel about Grant?" Nana asked.

Without hesitation, Caprice said, "I love him."

"Then you have to trust what you feel for him, and you have to trust what he feels for you."

"But I don't know for sure what he feels."

"Do you trust him to make the right decision, no matter what that is?"

Wasn't that a wise question? "Do you mean, do I think he's a good moral man who will do the best thing he knows how to do? Yes, I do."

Nana shrugged. "Then there you have it."

"So I have to let him walk away if he decides he wants to renew his marriage?"

"You can't deny what's already happened. You can't erase it, though you might have to try if you ever want to marry Grant in the church."

She'd never thought about that either. To marry Grant in the church, he'd have to obtain an annulment. She didn't agree with that, because he certainly had had a marriage, and there would have to be grounds. But it was the only way she and Grant could ever be married in the Catholic Church.

"Do you believe in the annulments, Nana?"

"I believe that you and Grant are going to have to do what's right for you. You might decide to elope to Las Vegas."

"If we ever get that far."

Nana put her arm around Caprice and gave her a squeeze. "Trust, honey. Trust."

But who should she trust? Herself? Grant? Fate? A higher power? Maybe she should start praying again instead of slipping affirmations into her silent butler. The thing was, she had to decide what to pray for. Probably just wisdom to know what to do next.

Caprice thought about what Nana had said all throughout lunch as she ladled out carrots and potatoes, as she made sure everyone who passed through the line had a bun as well as a burger. She noticed the diversity in the faces that went before her—black and brown, white and yellow. Large eyes, small eyes, big mouths, small mouths, long noses, short noses, glasses. All people just trying to make their way. She kept her eye on Mario too, so she could find him when she wanted him.

Finally after the last person had been served and she'd helped with some of the cleanup, Caprice saw Mario in the dining area wiping off a table with a cloth.

She approached him and asked, "Mr. Ruiz?"

"Mario," he said with a grin before he even saw who she was. Then he turned, and his smile became broader. "You're Mrs. De Luca's granddaughter."

"I am." She extended her hand. "Caprice De Luca."

"And I'm just Mario. Mr. Ruiz is my father, and my grandfather."

"Can I talk to you for a few minutes?"

"Sure." He looked puzzled. "Do you want to talk about the food we serve . . . something that can make it better?"

"No. Actually I want to talk about Drew Pierson."

At that, Mario's eyes widened, and he ran a hand through his tumbled curls. "What about Drew?" Mario asked, his eyes a bit narrowed now.

"My sister and I found him."

The wary expression left Mario's face for a moment. "I'm so sorry." He motioned to a little office where she spotted a computer and some bookshelves. "Maybe we should go in there where we have privacy."

She went to the office with him and stepped inside.

He closed the door. "What did you want to ask me?"

"I heard that you worked with Drew."

"Yes, we worked together in Washington, D.C. We were both sous chefs at the same hotel. But then the hotel was bought by a different corporation and we were let go."

"Did you come back to Kismet, expecting to work together again?"

Mario went to the desk and propped on the corner. "I'm not sure what we expected. We put in our résumés everywhere we could. If we applied somewhere and they needed more than one person, one of us recommended the other. I thought we were a team of sorts. At least in getting new jobs. But then I found the one in York. Drew drifted a bit until he decided to open his own catering business. If it weren't for helping out his grandmother, I think he would have gone back to D.C. and found work there again. But he was pretty insistent on staying here. He got tired of the short-order cook type jobs he was getting rather than the more prestigious ones."

"And what about you?"

"Me? I'm satisfied with what I've got. I respect the owner of the bistro I'm working for, and we serve good food. Would I rather be cooking in a

French restaurant in New York City? Possibly. But I'm giving this a try."

"Did Drew ever tell you he wanted to partner with my sister?"

There wasn't any hesitation when Mario answered. "Yes, he did. And I thought he was going to. But then their deal fell through. He never told me exactly why."

Caprice didn't see any harm in telling him, and she might learn more if she gave *him* information. "Nikki didn't feel a partnership with Drew would be in her best interest. I think she was right. He stole one of Nikki's recipes and served it at the wedding expo last weekend as his. He might have even stolen one of his grandmother's recipes."

Mario went silent for at least three heartbeats. Then he studied Caprice as if deciding what to tell her. Finally he said, "Do you know about the blackberry barbecue sauce he sold to the Rack O' Ribs chain?"

"I do. I saw him announce it on *Mornings with Mavis.* I tasted it, and it's darn good."

"Yeah, it's darn good. It was *mine.* I developed it before D.C. Drew knew I used it and he tasted it often. He'd seen me prepare it."

"Did you consider suing him?"

"I did. I actually saw a lawyer. But he said I simply don't have enough proof. Are you looking into this because you knew Drew?"

"I didn't know him, and I'm not sure Nikki did either. I'm looking into it because I'm afraid Nikki could be on the detectives' suspect list. She and Drew were rivals."

"Drew could put up a charming front when he wanted to, but he was a conniver underneath. Lots of people knew that, so I'm sure he had his host of enemies."

"Did you consider yourself his enemy?"

"My grandfather has a saying. When a wrong is done to you, don't let your anger make it develop into more than one wrong."

"That sounds like advice Nana would give me."

"I wouldn't consider Drew my enemy," Mario added. "I merely cut him out of my life."

That could be true. Or . . . Drew's lucrative deal to sell the barbecue sauce could have been a revenge motive for Mario to murder him.

Caprice found herself in Rowena Pierson's house again the following day. Nikki had decided it was better if she didn't show up for Drew's funeral. Between gossip and her motives being questioned, it just seemed the safer route to take. But Caprice said she would go for both of them . . . for the family. Nana decided to send a Mass card instead of attending. She knew Rowena in passing, but not well enough that her presence would be missed.

Caprice thought about Nana's Mass card, and Father Gregory saying a Mass to aid Drew's soul in finding heaven or growth or whatever actually happened after someone died. It couldn't hurt.

Not many people had attended the funeral and the graveside prayers. It hadn't seemed appropriate to speak to anyone at the church or at the cemetery, so she'd accepted the invitation from Rowena to attend the reception at her house afterward.

At the funeral Caprice had noticed something unusual. Jeanie didn't seem broken up about her brother's death. In fact, as she stood listening to Father Gregory at graveside, she'd appeared a little smug. Maybe that was the result of the way she had her lipstick applied. Caprice didn't know. But she did know that Jeanie didn't have the expression of a grieving sister. Was she a bit removed because she knew one day she'd inherit everything of her grandmother's, and Drew's death had given her that? Maybe she was just the type who couldn't show emotion easily, though she'd seemed to show plenty of emotion the day Bella and Caprice had gone into her shop.

Rowena's house wasn't large, and the funeral goers who came to the reception spread from the living room into the kitchen as well as the sitting room adjacent to the living room that once might have been a dining room. It was close quarters. Caprice caught sight of Jeanie again, and this time she was talking to an older man in a suit. She gestured toward the Tiffany floor lamp beside an armchair.

What was that all about? Just what secrets did those lamps hold?

Rowena, checking to make sure everyone had food or drink in their hands, approached Caprice. She was using her cane today.

She took Caprice's elbow. "I'm so glad you could come."

"Nikki sends her respects too . . . and Nana and my mom."

"I saw your Nana's Mass card. Tell her thank you. Kiki is going to help me with thank-you notes after all of it settles down. I don't know what I'd do without her. She's the one who took care of the food for today. I'm sure it's not as elegant as anything Drew might have prepared."

Caprice wasn't sure about that. As a lead-in, she said, "I don't know many people here. Do you know the gentleman who's talking to Jeanie?"

Rowena put a finger to her lips as she gazed at him. "I don't know who that is. Maybe it's one of her friends."

Just then, the man left Jeanie's side and stepped into the sitting room.

The front door suddenly opened and two men walked in.

Rowena turned their way. "Will you excuse me, Caprice? I need to welcome Drew's friends."

As Caprice studied the two men at the door, she realized they could be Bronson Chronister and Larry Penya. Just from their appearance, she could tell who was who. Bronson's suit shouted dollar signs. It was charcoal and impeccably made. His white shirt gleamed with a silk finish, and his tie looked like a designer one. His black leather wing-tips were spit-shined. Larry Penya, on the other hand, had a scruffier look. He would have been more handsome without the goatee, Caprice thought. His blue eyes were piercing, his dirty blond hair just a little too long. He looked uncomfortable in navy slacks and a white Oxford shirt. He and Bronson were about the same height, though Larry was thinner. For some reason, she got the idea that maybe Larry had borrowed his clothes from Bronson.

The two men were hugging Rowena, and she didn't want to intrude. So instead of lingering in the living room, she followed the Oriental runner into the sitting room. Jeanie was nowhere in sight. Caprice supposed she could have gone either upstairs or down to the basement. However, the man who had been talking to her stood there, and he wasn't mourning Drew. Rather, he was appraisingly studying a claw-foot table. As she watched, he took out his cell phone and snapped a photo of it. How odd.

Caprice approached him, saying, "That's a fine table, isn't it?"

As she studied him, he studied her. "It is. Are you interested in antiques?"

Extending her hand, she said, "I'm Caprice De Luca. My profession is home staging. I often use antiques to fill in. It's amazing how many places they fit, even with modern décor. I know Rowena, and I knew Drew. Were you a friend of Drew's?"

The man looked a little uneasy, but then he shrugged and pulled a business card from the inner pocket of his suit coat. "No, actually I didn't know Drew. My name's Carter Gottlieb. I'm an antique dealer from York. Jeanie and I are friends."

She glanced at the card and saw an address in the east end.

"I know you might think it's a little odd I'm snapping photos, but Jeanie asked me to come today. She wanted me to unobtrusively capture photos of her grandmother's antiques and evaluate them."

"Without Rowena knowing?" Caprice asked, wondering if this guy would be honest with her.

"She told her grandmother she was going to do it sometime. I guess she thought I could look around today and not have to bother her grandmother any other time. I think she's being sensitive to her grandmother's feelings, not wanting to talk about it so soon after Drew died."

"You mean her own inheritance?"

"I don't know about that. I'm only concerned with the antiques. The stars of the collection, of course, are the Tiffany lamps. And they are Tiffany, not reproductions or attempts at the same style. They are totally amazing."

He motioned to the claw-foot table, a bentwood rocker, a curio cupboard with engravings. "The rest of Jeanie's grandmother's antiques are quite ordinary. But that floor lamp in there alone is worth six figures. It's such a shame that the base to the other lamp is missing."

"The motive for Drew's murder might have been robbery, I suppose," Caprice offered, just to see what Carter Gottlieb would say.

"If this was robbery, it was a poor attempt at it. A robber who knew what those lamps were worth never would have left the shade."

That's exactly what Caprice had concluded. "So I guess Drew's murder had nothing to do with the lamps, even though they're worth what could be a small fortune to someone."

"Jeanie thought her grandmother might have another small Tiffany lamp upstairs. She went up to check. She showed me photos of the bedrooms upstairs, and I didn't see anything remarkable. For the most part, antiques are worth only the pleasure that they give, the memories and the history attached to them."

"I agree, but it sounds as if Jeanie's thinking about selling everything eventually."

"I don't know if she wants to sell it, but she's tallying it up. My guess is, she thinks her grandmother might move to a retirement facility and auction off all of this. She told me how much Drew helped Mrs. Pierson. I'm not sure she'll be able to handle the house if she stays here alone."

That could be true. On the other hand, there were services that could help someone in Rowena's position—Meals on Wheels, a cleaning lady once a week, a church network of volunteers who drive seniors to doctors' appointments. If Rowena wanted to stay in her house, there was a way to do it.

"I suppose it hurts Jeanie to think about selling the house. After all, she grew up here."

Gottlieb looked thoughtful. "From what she's told me, I'm not sure those times were happy times. She confided in me about her parents dying and she and Drew coming to live here. She doesn't seem attached to anything in the house, not even those lamps. Believe me, if I owned a Tiffany lamp like that, I'd be attached."

"Did she mention whether she and Drew were close? Only two years separated them."

"She really hadn't discussed that. But then again, I got the impression that she felt her grandmother was catering to Drew, letting him stay here, giving him free room and board. I suppose Jeanie felt a little bit left out of that, or like her grandmother wasn't being fair."

"I don't understand," Caprice said.

Carter lowered his voice. "I think Jeanie felt that Drew was manipulating their grandmother, trying to get into her good graces."

"Maybe he was just trying to redeem himself for all the problems he'd caused when he was a teenager."

"Perhaps that's true. I just got the feeling that Jeanie felt she was in competition with Drew."

And now that competition was over. Would Jeanie try to convince Rowena to move into a senior center? The most important question was, Did she kill her brother so she would inherit everything her grandmother left when she died?

Chapter Eleven

After Caprice rejoined the rest of the guests in the living room, Rowena was still talking to the two men. She'd settled on the sofa. The man in the suit was on the left of her, the blond-haired man on the right.

Rowena motioned to Caprice, and Caprice joined them, eager to find out if these were Drew's best friends. She sat on one of the folding chairs that had been set up near the sofa and caught a whiff of stale smoke. Apparently the man to Rowena's right was a smoker.

"I'd like you to meet friends of Drew's." Rowena looked proud that Drew had had friends. She introduced Bronson first.

Bronson shook Caprice's hand. "How did you know Drew?" he asked.

"Drew worked with my sister. I stage houses and she provides the food."

Bronson snapped his fingers. "I've heard of you. You're well-known for your shindigs . . . and for the marvelous food at them."

"And this is Larry Penya," Rowena said, maybe expecting Larry to extend his hand to Caprice as Bronson had. But Larry didn't. He just nodded, then glanced around the room.

Caprice decided to try to draw the two men out. "Were you friends of Drew's for a long time?"

To her surprise, Larry was the one who answered. "Since high school."

"It's amazing that you kept your friendships. They don't often last."

Bronson and Larry exchanged a look, and Caprice wondered what that was about.

But before she could get a better read on it, Rowena interjected, "I think I still have Drew's high school yearbook around here somewhere. After he moved back here, he was going to toss it. But I saved it. If I could just remember where I put it."

"It will come back, Mrs. Pierson." Again Larry surprised Caprice by patting the older woman's hand.

"I wish more things would come back," Rowena ruminated. "Like my ability to use my knees to go up and down stairs." Then she addressed Bronson directly. "I should have accepted your daddy's invitation to go camping for a weekend in one of his RV trailers while I still could have enjoyed it. Now trekking around in the outdoors is something I can't do."

"But you could still enjoy a campfire," Bronson suggested kindly.

Both of these men acted as if they were fond of Rowena. After all, they'd known her for years.

"You should go out to Happy Camper RV Center sometime and take a look at what Bronson sells," Rowena advised Caprice. "Some of those campers are amazing. Drew showed me pictures. The side actually extends from one of them, and it's almost as big as a house!"

"A home away from home on wheels," Bronson agreed. "That's what people want. Oh, they like to say they've gone camping. Real campers use a tent. People that come to our center . . . they want a few conveniences when they're camping, including heat, air, and bathroom facilities. Many camper vehicles can provide that now."

Caprice could see that Bronson was enthusiastic about the subject, and she supposed he had to be to make the business a success.

"My only experience camping was a tent in the backyard with my sisters and brother," Caprice said with a smile. "And I can't say it was the best time of my life, especially with Vince trying to scare us half to death in the middle of the night."

"Come on out to Happy Camper sometime. I'd be glad to show you around." Bronson's invitation sounded sincere. "And Mrs. Pierson," he added, "if you want to enjoy a camping experience, I would take you myself some weekend . . . and pick out the best camper to do it. You fed me and Larry often enough through the years, let alone let us sleep over here."

That explained the almost grandmotherly appeal that Rowena had for Bronson and Larry.

"You boys weren't always good for Drew, but you weren't always bad for him either. Don't think I didn't know about the trouble you often got into. But you stood by Drew and he stood by you . . . and that's what friends are for."

Caprice studied both of the men during Rowena's

little speech. Their expressions gave nothing away. She'd like to know a lot more about their friendships with Drew. Maybe she'd have the opportunity to talk to them separately.

A cell phone beeped.

Bronson slid his from inside his jacket pocket and studied the screen. Then he slanted toward Rowena. "That was a text from the manager at Happy Camper. I'm going to have to get back there. But Larry and I just wanted to stop and pay our respects.

"I'm glad you did," Rowena said, giving them both a hug.

The two men stood, and Bronson said to Caprice, "It was good to meet you. Remember what I said about coming out for a tour sometime."

As the two men moved toward the door, Rowena shook her head. "They didn't even have anything to eat."

"I think they were just glad to talk to you. Reviving memories always helps at a time like this."

"I suppose that's true. You know, I thought maybe the girl that Drew had dated would stop by his funeral . . . or here."

"He was dating someone?"

"Not lately. But he did in the spring. You know, I could see and hear better than he thought I could. He snuck her up to his room on weekends because he knew I'd never approve. I don't know who the girl was. But she was a redhead. I caught sight of her one night when I left my room to go to the bathroom for a drink. He and the girl were snuggling on the couch. But he never introduced her to me, and I thought that was a bit odd."

"Maybe he didn't want to introduce you to someone he didn't know if he was serious about."

"That's probably true."

To her surprise, Mario Ruiz came through the front door. He spotted Caprice sitting near Rowena and he came over to them. "Mrs. Pierson," he said. "I'm Mario Ruiz. I worked with Drew in D.C."

"Oh yes. Drew mentioned you."

Kiki, who had been supervising everything in the kitchen, called to Rowena from the doorway. "Rowena, can you show me where you keep your extra tea bags?"

Rowena stood, using her cane to support her. She said, "Thank you for coming, Mario. We'll talk after I solve this kitchen problem."

After Rowena had moved away, Caprice said to Mario, "I'm surprised to see you here."

"Drew and I were friends in D.C. At least, I thought we were. Maybe he stole my recipe because it was the only way he could get ahead. I have more talent than that one recipe. I have to get over it. I just wanted to pay my respects."

Studying Mario, Caprice tried to read him, to figure out if he was sincere. After all, he could have had a strong motive for murder. But maybe he really believed that grudges didn't serve him any purpose.

"Before you came in, Rowena was telling me that Drew had a girlfriend for a while. Rowena didn't know who she was, but she was a redhead. Do you know who he was dating?"

"A redhead? Oh, sure, I know who that was. That was Tabitha Dennis. She's the hostess at Rack O' Ribs and the daughter of the manager. Drew knew how to get ahead, and my guess is that's where he started when he wanted to sell the barbeque sauce. I could be all wrong. Maybe he started dating her and she put the idea in his head. Either way, he always had a reason for what he did."

"Are you saying he was ruthless?"

"I'm not sure about *ruthless.* I am sure about determined and motivated. At least, since I knew him."

Very different from the teenager he'd been, Caprice surmised. Could love of cooking make that kind of change in a person? Only if that's what they chose for their vocation. Only if there was more behind it than dollar signs.

That evening, Nikki stopped at Caprice's house around dinner time. She hadn't been able to stay away, and she wanted to know everything Caprice had learned.

After the reception at Rowena's, Caprice had driven to Grocery Fresh and bought tomatoes, a pepper, and a new bulb of garlic. When Nikki arrived, the aroma of garlic, onions, and simmering tomatoes permeated the air.

"A salad with this, or fresh broccoli?" Caprice asked her sister.

Nikki set a bag on the table. "I stopped at the Tasting Totem and got a bottle of that peach balsamic vinegar you like so much. Let's just do salad."

"Baby greens in the fridge," Caprice assured Nikki.

Nikki washed her hands and then went to the refrigerator to pull out ingredients for their salads.

"You're restraining yourself, aren't you?" Caprice asked with a smile.

"You bet I am."

Lady had run into the kitchen with Nikki, but Caprice shook her finger at her. "You already had your dinner. I promise that Nikki and I will play a game of chase with you after we eat if you let us talk now."

Lady cocked her head at Caprice, one ear flapping. Her big brown eyes seemed to say, *I'd like your attention now, but I understand if I have to wait.* After a little yip, she ran off toward Caprice's office, where Caprice knew Mirabelle was lounging on her chair.

"I'm glad she and the cats keep each other company," she said as she stirred the sauce another time. "Maybe their relationship will last as long as Drew's and Bronson's and Larry's."

"So you met them?"

"I did. And they seem to have a genuine fondness for Rowena."

"What did you learn?"

"Nothing concrete. But the three of them were fast friends. I could tell there was a bond between Larry and Bronson. You know, that "guy" thing? They exchanged looks a couple of times, and I got the impression they knew what the other was thinking."

"Sort of like sisters?" Nikki jibbed.

"Actually, yes. It was sort of like that. Bronson invited me to tour Happy Camper whenever I'd like. I might take him up on it."

"Rowena had told us that Larry had fallen on hard times. So how does he fit into Bronson's world? Their lifestyles are so different," Nikki mused.

"I don't know. Maybe Bronson's helping him out."

"And what does Bronson get in return?"

"If they're like brothers, maybe he doesn't need anything in return. Or maybe it strokes his ego to be the big man on campus, so to speak, and help out his friends. I did learn that Drew had dated Tabitha Dennis."

Nikki looked puzzled. "Should I know the name?"

"She's the daughter of the Rack O' Ribs manager, and the hostess there."

Nikki whistled through her teeth. "Do you think that has something to do with the barbeque sauce?"

"I don't know, but it's certainly an avenue to pursue. He didn't introduce her to Rowena, though. He just sort of snuck her in at night. That makes me wonder why. If he liked her and he was dating her, why wouldn't he bring her to meet Rowena?"

"Maybe he was dating her for a purpose. You know, the same way he made a pass at me for a purpose."

"His purpose with you was that he found you attractive."

"I'm not saying that doesn't go along with it. But I'm beginning to think Drew was a lot more calculating than I ever gave him credit for."

"Except he messed up with you," Caprice pointed out.

"He underestimated me. Before I drove over here, I got a call from Detective Carstead. I have to go to the police station again tomorrow for more questioning."

"On a Sunday? Do you want me to come along?" She was supposed to meet Juan at a house they'd be staging, but he could take a preliminary tour without her. She knew if she went with Nikki, she'd probably have to sit on that hard bench in the lobby. But if Nikki needed the support, she'd be there.

"There's no point in you coming along," Nikki muttered. "I know they're going to want to question me alone. I really think Detective Carstead is a good guy who just wants to find the truth."

Caprice's conversations with the detective had led her to the same conclusion. Still, this was her sister's freedom that was at stake. "You should take Vince along."

Nikki went to the pantry for Caprice's salad spinner. When she came back out, she dumped the salad greens into it and added water to wash them. "I'm not going to ask Vince. I think Detective Carstead is right. Taking a lawyer along makes me look guilty. I don't have anything to hide."

Even if that was true on some level, Caprice didn't like the idea of Nikki talking to the police without her brother present. Carstead might be a good guy, but just like Jones he wanted to pin the murder on someone.

She just hoped it wasn't Nikki.

The house was amazing. Caprice toured it slowly on Sunday, appreciating every detail. Then she went outside to the front yard again to wait for Juan. Plans for staging it seemed to materialize before her eyes.

She'd staged many houses, and each had its own beauty. That's why she gave them unique themes. But this one, with its Spanish-style design and architecture—

Her theme for this house staging was easy to devise—Hacienda Haven. The 5,500-square-foot, two-story edifice, including a four-car garage, had a wondrous story to tell. At least that's the impression Caprice wanted to give any buyer who might come in. She wanted them to see a possible home that was all about hearth, family, rusticity, and old-world charm.

The house was empty now, except for the beauty that was innate. But she could envision exactly what she wanted to do with it. This structure was about more than a Mediterranean feel. She wanted Hacienda Haven to manifest a culturally rich home that invited family to gather, talk, and play.

As she faced the front entrance, the sun shone on the sprawling home with its red-tiled roof. Its villa ambience was made unique by interesting angles. Rooms weren't just square or rectangular. There were rounded walls, high ceilings, arches, and wrought-iron lacy grillwork. With five bedrooms— three downstairs and two upstairs—a loft, a media room, and even a meditation room, the house could appeal to a host of prospective buyers. The exposed beams, the dark wood flooring and unique tiling, the brick and stone, terra-cotta tiles, rough edges, and textured plaster gave the illusion of comfort and ease, even though every detail had been done to perfection.

No, Caprice could never afford a home like this, but she knew exactly what she would do with it if she could.

Juan arrived, parked in the circular drive, and met her at the heavy dark wood door. When they walked inside, he gave a loud whistle. The entranceway was magnificent with its thirty-foot ceiling.

"Have we ever staged anything like this before?" he asked her.

"Remember the castle house that Roz owned?"

"That's different. Nobody would want to live in that one. But this . . ." He sounded in awe of the architecture, the style, and the materials.

On the left, a doorway opened into a den or study. It was almost a trapezoid shape with a hexagonal front window and a rounded roof. If they went down the hallway in that direction—the left wing of the house—they would find the master bedroom and bath, a powder room, and a set of stairs to an upper level. If they walked straight ahead, they would find the seven-sided family room. If they stepped through the doorway on their right, they'd enter the dining room that led into a grand kitchen with a breakfast nook and family eat-in area large enough for a dinner party. The staircase that led to the loft was incredibly beautiful with traditional tiling used in Spanish homes. The tiles ranged in design colors from orange to blue, taupe and fuchsia . . . handmade, no two identical. She wouldn't change the multilayered wrought-iron chandeliers swinging from the vaulted ceilings.

"I want to stage this house with color," she offered. "Vibrant color. No neutrals here. There's enough of that in the stonework and the tile and the brick. Think yellow and orange, pink and blue."

Juan ran his hand over a wall. "Plaster skimmed with a whitewash?"

"Specialized paint, for sure. It looks like something you might find in a Mediterranean villa, but this will withstand the cold and heat of Pennsylvania. I want to find woven rugs in the same colors as those tiles on the staircase."

"You're not asking for much."

"Do I ever?"

Juan laughed as they climbed the curved staircase leading to the second floor. Once there, they stood at the loft railing looking down on the floor below. "We're both going to have to look through Spanish artwork and even videos of flamenco dance, maybe study paintings by Dali, Goya, and Picasso. Those will give us design images. I'll look through the rental company's Web site for pieces in that flavor. But I also want to use pottery—lots of it—as well as sconces, unusual headboards, dark wood, and wrought iron."

"How about leather? Think metalwork too. And Spanish landscapes," Juan advised.

She nodded, already picturing it all. "Most of all, I want each space functional with not too many items. The covered porch on the back is going to need its own treatment as if it were inside the house instead of outside."

As Juan stared down below, he said, "I can imagine sectionals . . . maybe leather trimmed with wood. Possibly a couple of large mirrors to reflect those chandeliers."

"We might also want to think about framed tapestries with bold designs. Greenery too in the arched crooks and crannies. Soft wool throws in whatever color we decide is dominant."

"When do we have to be ready to put this on the market?"

"I think it will take us at least a couple of weeks

to collect everything. So let's give it a two-week time frame."

"Aren't you going to be tied up with a new murder investigation?"

She remembered all too well her last investigation and what had almost happened. In fact, she'd found herself in danger every time she'd insinuated herself into an investigation. That's why Grant and her family wanted her to stay out of it. But with Nikki at the police station again right now—

She wasn't exactly sure what she wanted to do next. "I want Nikki to be in the clear, but I don't want to create enemies for her or for me. I'm waiting for some kind of lead. Do you know what I mean?"

"One of your signs," Juan determined wryly.

"I guess so. Let's face it. In the past, I've jumped in and started wading around and made gigantic waves. I didn't know what I was doing. I still don't. But this time I want to make sure I don't put anybody in danger . . . including myself . . . and especially not Nikki. I have to be as unobtrusive as possible."

"That's kind of tough when you go around wearing lime green bell-bottoms and tie-dyed T-shirts, never mind the jeweled flip-flops."

She wrinkled her nose at him. "You sound like Bella."

He laughed. "So what are you going to do next?"

"Grocery Fresh is hosting a raspberry festival on Saturday. Since Nikki is involved in the investigation and word is going to spread that she and I found Drew's body, I would expect if we just mingled there, go from stand to stand, chat people up, we could find out tidbits without even trying. I don't have to ruffle feathers that way if I just listen. As it is, I think Bella and I ruffled Jeanie's feathers—Drew Pierson's sister. She believes Nikki did it. And if she goes spreading that rumor all over town, it could catch more fire. More fire, more pressure on the police department to solve this."

"Is Nikki going to be serving anything at this raspberry festival?"

"I don't think so. It's better if she keeps a low profile. But Nana's entering the raspberry dessert contest. I might too."

"Speaking of food, do you have any ideas what you want to serve at this open house?"

"I'll leave that up to Nikki. Maybe churros—Spanish fritters. While I was waiting for you, I also read something about a garbanzo and chorizo stew. I saw a picture of these long cigar-shaped sweetbreads too, which originated in the region of Valencia. I'm sure Nikki will have a ton of ideas. This house is going to generate one idea after the other. Can't you just see it, Juan?"

He gave her an affectionate smile. "Can I see your vision? Sure, I can. Down to a tall acilino on a credenza."

The strands of "Let It Be" played from Caprice's pocket. She slipped her phone out and saw Nikki's photo. "I have to take this," she said to Juan. "It's Nikki."

"I'll go downstairs and explore outside. Maybe the landscaping will provide ideas for the covered porch furniture."

As he loped down the stairs, Caprice connected

with Nikki. "Are you finished at the police station?" she asked her sister.

"I'm done for now. I doubt I'm finished for good. They took me over the same ground repeatedly. Finally Detective Jones left and it was just me and Detective Carstead."

"Are you wishing Vince had been there?"

"No. They didn't try to trip me up or anything. They're just checking every little detail. Detective Carstead had a list. When did I meet Drew? How often did I work with him? When did I stop working with him? It's a good thing I keep accurate work notes on my tablet so I could tell him the exact dates."

"But you had told him all that before."

"Yes, I had. And, at times, he seemed almost apologetic for asking again. You know, he's really kind of cute."

"Brett Carstead? Cute?" Every woman had her own idea of *cute*. "You didn't flirt with him, did you? That could get you into big trouble."

"No flirting. I controlled myself. It's too serious a situation to even think about it. But after this is all over, who knows what could happen?"

Caprice thought she heard hope in Nikki's voice. Her sister had been so down . . . first about Drew's competition and then about what had happened. She was glad to hear positive energy from Nikki, even if it had to do with the hunkiness of Detective Carstead.

Do you know anything about him?" Nikki asked. "Like, is he married?"

"Don't know," Caprice said. "Never asked."

"He doesn't wear a ring. But that might have to do with his work."

"Or not," Caprice suggested blandly. "Grant might know." Then she remembered what was going on with her and Grant. "But now isn't a good time to ask him . . . anything." She'd already told Nikki about Grant's ex-wife and what he planned to do.

"Aren't you two talking?" Nikki asked, sounding surprised.

"There's nothing to talk about right now. Not until this is all over. Not until he makes decisions."

"Whether he wants a serious relationship with you?"

"Even more important, he has to decide whether his bonds with his ex-wife are cut or if he wants to keep those threads."

"And if he does?" Nikki asked.

"I don't know. I don't know what that will mean for either of us or for both of us together."

"Don't give up," Nikki counseled her.

"I'm not giving up. I'm just afraid to hope. I'm going to concentrate on staging this Spanish-themed house. And figuring out who might have murdered Drew. I want you to mingle with me at the raspberry festival and see what we can learn.

"At least we'll have raspberry delights to munch on while we snoop."

Raspberry delights. She'd like to be sharing them with Grant.

Chapter Twelve

Caprice had been keeping tabs on Dulcina and her new adoptee through text messages. But she wanted to see for herself how Halo was faring. She knew Dulcina was a kind, gentle person. But not everyone was a cat person. Maybe she'd thought more about the responsibility of caring for a cat with kittens and had changed her mind.

On Monday morning while Lady played with her kibble release toy and Sophia and Mirabelle napped, Caprice crossed the street to Dulcina's house. After she rang the bell, it took her neighbor a few minutes to come to the door. Caprice was almost ready to text her to see if she was home when Dulcina opened it. She looked a bit harried. Instead of her hair being tied back, it was loose around her face and a bit flyaway.

"I was in the closet upstairs looking for old towels," she explained. "They're fine for Halo but not for the kittens. I think receiving blankets would be better, from what I've read on the Internet. Their little claws won't get caught in them."

Caprice had to smile as Dulcina motioned her inside. "So you're going to visit the baby store?"

"No, I found a good deal online. They'll be here in two days. I'll have everything washed up and ready. I have one of those storage bins. I'm going to line it with newspaper and put the receiving blankets on top."

Caprice followed Dulcina into her sunroom, where Halo was sitting on a new condo in front of the window. "How's she doing?"

"This morning she let me pet her. She didn't back away from my hand."

"That's a good sign. Is she eating for you?"

"She gobbles everything down like she hasn't eaten for months."

"Marcus said she was malnourished. She might eat like that the whole way through her pregnancy and while she's nursing. Are you still willing to do all of this?"

"Yes, I am. I downloaded a book about cats having kittens, and I've watched a few videos. I know there's a possibility that things can go wrong. If for some reason she's not a good mother, I might have to hand-feed the kittens every two hours. But, Caprice, it feels so good to be giving time to nurturing this little being. Do you know what I mean?"

"I know exactly what you mean." Slowly approaching the condo, Caprice said, "Hi there, Halo. Do you like it here?"

The purring cat gave her a slanted-eye look that wasn't either cautious or accepting. It was quite serene, really.

"That first night I wasn't too sure how she'd be in here," Dulcina explained. "She went from window to window and looked like she wanted to go back out. She meowed. But I just talked to her softly and kept showing her the litter box. I closed the blinds and stayed in here with her and read. Finally she just sat too and then fell asleep. She looked exhausted."

"The trauma of being captured and taken to the vet could have exhausted her. But you have to remember, being outside, she was never safe where she slept. She probably always slept with one eye open. Feral or stray cats have to be vigilant constantly. Are you going to keep her in here?"

"Just for today yet. The flea treatment should have done its thing by now, according to the pamphlets the vet gave you. I'll wash up the sunroom really well and then let her explore. I'll watch to see her favorite places and then put a bin nearby. Maybe I'll put one in two different places."

"She might like someplace darker than the sunroom to have her babies."

"That's what I read. I'm thinking in the kitchen. I can move the chair away from my little desk nook and put the bin under there. She should feel safe."

"It sounds as if you have all the bases covered." Caprice walked closer to Halo and then stretched out her hand, very slowly. The cat eyed her warily but didn't jump or move away. She sniffed a few times, then folded her paws underneath her.

"You're a beautiful girl," Caprice said to her. "After good food and loving, you'll make a great companion."

"I talked to Rod last night and told him about her."

"And?" Caprice prompted.

"And he told his girls right while we were on the

phone. Vanna even got on the phone to ask me about her. She's the younger one."

"So kittens could be a bonding experience with them too."

"I can hope. Nothing else has been. The concert on Sunday might be, but I won't know how they're going to react until we're there. On the other hand, who can resist kittens?"

Caprice laughed. "Lots of people can."

"I still have so much to learn. From what I read, I shouldn't handle them if I don't have to for two weeks, except to weigh them and that kind of thing. And I don't think I'd let anybody else touch them for a month, especially not anyone who hasn't been around animals."

"That sounds about right."

"I am nervous about being a midwife, though."

"You don't have to do it on your own. I can give you Marcus's number. And you can call me if you need me. I've never delivered kittens, but I've helped to deliver pups."

That brought back bittersweet memories. She and Grant . . . delivering Lady's litter. Caprice had found Lady's mom in *her* mother's tomato garden. She'd named her Shasta because she was the color of Caprice's daisies. When Caprice had found her owners, however, she learned that Shasta's real name was Honey.

"I thought of asking around to see if anyone wanted a kitten," Dulcina said, studying Halo. "But I don't want to be superstitious about this. I'm just going to wait until they're born. Then I'll go from there. I know for sure I want to keep one of them with Halo."

For Halo's sake, as well as Dulcina's, Caprice hoped all went well. Dulcina was definitely invested in the process.

Caprice lowered herself into one of the lawn chairs Dulcina had arranged in the sunroom. The blue-and-green-flowered cushion was comfortable.

Dulcina sat in the chair beside her. "Would you like coffee? Vanilla hazelnut."

Caprice laughed. "You've convinced me."

Dulcina was already on her feet. "You just stay there and commune with Halo. I'll get us some."

About five minutes later, Dulcina returned with two mugs. She handed one to Caprice. "I hope it's right. A dab of sugar and a couple of teaspoons of milk."

"You've got it."

After Dulcina was seated, Caprice asked, "Are you going to the raspberry festival?"

"I don't know. I think I'm going to stay close to home for the next month, except for short errands . . . and the concert. I want to make sure Halo is okay."

"How about Rod?"

"I don't see him that often as it is. It's rare that the girls don't have to be run here, there, and everywhere on a weekend. He doesn't like me to be too involved in that, or else the girls don't want me to be involved. I'm not sure which it is."

"They play soccer, right?"

"They do."

"Maybe he feels it would be boring for you to sit at their games. Have you told him you want to go?"

"Not really. I didn't want to push in where I wasn't wanted."

"If you don't ask or push, he might not know you're interested in the girls' welfare as well as his."

"That's a thought." She paused, looked at Halo and then out the window at the sunny end-of-June day. "Even though he's been divorced for a long time, I don't know if he's ready for a relationship."

"I can relate to that," Caprice said before she thought better of it.

"But you're dating Grant now. Aren't you two becoming more serious?"

"I thought we were. But his ex-wife's coming to town and he's going to see her. He feels as if he has to."

"And you're worried he's not ending anything."

"Something like that. There's this wall up between us now. And until she comes and goes, I can't see either of us jumping over it."

"Don't be out of touch with him," Dulcina counseled. "You need to stay connected."

"But that hurts when I don't know what he wants," Caprice admitted to Dulcina and herself.

"Maybe you could text him 'Thinking of you' or something like that."

"With a little heart?" Caprice almost joked.

"Don't get too flowery about it. But just let him know you want it to work."

"Are you doing that with Rod?" Caprice asked slyly. "Does he know you want to get close to his girls? Not just because you want to date him, but because you want to mother them?"

"I don't know if they want to be mothered."

"Everyone wants to be mothered whether they'll admit it or not," Caprice suggested.

"A lot will depend on their going to the concert and their reaction to it."

"Don't put any expectations on it, or you won't have fun yourself. If they see you and Rod having fun, that can make a difference too. Surely they want their dad to be happy."

"Are girls that age that unselfish?"

"If he's raised them to care about others, they might be."

Halo suddenly rose, stretched, then studied the two of them.

"She has such long legs," Caprice said.

"If you watch how she sits there," Dulcina noted, "you can see that she's crooked. That one back leg folds up higher than the other one. And when she walks, there's a slight limp there."

"She's a lucky kitty to have survived some kind of accident. The wonderful thing is that she's not wild or nasty. Even at the clinic, she let Marcus examine her and didn't put up a fuss. There's a resignation about her. Or maybe it's just serenity. I don't know."

Halo jumped down off the condo and went to a bowl that held a few kitten crunchies. She gobbled them up quickly as if someone might take them if she didn't.

"She hasn't sat on the chairs yet," Dulcina observed. "It's as if she's just used to the ground, and maybe trees. I guess that's why she likes the condo."

Halo made a turn around the room, stopped at the door leading into the kitchen and living room, then went to sit on the rug that Dulcina had laid in front of the French door.

"Have you found out anything more about who might have killed Drew Pierson?"

"I met a couple of his friends at the funeral reception. And his sister seems to already be numbering her grandmother's possessions for when she inherits." Caprice shook her head. "I shouldn't have said that. You didn't hear me say that."

Dulcina laughed. "If it's true, then maybe she has a motive. What kind of person is she?"

"I'm not exactly sure. She seemed volatile. On the other hand, inviting an antiques dealer to the funeral reception is calculating."

"And Drew's friends?"

"From what I could tell after spending just a few minutes with them, Bronson Chronister seems like an interesting guy. He comes from money. His father made Happy Camper RV Center into a huge success. Bronson's taken over now."

"Camping," Dulcina said with disgust. "Not something I want to contemplate."

"From what Bronson says, the newest campers have every convenience. It's not the *camping in a tent* experience. It's more like *staying in your own hotel room on wheels and seeing the surrounding sights* experience."

"I wonder if Rod has ever thought about doing that with his daughters. Do you think you can rent them?" Dulcina asked.

"You want to be cooped up with Rod, a teen, and a preteen for a weekend?" Caprice returned.

"That does sound pretty unsettling. And once the kittens are born, they'll probably need me twenty-four hours a day."

Caprice wondered if Dulcina wasn't using the

idea of Halo and her kittens to give herself an out with Rod in case things didn't work out. Could they be an excuse for her not to get more involved? Maybe she wasn't any more ready than he was.

"If I'm prying, just tell me to butt out. But you never talk about your first marriage." Caprice knew Dulcina had been a young widow but not the details of what had happened.

"It was a wonderful marriage," Dulcina assured Caprice. "And I don't say that looking back with rose-colored glasses. Johnny was perfect for me, and I seemed perfect for him. Once we met in high school, we knew we were going to be together forever. But I learned the hard way that forever is for fairy tales. An icy road and a drunk driver coming at him . . . he didn't have a chance for forever . . . and neither did I."

"I'm sorry."

"I try not to think about it anymore," Dulcina said with a sudden catch in her voice. "I still miss him so much. And the truth is, I don't think I'll ever find anything like that relationship again. We were soul mates. How do you have a second act to that?"

"I guess you start by deciding if you *want* a second act. Do you?"

"I think I do. Being alone sucks after a while. I'm not afraid to be alone but, on the other hand, I don't want to settle for less than I had." She sighed. "If you play armchair psychologist with me, you'll have a field day. You'd say I'm not pushing things with Rod because I might not want to."

Dulcina didn't need *her* to play psychologist. She'd already come to important realizations on her own. "Right now, I'm not the one to give any advice."

"Maybe I should help you solve a murder instead of worrying about my relationship woes."

"I have a feeling when those kittens arrive, you won't have much time for anything else."

"I see that as a good thing," Dulcina decided. "If I lower my expectations with Rod and concentrate on the kittens, maybe karma will take care of itself."

That was the thing with karma. The universe was made up of actions and reactions. Every action caused a reaction. So if you did nothing, were there no reactions?

Either the murder or worrying about Grant was getting to her. "I have a feeling I'm going to be over here watching those kittens a lot. Then both of us can forget about everything else."

Was that possible?

In about a month she'd find out.

Raspberries were definitely in the air on Saturday. Grocery Fresh had commandeered the town park for their festival. Their stand with quart boxes of raspberries sent the sweet aroma into the whole area, or so it seemed.

Caprice held Lady's leash loosely as she watched everyone with interest. Lady trotted along beside her, nosing the ground around the food and craft stands.

Caprice, Bella, and Nana submitted their desserts to a tent for judging in the late afternoon. Bella's raspberry trifle, Caprice's raspberry bread, and Nana's raspberry shortcake were given numbers.

The judges would have no idea who had prepared the desserts. Winners would be announced right before the chicken barbecue stand began serving dinners.

As they were leaving the tent, Nikki ran up to them. "Sorry I'm late. I was doing cold calls, trying to line up more clients."

"Did any pan out?" Caprice asked.

"One out of twenty," Nikki admitted.

Bella patted her shoulder. "Ace Richland's concert tomorrow might be good for all of us. Joe and I badly need a date night. And you need to forget about work and Drew Pierson's murder." She checked her watch. "I'm going to meet Joe at the playground so I can watch Benny while he and the kids can have a little fun," Bella told her. "I'll catch up to you later." She waved to them and headed off toward the swings.

Nana squeezed Nikki's hand. "How are you holding up?"

"I'm fine. Caprice and I are going to do a little sleuthing."

Nana narrowed her eyes at them. "Nothing that will catch too much attention, I hope."

"Caprice always attracts attention," Nikki teased. "Look at her outfit."

Juan had said the same thing! Was she that conspicuous? Today she'd worn a flowing, beaded paisley Bohemian-style top over white clamdiggers reminiscent of the fifties. She'd left her jeweled flip-flops at home and chosen a pair of white leather sandals instead. This was a fairly conservative outfit for her.

"You can see the lime green and fuchsia in that top coming and going," Nana continued to joke.

"You're all taking lessons from Bella, and I don't like it," Caprice complained.

Nana gave her a hug. "You know we're just teasing. We love the way you dress. I suppose you're just going to mingle and ask questions, and that's fine. Nobody has to know you're doing the detectives' work."

"We're not doing the detectives' work," Nikki protested. "I'm sure Brett is doing a fine job on his own."

Nana eyed Nikki thoughtfully. "Brett, is it?"

Nikki blushed. "We're not on a first name basis, but I wouldn't mind if we would be. The title *Detective Carstead* just seems so formal."

Caprice dropped to a crouch to give Lady attention. The pup looked up at her adoringly. "Murder investigations are always formal."

Nana gave Nikki a kiss on the cheek. "I'll talk to you about this Detective Carstead when you're no longer on his list of persons of interest to be questioned. I'm meeting Darla Watson over at her knitting stand. She makes these adorable little hats for babies. She's going to show me how. See you in a while."

Straightening up, Caprice watched Nana walk toward the knitters' stand. "Where do you want to start?" Caprice asked Nikki after Nana had strolled away.

"Let's just make the rounds. If we see anybody we know, we'll stop and chat. The murder will probably crop up."

They meandered from one stand to another

slowly, appreciating the hanging baskets filled with geraniums, the craft stand with raspberry-patterned runners for tables, and another with shawls that had embroidered raspberries dotting the wool.

Caprice thought she recognized someone trying on a shawl. When the brunette with the pageboy turned around, Caprice smiled. "Hey, Helen. I haven't seen you for a while." Helen Parcelli had been in her high school class.

Helen twirled in the shawl and asked Caprice, "What do you think?"

"I think it's pretty and would keep you warm on a cool night. How are you doing?" The last she'd heard, Helen was in charge of advertising at the *Kismet Crier.*

"My hours were cut again. I only want to work part-time because of the kids, but pretty soon I'm going to have to look for something else. Eight hours a week just isn't enough."

"I'm sorry to hear that," Nikki said. "Could you get a job on the York newspaper?"

"It's possible. But my salary isn't that great, and I'm beginning to think maybe I'd like to try something else."

"What kind of something else?" Caprice asked.

Lady nosed around Helen's shoes and Helen dropped down to pet her. "Hey, girl." Then she gave her attention back to Caprice. "Maybe marketing. It's a whole new world out there now, incorporating social media into advertising. I was thinking of becoming a social media consultant for businesses. It's not just celebrities who need them anymore."

"That's an interesting concept," Caprice responded, meaning it. "Nikki and I are trying to grow her business, and we've tapped into the social media world. But it's rough getting a foothold."

"You have to know the right outlets to push the word out. Do you want me to try to secure a couple of well-placed ads for your catering business?" Helen asked Nikki.

"I don't have much of a budget," Nikki warned her.

"Let me see what I can find out." After Helen and Nikki exchanged numbers, Helen studied the shawl again that she'd thrown around her shoulders. "This might be nice topping a sundress for the reunion. Are you going?" she asked Caprice.

"I'm on the development committee, so yes, I'll be there." Originally she'd expected the reunion to be a happy occasion, that she'd take Grant as her guest. But now, Grant might not be accompanying her.

"You know the gossip will be all over the reunion about Drew Pierson," Helen said. "Isn't it just awful? Killed in his grandmother's house."

"It is terrible," Caprice agreed. "Did you know him?"

"He went to school with my sister. She had a crush on his friend Bronson Chronister, but he only dated girls who came from well-to-do families like his own."

"I understand Bronson is successful in his own right now," Caprice prompted, hoping to learn more.

"That's true," Helen admitted. "He's on several boards including the hospital in York, the school board in Kismet, and Kismet's new Chamber of

Commerce tourism board. He thinks his business influence can pull businesses into the area."

"He did expand his RV centers," Nikki said. "And think about his client base. They come from far and wide, and they go far and wide."

"Each one of those customers could be a voter," Helen explained. "I heard he might be stepping into politics soon. Since he's a bachelor, my sister still has her eye on him. She even got a part-time job at the pro shop at the Country Squire Golf and Recreation Club hoping to chat him up. He plays a lot of tennis."

Caprice's mind started spinning. She knew Bronson had invited her to Happy Camper to tour the property and the recreational vehicles, but she'd really like a conversation on turf other than his. Maybe it was time she used her own contacts. Roz had a membership at Country Squire. They could both play tennis if Caprice went as her guest.

"Would you vote for Bronson?" Caprice asked Helen.

"I might. He has a lot going for him. He's intelligent, he has connections, and he's traveled around the world. With family money backing him, he could be good." Helen turned to Caprice. "Since you're on the development committee, is this going to be a dressy reunion? It's at the high school, so I kinda figured it wouldn't be."

"If you want to go glitzy, you're free to go glitzy. We're old enough to be and dress the way we want to, don't you think? We haven't defined a wardrobe code. Nikki's catering it, so the food will be exceptional. One of the guys is springing for bottles of champagne, and someone else's family owns a winery, so he's bringing wine. We have a DJ who can play anything from the forties to now. I am hoping the guys wear suits, and I'll push that if anybody asks."

"That sundress I mentioned might be just right," Helen said thoughtfully. "It has a cute sequined top. I can sparkle that night."

They all laughed. After a few more exchanged pleasantries and talk about the July Fourth fireworks over the reservoir that night, Helen took the shawl she'd thrown over her shoulders to the cashier and paid for it.

After she walked away, Caprice turned to her sister. "So Bronson wants to run for something."

Nikki shrugged. "He probably has aspirations that will take him beyond Kismet."

As Caprice glanced toward the judging tent, she suddenly froze. Something odd must have shone in her expression, because Nikki grabbed her elbow. "What's wrong?"

"Look," Caprice said morosely.

Her sister looked in the same direction. Grant stood at one of the baked goods stands holding Patches's leash . . . and next to him was a very attractive blonde.

"Do you think that's his ex?" Nikki asked with compassion in her voice.

"I don't know who else it would be."

Caprice took a step forward to get a better look.

As she did, both Grant and the woman turned around and headed in their direction.

Caprice wanted to duck behind one of the stands, or at least behind Nikki. But that would be a coward's way out.

Nikki leaned close to her and said, "They're just walking beside each other, not arm in arm, or holding hands, or anything like that."

What Nikki said was true, but Caprice could see how their elbows brushed, and the body language said they'd done this before. There was a certain familiarity there that exes have. As she watched them come nearer, she saw her dreams going up in smoke. To think, only two weeks before, she'd been contemplating scouting vintage wedding gowns online.

Scanning the area in front of him with Patches nosing ahead, Grant suddenly spied her.

Patches spotted Lady and pulled on his leash. Lady, recognizing her doggie friend, did the same. Caprice had no choice but to walk forward and let the two dogs meet.

Could any situation be more awkward?

Grant crouched down with Lady and Patches, maybe to calm them a bit. Caprice felt she needed to be calmed too, but that wasn't going to happen.

Caprice noticed the look Naomi gave the dogs. It wasn't an I-want-to-pet-them-too look. It was an I-wish-they-weren't-here look. Possibly she wasn't an animal lover.

After Grant rose to his feet, he said to Naomi, "These are the De Luca sisters. Caprice and Nikki, this is my ex-wife, Naomi. She just flew in today. I thought the Raspberry Festival was a good way to introduce her to Kismet."

The De Luca sisters? That was how he was going to introduce her? Of course, what could he say? "I've been dating Caprice, but now you've interrupted our relationship. Caprice was getting serious about me, but I don't know what I'm feeling about her."

She told herself to get a grip. This was awkward for everybody, because she had the feeling that Naomi did know who she was from the look and assessment the blonde gave her. From Naomi's well-tailored slacks and her fashion-forward blouse, Caprice suspected she didn't appreciate Bohemian chic.

Trying to be polite as well as civil, Caprice forced herself to make conversation. "How do you like the raspberry desserts?"

Nikki gave her a *can-you-think-of-anything-lamer?* look. Oh well.

Naomi sent her a practiced smile. "Those dessert stands are a dieter's nightmare."

Grant interjected, "But the raspberries look really luscious, don't you think?"

All Caprice could think of was sharing a bowl of fresh raspberries topped with whipped cream with him. This wasn't going well.

"Bella, Joe, and the kids are over at the swings," she mentioned. "I'm sure they'd love to see Patches. I'm going to take Lady over there in a little while, after the dessert judging announcements."

"Did you enter?" His attention was all on Caprice, and she could feel his regret and longing.

"I did, but so did Nana and Bella, and about thirty other people."

Patches and Lady somehow got tangled around

Naomi's legs. She did a little two-step to extricate herself and frowned. "They must be quite rambunctious when they're together."

Grant answered before Caprice could. "After their first burst of excitement, they get along really well and calm each other down. But neither of them is crazy about football. They snooze when it's on."

Caprice knew he was trying to stay connected to her by referring to the time when he pup-sat Lady with Patches and they'd joked about what TV show they should be watching.

But Naomi had her own ammunition. "Seems to me *you* used to snooze through football too."

Oh, yes, get that history in, Caprice thought.

Nikki's shoulder bumped Caprice's. "Everyone's gathering over at the dessert judging tent. We'd better get over there in case you won."

Caprice saw the expression on Grant's face. He looked as if he wanted to stop her from leaving. Yet there was no point in her staying.

"Have a good time at the festival," she told the couple. Then she patted her hip and called to Lady to follow her. But Lady was reluctant to leave Patches.

Caprice took a treat from her fanny pack and patted her hip again. When Lady went to her, she gave her the treat.

Before she could move away, Grant said, "Good luck. I hope your dessert wins."

Caprice threw a "thank you" his way and a "nice to have met you" over her shoulder to Naomi. Then she hurried off with Lady to find out if she'd won the dessert competition.

But she couldn't help taking a last glance over

her shoulder to see Naomi and Grant walking away. She already felt as if she'd lost him.

"She doesn't like dogs." Nikki sounded sure of that as they approached the dessert tent.

"She just didn't want to get those pretty slacks slobbered on."

"Me-ow," Nikki said, giving her a *you're-not-usually-catty* look.

Caprice shook her head. "I don't know what's gotten into me."

"True love."

"It can't be true if he's looking in another direction."

"He's looking back. That doesn't mean he can't look forward again."

Out of nowhere, Caprice heard a beeping. Her phone didn't beep.

Nikki slipped hers from her pocket. She said, "I recognize this name. She inquired about my services. I should take this."

Caprice gave her a nod and went toward the tables where the judges and onlookers were gathered. The judges, however, weren't ready to announce. Caprice dropped to the ground giving attention to Lady until Nikki came back, a worried expression on her face.

Before Caprice could ask, she said, "I have a decision to make."

"It doesn't sound like one you want to make."

"The call was from Trudi Swenson. She wants me to cater her wedding reception."

"What's wrong with that?"

"Drew was supposed to cater it. Her wedding is Tuesday evening and she can't find anyone else. I had even met with them, and they decided to go with Drew instead."

"What did you say?"

"I said I'd call her back. She was in tears, Caprice. If I don't cater it, she's going to have to cancel her reception. But if I do it, how's that going to look to the police?"

"You can't live your life worried about what the police are going to think. You also have to make an income. On the other hand, if the powers that be need just one little excuse to go after you, I don't know if that could give it to them. Why don't you call Vince and ask his opinion."

"I don't want someone else making decisions for me."

"This could be an important one, Nik."

"Instead of thinking about the police or consulting Vince, I'm just going to put myself in her shoes. Her wedding is a few days away and she can't find a caterer. What would I want someone to do for me?"

"And the answer is?" Caprice knew what Nikki was going to say.

"I'm going to cater it, and I'll deal with the fallout later."

That fallout could be a murder charge that Nikki wasn't ready for.

Someone tapped on the microphone at the head of the tent, and Caprice heard a man's booming voice say, "We have the results. We're ready to disclose the winners of this year's Grocery Fresh Raspberry Festival."

The manager of the store, Irving Bradford, was doing the announcing. Caprice could see he was enthusiastic about what he did and how he did it.

That's why Grocery Fresh was one of her favorite places to shop.

There was a round of applause, and Irving raised his hand. "Here we go. In third place, for a twenty-five dollar gift certificate from Grocery Fresh, the winner is Caprice De Luca's raspberry bread."

Nikki gave her a hug and Nana waved from across the tent.

"In second place, for a fifty-dollar Grocery Fresh certificate, the winner is Teresa Arcuri with her raspberry rhubarb cobbler."

Caprice knew Teresa. She'd redecorated her living room and dining room not so long ago. She was her mom's age and took baking as seriously as anyone in the De Luca family.

"And for our grand prize, a one hundred dollar Grocery Fresh gift certificate, the winner of this year's dessert raspberry competition is Celia De Luca with her raspberry shortcake. I've got to tell you, Celia, there isn't much of it left. The judges gobbled it all."

Everyone laughed, and Caprice and Nikki rushed to Nana to give her a hug. At least something good had come from today.

Then Caprice remembered talking to Helen and learning about Bronson's tennis matches. As soon as she found a quiet spot, she'd call Roz and see if her friend could pull a few strings to reserve a court next to his.

She couldn't do anything about Grant and his ex-wife, but she could solve Drew's murder. It was time she put more effort into that endeavor.

Chapter Thirteen

Caprice was so excited as she and all of her family, as well as Roz trailed from the parking area toward the Giant Center on Sunday evening. They entered as soon as the doors opened and went to a special window. Dulcina, Rod, and the girls met them there. After introductions, Caprice could see Dulcina was excited too.

"I can't believe he did this for all of us."

Leslie said, "He's a rock star. He can do whatever he wants."

Caprice spoke up. "Ace might be a rock star, but he's just a nice guy too. He likes lasagna and times with his family, and most of all he loves music. You'll see that tonight."

When Leslie looked as if she might have a retort, her father hung his arm around her shoulders. Rod was about five-ten, with sandy brown hair and hazel eyes. All of his attention was on his daughters, and Caprice supposed that's how it should be. But he was dating Dulcina. He should be giving her some attention too.

After Caprice presented their tickets and their backstage passes at the window, the clerk made a call. A security guard came to escort them to the area where they'd be meeting Ace. Caprice's uncle Dom and Dulcina began discussing Halo as they followed the security guard. They all clambored into an elevator that took them to the ground floor.

Excitement practically hummed in the air as they followed the security guard . . . or bodyguard. This was the home of the Hershey Bears Hockey Club. It also sponsored other sports events. Soon the place would be filled with an enormous concert crowd that could number more than ten thousand fans who wanted to hear Ace's music. This was a huge venue for Ace, and she wished him every success.

Caprice kept her gaze on her Nana as they went down a hall. They seemed to be headed to the hockey players' dressing rooms. This had been a long walk for Nana from the entrance of the arena where they left her off to where they were now. Although Nana was a spry seventy-six, Caprice worried about her.

She tapped her nana's arm, leaned close, and whispered, "Are you okay?"

"Don't you start," Nana retorted. "That security guard asked me if I wanted a wheelchair. Seriously? Just look at my sneakers. I walk every day. I'm fit for more than this."

Caprice had to smile. That was Nana. Raring to go.

Soon they were shown to an area that was set up for Ace's Meet-and-Greet. Ace was waiting at a table for them. Caprice caught sight of Marsha, Ace's ex-wife, and his daughter, Trista, talking to the band members, who were also milling about. Marsha waved and Trista ran over to give Caprice a hug.

"Isn't this so exciting?" Trista asked. "I've never seen Dad perform in a place like this before. And Mom and I might be moving to Kismet to be near him."

"That's wonderful. Then I can see you more often too." She saw that Marsha was smiling as she spoke to Zeke Stoltz, Ace's bass player. Zeke had almost quit the tour, but he and Ace had resolved the misunderstandings between them.

Caprice noticed Ace give Marsha's arm a squeeze before he came over to them, and she seemed to be looking at him adoringly once more. Was it possible the two of them would reunite?

Ace was a different man now than he'd been before his divorce. He'd taken responsibility for his daughter and a past road-life he didn't want to repeat with his comeback tour. Whether or not he and Marsha got back together again, their renewed relationship could only be good for Trista.

Although she and Ace had become friends and he'd met Nikki, he'd never been introduced to all of her family until now.

He gave Nana a big hug, and Caprice heard him say to her, "From what Caprice tells me, you remind me a lot of my own grandmother. She was a big influence in my life growing up. I consider her my guardian angel now."

Nana whispered something in his ear, and Ace laughed.

The evening seemed to take wings as there were

photos all around, for her and her family, and for
Dulcina, Rod, and the girls. The Meet-and-Greet
fun was over way too soon. But Caprice knew Ace
had other fans to greet, some who had won an
autograph session from a nearby radio station, and
others who had won a contest via e-mail through his
fan club.

The guard walked everyone back out to the main
arena and showed them to their seats in the front
row. The ground floor seating was slowly filling up.
The bright lights would be dimmed at concert
time, but for now it was easy to see the flow of
people, all age groups, who had come to hear Ace
and his band perform.

Caprice's attention wandered to Bella and Joe
down the row from her. Joe's arm was around his
wife's shoulders, and they both looked happy to be
here. With a baby, date night was a special thing for
them. Maybe she and Nikki could hold down the
fort for them some night soon so they could go out
again. Caprice didn't feel quite capable of handling
an infant and two kids on her own. She was about
to say something to Nikki in the seat beside her
when Nikki snagged her attention first.

"Caprice, look over there." She pointed to a row
of seats behind a railing, up the first few steps from
the ground floor. Caprice didn't even need the
binoculars she'd brought along to see who it was.

"Is that Judy Clapsaddle and Jeanie Boswell?"
Nikki asked.

"Sure looks like it."

Judy Clapsaddle owned the Nail Yard in Kismet
where Caprice had had her nails done and had

bought a gift certificate for her mom. Judy had given her good information when Caprice looked into the murder of her mom's best friend.

"Maybe I'll just wander over there and talk to them," Caprice said. "I've got plenty of time before the concert starts."

"Do you want me to come with you?" Nikki asked.

"No, you stay here. I won't be long."

But as she made her way over to the steps and started climbing them, she noticed Jeanie leave the row and head toward a concession stand in the back. Apparently she wanted an Ace Richland T-shirt more than she wanted to talk to Caprice.

Judy, however, aimed a welcoming smile at Caprice. "Imagine seeing you here. I'll bet we'd notice a lot more Kismet residents if we take stock of everybody who walks in."

"Probably. I thought I'd come over and say hi. I was going to talk to Jeanie too, but she ran off."

The din in the arena was growing louder with more people talking now. Music was playing in the background over the speakers.

Judy leaned into Caprice so she could hear her. "I think she's just embarrassed. She wasn't sure she should come tonight, you know, after Drew's death and all. But she had the tickets, and what good would it do her to stay home? When she mentioned it to me, I said we could come together."

"That's really nice of you. How is she doing?"

Judy seemed hesitant to answer. "Are you looking into Drew's murder?"

"Let's just say I'm keeping my ears open."

"You really helped the police when Louise was killed."

"Some of that was inadvertent," Caprice admitted, remembering how she'd come face-to-face with the murderer but had ended up winning out.

Recalling all that, and apparently the information she'd given Caprice before, Judy said, "It's always been hard to get to know Jeanie. But because we have businesses practically across from each other, we often bump into each other at the Koffee Klatch or at the deli. So we've had a few conversations. That's how I learned she was coming up here tonight when I ran into her at the deli yesterday."

"Did she take any time off?"

"Just for Drew's funeral. And to tell you the truth, she doesn't seem all that affected by Drew's death. It's crazy. I mean, I have a brother. If anything happened to him, I'd be devastated."

The same was true for Caprice. "What was her mood driving up here tonight?"

"She was all light and excited as if nothing unusual had happened. I don't know. Maybe I'm reading her all wrong. Maybe she's just really good at covering up what she's feeling."

After a few more exchanged pleasantries with Judy, Caprice returned to her seat beside Nikki.

Nikki asked, "Did you find anything out?"

Caprice just shook her head.

Not long after, as the lights in the arena dimmed, as the excitement and the buzz and then the applause grew, as Ace's opening act appeared on the stage and swung into an introduction, Caprice's thoughts couldn't stop tripping over one hurdle. What if Jeanie Boswell wasn't just hiding her feelings?

What if she was a cold-blooded murderess?

Caprice swam laps on Monday afternoon as if her life depended on it, and maybe it did. She needed to burn off excess energy. If she did, maybe she could think more clearly. Her thoughts were disrupted with worry about what Grant and Naomi were saying . . . and doing. *Especially* doing. They were also disrupted by everything she had learned and not learned about Drew Pierson, as well as his sister's attitude. Just what direction should she go next?

The gym part of Shape Up was a busy place this afternoon. The pool, not so much. Because she didn't dawdle, her swim took about a half hour, her shower and hair dry about another fifteen minutes. She'd be home to her animals to spend time with them before an evening tennis game with Nikki. Maybe she'd take Lady along. Animals were like kids. You couldn't leave them for hours on end without them missing you. If they missed you too much, they misbehaved, or tried to get your attention in unusual ways. She tried to prevent that.

She pushed open the women's locker room door, about to head straight through the gym area to the front of Shape Up. But as she passed the elliptical trainers, she spotted Larry Penya.

Nana would tell her that was a sign.

Away from Bronson, would he open up more

than he had at Rowena's? There was only one way to find out.

She "accidentally" brushed against his machine, her bag catching on the corner. As she stopped to apologize, their gazes met.

"I'm really sorry," she said. "I wasn't watching where I was going." Then as if a lightbulb had gone on in her head, she said, "I met you at Rowena's. Larry Penya, isn't it?"

"You have a good memory. You're Nikki De Luca's sister."

"You know Nikki?"

"No, I don't know her. I was at the Valentine's Day dance. Drew pointed you out to me, along with Nikki while he was working with her."

Almost everybody in Kismet had been at that dance. She'd been preoccupied that night with Grant . . . and with Seth. But now she wasn't preoccupied.

She moved a little bit closer to Larry. "Because my sister and I found Drew, as well as for Rowena's sake, I'd like to get to the bottom of what happened if the police don't. So maybe you could help me with something."

He looked reluctant to do so, then asked, "What do you need help with?"

"It's a personal thing, really. Can you tell me if Drew really liked Nikki? He gave her the impression he did, but she didn't want to mix business with pleasure. I'm not sure if she regrets that now."

Larry took the towel from around his neck and wiped sweat from his brow. "I guess it doesn't much matter anymore what I say, so I guess I can tell you the truth."

Caprice held her breath. It was rare that someone actually spoke the truth.

"Drew knew Nikki was experienced with her business and a good chef. He intended to work with her to learn what he could from her—about running a catering business and about the type of food she cooked. He made a play for her because he thought if they got serious, they could partner up, and he'd be on his way to what he wanted."

"What did he want?"

"To make some money, to be a success, to ride on somebody else's coattails without putting a lot of effort into it."

Caprice didn't want to respond out of pique, so she waited a few beats before she said, "But it didn't work out with Nikki. So he must have been motivated. He ventured out on his own and then he managed that lucrative deal with Rack O' Ribs."

"Drew was motivated, all right. He wanted the good life like Bronson has. He just wasn't exactly sure how to get it. There's a reason he got that deal with Rack O' Ribs."

"A reason other than the barbecue sauce tasting good?"

"Lots of barbecue sauces taste good. Drew got serious with the manager's daughter, and she put in a good word for him with her dad. Drew knew that manager was friends with the CEO of the chain. That's the kind of conniving Drew did."

Caprice put the manager on her list of people to talk to next. Maybe Drew's conniving is what had gotten him killed.

Larry said, "I'm going to hit the showers. Good

luck screening Drew's enemies. He was racking them up."

Before Caprice could inquire about more of them, Larry had climbed from the machine and disappeared into the men's locker room. Did he have more information she could tap, or did he have something to hide?

On Monday evening, Caprice knew she had to practice her swing before she and Roz *accidentally* ran into Bronson on the tennis courts at the country club, she hoped by the end of the week. So she'd asked Nikki to join her at a playground near her sister's condo tonight. There were four tennis courts here for the general public. Caprice had to admit she didn't like swatting around tennis balls and sweating. The only good thing was, she'd brought Lady along too. Lady, of course, happily wanted to run and catch each tennis ball. But after about fifteen minutes of that, Caprice had given her a chew toy and now she sat under a bench while Nikki served the ball to Caprice once more.

Her sister lobbed it just over the net. Caprice ran forward, swung under the ball, and managed to fish it up so it bounced back to her sister.

Nikki called, "I didn't think you'd get that."

She'd gotten it with luck, not skill. After another fifteen minutes of running and missing and practically falling over her own feet, she pointed to the bench.

Nikki joined her there, and they both opened bottles of water Nikki had brought along. "I can't believe you even managed to look vintage when playing tennis."

Caprice had worn a skort in pink gingham and a pink tank with a little fringe. Her sneakers were printed with peace signs in fuchsia. "I don't look vintage. I just look cool, or groovy, whichever word you want to choose."

Nikki groaned. Her own blue tank and running shorts were skimpy, but that's what she liked to wear to move around the tennis court. Her outfit looked great on her, since Nikki was more slender than Caprice. If Caprice lost about ten pounds . . . That had been her wish for the past few years.

"I have a favor to ask," Nikki said. "I already asked Bella and she said yes."

That always applied subtle pressure when two sisters were on board.

"What favor?"

"Bella doesn't work at All About You tomorrow night, and she agreed to help serve with me and Serena at the wedding reception. Can you help too? Since this is last minute, I'm having trouble finding waitresses. The four of us would work together well. You've been around Serena at the open houses."

Serena was friendly and efficient, and Caprice liked her. "Sure I can help. I'll see if Uncle Dom can sit with Lady. If not, maybe Mom can keep her company."

As they sipped water and caught their breath, Caprice thought about what she should tell Nikki, and what she shouldn't, about the information on Drew she'd ferreted out so far. They were friends as much as sisters. Because of the friendship as well as the sisterhood, they didn't keep secrets.

She took another long swig of water. "I ran into Larry Penya at Shape Up today."

"You did? Did you learn anything?"

When she was slow to answer, Nikki eyed her with a shrewd sisterly look. "You should have called me if you learned something."

"Why call when I was seeing you tonight."

"Okay, now you're seeing me. Talk."

"You're not going to like it."

"What else is new these days? What did he have to say?"

Lady must have heard the tension in their voices, because she stopped chewing, dropped the toy to the ground, wiggled herself between Caprice's and Nikki's legs, and put her paws up on the bench.

Caprice stroked her dog's neck. "It's okay, baby, we're just talking."

"Not yet we're not," Nikki murmured, then gave Lady a pat too.

"First of all," Caprice began, "Larry told me that Drew pointed us out when he was working at the Valentine's Day dance."

"That's not toxic. So tell me what is."

"I asked him if Drew really liked you, as a woman, not as a chef."

Nikki's face, already flushed from exercise, grew a little pinker. "And?"

"And, he told me Drew wanted to work with you to learn what he could from you—about running a catering business, about the type of food you cooked."

"That's what sous chefs do."

"Larry also confided that Drew thought if the two of you got serious, then you'd partner up and he'd be on his way."

"I'd already guessed that, but it isn't easy to hear."

"I didn't just learn about his attitude toward you, though. Apparently Drew was a conniver. Larry maintains that Drew got serious with the manager's daughter at Rack O' Ribs because the manager could put in a good word for him. Mr. Dennis was friends with the CEO of the chain. That's how the barbecue sauce got its tasting, and that's how it got put into the pipeline. I'm putting that manager on my short list of people to talk to."

"You've decided to go after this full throttle, haven't you? Vince isn't going to like it. Grant's not going to like it."

"Vince can live with it. He has before. And as far as Grant goes? He doesn't have any say over my life."

"Caprice?" Nikki's voice held a cautious note that warned Caprice to be cautious too.

"How am I supposed to think about this, Nikki? He's doing what he needs to do. I need to do what I need to do. Quid pro quo, or something like that, if we have to put it in lawyer's terms."

"We don't have to put it in lawyer's terms, and I don't think Grant would either. Just because he's spending some time with Naomi doesn't mean he doesn't care about you. Can't you get that through your head?"

"I only know what I'm feeling, and if I have insecurities, well, so be it. I'm not confident about our relationship because of his background."

"Your own background doesn't help much either.

Maybe you could trust Grant if you hadn't been dumped by two men."

"Thanks a lot for the reminder."

Nikki nudged her shoulder. "I meant it in the nicest way. You deserve better than a man who could forget about you because of a long-distance relationship, or because of a man who wasn't finished with his ex-wife."

"Gee, who does that sound like?" Caprice muttered.

"You usually have a better attitude."

Caprice was saved from a response when a black sedan pulled up along the curb beside the tennis courts. It was shiny and just washed and caught their attention. Both were surprised when Detective Carstead climbed out.

He wasn't wearing a suit tonight, but rather navy dress slacks and a wrinkled cream Oxford shirt. No tie was in evidence. Had he spotted them when he was driving by and just decided to stop and chat?

As the detective strode closer, Lady yipped at him. It wasn't a stay-away yip. It was sort of a "hello" yip. After all, Lady was friendly.

Her soft bark didn't seem to bother the detective. He stepped right up to the bench and looked down at the cocker. She looked up at him as if she wanted a head pat. Caprice reminded herself that her dog was a good judge of character.

"Hello, ladies." His glance toward Nikki seemed to take in her tennis attire. But then he turned to Caprice. "Does she belong to you?"

"Yes, she does. She's all mine."

"Is she friendly?"

Feeling a bit out of sorts this evening, Caprice returned, "Friendlier than I am."

The corner of his lip twitched up as if he wanted to smile but wasn't going to. Holding out his hand to the cocker, he let Lady sniff it. She rubbed her ear against it, then she rolled over for a tummy rub.

Caprice just shook her head. What if Detective Carstead wasn't a friend, but rather the enemy? Could she trust her dog to decide which he was?

Receiving the message, the detective rubbed her tummy for a while, said, "You're a beauty," then rose to his feet again. "I recognized you when I drove by. I was going to give you a call in the morning, but this is just serendipity."

"Serendipity," Caprice repeated. "What were you going to call me about?"

"I heard you went to Drew Pierson's funeral."

"I did. Nikki didn't."

He glanced at her sister again. "I know that."

Of course he did. After all, he was an investigator.

"You knew Drew Pierson's grandmother well enough to pay your respects?" he asked with a probing look.

"First of all, we were there the day he was murdered. Second of all, my mom and Nana know her from church. Third of all, it only seemed right."

His expression was totally neutral, and she clamped her lips shut before she said anything else. Nikki had remained silent, which was a good thing.

Brett Carstead shifted on his wing-tipped shoes, then he asked, "Are you investigating the murder?"

Caprice knew when the Fifth Amendment had to apply. She wasn't going to answer that one.

He gave a resigned sigh. "I warned you before,

and I'm going to warn you again. Keep out of it. You're putting yourself in danger, and it's not necessary."

She knew he was thinking about the last murder she inadvertently solved at the same time the police were closing in.

Now Nikki spoke up. "Am I a suspect?"

The look the detective gave her sister was a bit longer than necessary. "I can't discuss the investigation, and you shouldn't be either."

Nikki held up her hands like stop signs. "I'm not discussing the investigation, at least not with anybody other than Caprice . . . and of course Vince."

Carstead gave a little grunt. He couldn't fault her for that answer. Caprice noticed the way Brett Carstead was gazing at her sister. He didn't want to fault her at all. He didn't want to charge her with a murder. In fact, he *could* want to date her.

And the way Nikki was gazing at him—

Carstead broke his eye contact with Nikki. "Enjoy your game of tennis. I'm glad I stopped. This saved me a phone call." Not forgetting about Lady, he gave her another pat on the head, then he turned and walked away.

Nikki watched his long-legged stride, the way he rounded the car, then opened his door and climbed inside.

"What are you thinking?" she asked Nikki.

"I'm thinking he's pretty hot for a detective."

Caprice groaned. As if they didn't have trouble enough.

Chapter Fourteen

For Caprice, dressing on Tuesday evening as a server—which meant conservatively—was almost painful. She smoothed down her white apron tied over black slacks and a white blouse. The wedding reception was being held in the social hall adjacent to the Kismet United Methodist Church. Although Nikki had been nervous about catering this event, she needed the income, and she also needed the recommendations if the reception went well.

Bella nudged Caprice and nodded toward the wedding cake. It was Nikki's new specialty—a square carrot cake with two connected crystal hearts perched on top. Silver swirls ran down the sides. It was quite attractive.

"Would you want that at your wedding?"

Bella was just making conversation, helping the time go faster while they served the meal. But Caprice didn't want to talk about weddings. Still she answered cheerily, "I love Nikki's carrot cake."

Bella gave her a long look. "Are you and Grant still on the outs?"

218 *Karen Rose Smith*

Caprice shrugged. "I haven't heard from him."

"He stopped by the swings with Patches at the Raspberry Festival to say hello. His ex didn't look too pleased," Bella said with a wink.

Caprice was silent.

"I know from my counseling sessions with Joe, you shouldn't let things fester," Bella added more seriously.

"Nothing's festering. He has to make a decision."

"Or, you have to stand by him," Bella warned sagely.

Caprice knew Bella had learned a lot about standing by Joe when she and her husband had been going through their problems. Was she looking at this all wrong? Should she just *be there* for Grant?

It was time for the couple to cut the beautiful cake. The billowing wedding gown sparkled under the lights as the groom took the bride's hand and they strolled toward the cake stand together. Nikki was waiting for them with an engraved cake knife that the bride had provided. As soon as the bride and groom cut those first slices, Bella and Caprice would swoop in with trays and dishes. Nikki would push the cake into the kitchen and Serena would quickly slice pieces for the guests.

Trudi placed her hand on top of her groom's on the knife. They were so young, Caprice thought, probably in their midtwenties. They looked as if they expected their lives to turn out just the way they wanted them to. Maybe they would.

Nikki was there with a silver-trimmed white plate to collect the slice the couple cut. Then she held it up for each of them to take a piece to feed each other. Trudi fed her groom first, and he had icing all over his mouth. He fed her a bit more daintily. Everyone applauded when they were finished.

Nikki was about to wheel the cake toward Bella and Caprice when one of the guests approached her. The woman was older than Caprice, but it was hard to tell how old with her bleached blond hair and her polished red fingernails. She wore loads of makeup too, and she caught Caprice's attention because of it. Caprice didn't wear much makeup, and when she saw someone who did, Caprice took notice and wondered what she was trying to prove . . . or what she was trying to hide. In this case, she was probably trying to hide wrinkles.

The woman pointed to Nikki's wedding cake. "I saw you at the wedding expo when I was there with Trudi. She was supposed to be using Drew Pierson. They would have had a chocolate walnut groom's cake then."

"I'm sorry if you would have preferred that," Nikki said blandly, and Caprice could tell she didn't intend to give in to an argument with this woman.

"Maybe you shouldn't have taken over this wedding reception. Maybe you should have let someone else handle it."

Caprice could tell that Nikki just wanted to go hide somewhere, but her sister was made of sterner stuff than that. "Drew and I were in competition for business. I saw no reason to turn down this job when Trudi couldn't find anyone else. She would have had to cancel the reception. Is that what you would have wanted her to do?"

The woman who had accosted Nikki took a step

back. "She could have had a deli cater it. There were alternatives."

"Not according to Trudi. Maybe you should ask her. Maybe you should ask her why she chose me."

Just then, Trudi came over to Nikki and said, "Everyone's raving about the food. You've done a marvelous job here tonight." She looked at the guest who was a relative or a friend. "Delia, are you telling Nikki how pretty her cake is?"

"No," the woman snapped. "Pretty doesn't matter if she had a motive for murder."

Instead of being embarrassed, Trudi patted the woman's arm. "Delia, I think you've been reading too many mystery novels. Nikki's trying to do her job just like everyone else. That chocolate walnut groom's cake attracted us to Drew Pierson's menu, but Nikki's meal tonight was flawless, and we should have just gone with her in the first place. Please try her carrot cake and see how good it is. That's all that matters."

Caprice had been about to step in, but Trudi had done it for her, and very adroitly too.

Delia took a last look at Nikki and huffed away.

Her bridal gown rustling from here to next year, Trudi pushed her veil over her shoulder and gave Nikki a huge hug. She said, "My husband's the one who wanted to go with Drew in the first place. I would have chosen you. You've done a fabulous job tonight. So don't let what Delia said bother you one little bit. No one else is thinking it."

Bella leaned close to Caprice and nodded to some of the other guests who were looking their way. "That's a nice sentiment, and I'm sure Trudi means it. But I have a feeling there's more than one person in this room thinking that Nikki might have done it."

Caprice was absolutely sure that Bella was right.

"You need to get yourself a police scanner."

Caprice had been in the middle of working up figures for a proposal for a house staging when she'd answered Isaac Hobbs's call Wednesday evening.

"Why should I get a police scanner when you have one and Lloyd Butterworth at the Koffee Klatch has one. I usually hear the news before it makes it down the street."

Isaac gave a grunt. "I just have one for entertainment value when I don't have any customers in the shop. Lloyd Butterworth milks his for all it's worth and thinks it brings him business."

"He could be right about that. His coffee's darn good too."

"And mine isn't?"

Isaac let his pot of coffee sit all day. Sometimes when she went to visit in the afternoon, it tasted as if it had been burnt to a crisp, and that was hard to do with coffee. "Your coffee provides great conversation." She went back to their original subject. "Why do I need a scanner?"

"Because Rowena Pierson's house was burglarized last night."

"What?"

"You heard me. This is small-town Kismet. You don't just go by codes. I listen to chatter too. The police were called to that address for an attempted break-in. That's basically all I know, except . . . I called a friend of a friend who knows one of the officers. She said they don't think anything was taken."

"Then why the break-in?" Caprice mused.

"I don't know. I did find the paperwork on her lamps. The table lamp is worth around $200,000 and the floor lamp around $400,000. But those prices swing around at auctions. One auction house I know of deals mainly with Tiffany lamps. They have a list of private collectors always on the lookout. Then, of course, there is Christie's."

The most high-end auction house, Caprice thought.

Isaac added, "There are lots of forgeries. Provenance often tells the tale. Rowena's lamps have provenance dating back to 1929. Are you going to pay Rowena a visit and nose around?"

"I can't very well do that tonight. I have work with deadlines. Besides, a visit this soon would be unseemly."

"Like you were nosing around," he agreed.

"I have to be careful, Isaac. Detective Jones's eyes are on me."

"Is Rowena Pierson's place within walking distance?"

"It could be if I wanted the exercise. Why?"

"So take Lady for a walk tomorrow and Jones won't be the wiser."

Not only her work van but her yellow Camaro was recognizable, and Isaac might have a valid point. "I'll think about it."

"If you snooze, you lose."

She laughed. "I get the idea, Isaac. If you hear anything else, will you let me know?"

"Sure will. And if you need my services, you know where to find me."

Isaac and the paperwork at his shop had helped her out before. "You're a good friend, Isaac."

"And you're a great customer."

She knew Isaac tried to be hard-boiled on the outside, but he was a softie on the inside. After all, he'd attended her birthday party in April and brought her the cutest little vintage cat creamer.

"I'll take your advice to heart," she told him.

"And you'll let me know what happened with the break-in?"

Caprice had to smile. "I promise I'll let you know. Thanks for the tip."

"Anytime."

As she ended the call with Isaac, Caprice realized that he was a good friend, not just a contact. She'd have to invite him over for dinner sometime so they could really chat, or maybe invite him to one of the De Luca family dinners. He'd get a kick out of that.

She was thinking about the next family dinner, what she'd make, whether Grant would be there, as she walked Lady the following morning and headed for Rowena's. Midmorning in early July, heat was already setting in. She'd chosen to wear fifties-style turquoise pedal pushers and a white blouse with turquoise pinstripes. Her sneakers were comfortable for walking.

Lady didn't seem in any hurry as she snuffled the grass along the sidewalk and then looked up at Caprice inquiringly. *Does this walk have a destination?*

"Yes, it does," Caprice told her. "I don't know if Rowena likes dogs, though, so we might be staying outside on the porch.

Lady tilted her head as if considering that.

Caprice rubbed her, and Lady heeled perfectly for the rest of the walk. She responded to praise so well, and treats worked too, though Caprice used them less now than she used to. At ten months old, Lady was growing into her beautiful self. Her golden color was rich and deep, and the cream along her ears reminded Caprice of the golden highlights in Nikki's hair. Nikki probably wouldn't like being compared to Lady.

As Caprice reached Rowena's block, she noticed the flowers dotting the yards—purple and white petunias, red roses in full glory, marigolds a neighbor had planted along a border. Caprice wondered if Rowena would even be staying at her house or if she would be staying with Kiki again because of the break-in.

The next minute, her question was answered. A white van had parked at the curb outside of Rowena's house. Two men hurried down the steps and climbed into the vehicle, slamming the doors. As Caprice and Lady approached, she heard the van start up, then it pulled away from the curb and sped down the street.

Maybe repairs had been necessary if someone had broken in. Had Rowena been here when it happened?

She was hoping she'd soon have her questions answered.

Lady ran up the steps beside Caprice. Caprice put her finger to the doorbell, but before she could even press it, Rowena was at the door.

"Hi, Caprice, what brings you here?"

Caprice nodded to Lady. "I was taking her for a walk and just headed in your direction."

"Oh my. I missed her at first."

"I understand if you don't want a dog inside. I just came to check on you and see how you're doing."

"I've never had a dog, but I don't mind yours coming in as long as she doesn't run around and knock everything over."

"She's usually pretty well behaved," Caprice assured Rowena. "If she gets rambunctious I'll bring her back outside again. I brought one of her toys that she can chew on while we're talking."

"That sounds good."

"Was that a repair truck I saw leaving?"

Rowena waited until Caprice and Lady were inside before she answered. "Not exactly a repair truck. One of those was here yesterday to fix my basement window. Someone broke in night before last."

"Were you here?"

"Yes, I was here. I was all settled in my bedroom when I heard a noise. I didn't know what it was. Apparently it was someone breaking in that basement window. They made it up to the living room, but I had my four-pronged cane and I went after whoever it was. The person wore a hoodie, so I couldn't tell if the intruder was male or female. I wish my sight was as good as it once was. Anyway, I chased whoever it was back down the basement and shut the door and put a chair in front of it. Then I called the police."

"I can't believe you did that! You're fortunate the burglar ran."

"I am, aren't I? That's what the police said too. They think whoever it was wanted to steal something. Maybe the Tiffany lamps. But I don't know. I did see that the burglar had something on his hands. They looked white. The police think those were latex gloves. From what I could tell, nothing was taken. I guess I surprised him. Maybe he expected me to still be at Kiki's."

That was a reasonable supposition.

"So the police didn't find any evidence of who was here?"

"Only the broken glass from the basement window. The men you saw leaving were installing my burglar alarm system. I should have had it done a long time ago because of the Tiffany lamps if nothing else. But nobody knew their worth. Not really."

Was that true? *Were* the lamps the object of the break in? Or did Rowena have something of Drew's that the burglar might have wanted? Even more possible, what if the burglar knew about the recipes inside the light? Did he or she want those?

Rowena motioned to the sofa. "Please sit."

Caprice undid Lady's leash and gave her the toy she'd brought along.

"Your nana called me to talk awhile. I so appreciated that. It seems since my grandson was murdered I'm persona non grata in Kismet."

"What do you mean?" Caprice could guess, but it seemed Rowena needed a listening ear.

"I thought I had friends in this town. I've lived here all my life. I raised Drew and Jeanie the best way I knew how. They went through the public school system, and I made friends with other parents even though they were younger than I was. Granted, since I haven't been able to get out and about as much, I've let a lot of friendships slide. When you can't go and do, people forget you're around. All except for Kiki. She's been a true friend. The others—they're all keeping their distance. It's as if I have the plague."

Caprice didn't know if she could help Rowena, but she could try. "I don't know if I can find out who killed Drew, but I might be able to find some tidbits of information that could help the police. What I want *you* to know is that the general public does look on murder as if it's something that's catching. It's not fair, but they don't want to be tainted by it. They don't want to think that they could bring something like that on themselves. They want to believe they're different. They're not, of course. Violence can touch anyone."

"I just feel . . . so alone now."

Caprice knew Rowena was missing Drew desperately, and she was hurt by her friends ignoring her and putting her in a "do not touch" category.

"Is there anything I can do to help?"

"Just your visits help. You don't know how much they mean to me. Your grandmother said she'd visit too. She didn't want to barge in too soon, but I don't think there is a too soon with this. I'm never going to get over Drew being taken from me. All I can do is learn to live with it."

"Has Jeanie been by to visit?"

"She's at her store all the time, and she tells me she can't get away. But from what I've seen of write-ups about you in the newspaper, and what your nana says, you work a lot too. Yet here you are."

Yes, here she was. And she wasn't going to ask any more questions. She was going to keep Rowena company and just let her talk about Drew. She had the feeling that that's what the woman wanted to do most, and Caprice was going to let her.

That evening Caprice had just ended a video conferencing call with a client when Roz texted her.

Are you busy? Can I come over?

Caprice texted back, Sure. Anything wrong?

Roz texted back, We'll talk.

Hmmm. That didn't sound good. A problem with Bella working for her? A pothole in the road with Vince?

Caprice was wearing her favorite pair of lounging pants, patterned with kittens, and a bright pink T-shirt that matched part of the design. She briefly thought about changing, but this was Roz. She could be comfortable.

After almost exactly fifteen minutes, her doorbell rang. She checked the monitor next to her computer. Yep, that was Roz standing under her porch light, and she had Dylan with her.

Caprice opened the door and invited them inside. Dylan yipped, danced around the foyer, then met Lady in the dining room and took off for the kitchen.

"I made decaf coffee," Caprice told her friend. "It's a new flavor—butternut rum."

"Do you have a bottle of wine? I think that's more my speed tonight."

She and Roz had shared wine before, but it

wasn't usually their beverage of choice. Something was wrong.

"I think I have Tears of Gettysburg that Vince brought me from Adams County Winery." It was a sweet white wine that went down easy.

"That might be appropriate," Roz agreed, going into the living room and plopping down on the sofa.

Roz's golden-blond hair was always perfectly coifed. She usually wore gold earrings or jewels even when she was dressed casually. Casual for Roz was a well-tailored, probably designer top and slacks. Tonight she wore a pale green set with emeralds at her ears.

"Do you want to tell me what's wrong *before* we have the wine or afterward?" Caprice asked.

"First of all, I want to tell you we have a tennis court date for tomorrow at four-thirty. We'll be on the court next to Bronson."

"That's great. How did you manage it?"

"That wasn't hard. I just dropped in at the Country Squire pro shop. I asked about court availability. I hinted that I might want to do some business with Bronson, and the manager set me up."

"It's good to have friends in high places," Caprice joked.

"Or at the computer in the pro shop. When Ted was alive—" She stopped abruptly.

"Go on," Caprice prompted. "You can talk about him, you know. You were married to him."

"And what a sham that was," Roz said. "He often had the manager rearrange court times or court schedules to suit him when he wanted to discuss business over a tennis game. I felt it was manipulative, and here I am doing the same thing."

"Does it make a difference that I'm trying to catch a murderer?"

Roz's gaze met hers. "Of course, it does. I just . . . I just regret so many things about my marriage to him."

"Where is this coming from now?"

"Let's open the wine."

Caprice brought out two crystal wineglasses. Vince had given them to her as a housewarming present when she'd bought this house. They were blown glass with an etched flower pattern. She suspected he'd gone to Isaac's shop to find them.

After Caprice sliced cheddar cheese and paired it with one of her favorite crackers, she arranged a plate for the two of them. When she returned to the living room with the dish and the open wine, Roz was staring into space. Something had her spooked.

After Caprice poured the wine, she handed Roz a glass. "Okay, spill it. What's going on?"

"It's your brother. It's Ted. It's my history with men. I'm confused about all of it, and I'm not sure what I should do or shouldn't do."

"That's one very broad topic. Can we narrow it down?"

Roz drank at least half her glass of wine. "I haven't always made the best choices when I've tried to have relationships in my life. I dated a few men after Mom died . . . before Ted."

Although Roz was rich now, she'd had few advantages growing up. Her mom had raised her on her own. When Roz was a senior in high school, her mother had been diagnosed with breast cancer. The summer after graduation, out of necessity, Roz had had to put her dream of being a flight attendant on hold and waitress while she'd taken care of her mom. Before her mother died, Joan Hulsey had made Roz promise not to put her dreams on hold again. So after the funeral, Roz had trained for her job, flown everywhere, and then met Ted Winslow. Roz's traveling and then her marriage to Ted had interfered with their friendship. They'd kept in touch, but weren't the good friends they'd been in high school. Not until after her husband's murder. Roz had been accused of killing Ted, and Caprice had stepped in. Now she and Roz were close again, close enough to be honest with each other and tell each other the truth.

"The men you dated before Ted. Were they really serious relationships?"

Roz thought about it. "I didn't let them get too serious, I guess, because of my traveling. As you found out, it's hard to have a long-distance relationship."

"But Ted was different because he promised you the sun and the moon and the stars?" Caprice asked without judgment.

"I guess you could say that. He was rich, powerful, and confident. He swept me off my feet. He wouldn't take no for an answer. I was blinded by what Ted could give me, by the facade he showed me. He wasn't who he seemed."

"You don't really know a person until you're with him for a while." Caprice couldn't help but think about her own situation with Grant. She thought she knew him. But did she really?

"What are you afraid of most?" Caprice took a few sips of her wine and thought about the answer she would give.

Roz drained her glass, set it on the coffee table, and poured herself another. "I'm afraid of getting hurt again. I'm afraid I'll hurt Vince. Up until now, we've had fun together. We've enjoyed each other's company. We've given in to a romance that just happened. If my relationship with him goes south, what happens to my friendship with you . . . with your family? If he and I really don't belong together, what damage are we going to do to each other?"

"I've misplaced my crystal ball," Caprice said. "You can't possibly think you're going to answer these questions, do you?"

Roz sipped more wine, then laid her head back against the sofa cushion. "Here I thought you'd have some answers."

"Not to those questions. I can tell you no matter what happens between you and Vince, it's not going to affect our friendship. We've been through too much together." She motioned to the dish of cheese. "Eat something before all that alcohol goes to your head."

"My head's already spinning, so it's not going to make much difference."

As Roz assembled cheese on a cracker and popped it into her mouth, Caprice asked, "What brought all this on?"

Roz chewed, swallowed, and took another sip of wine.

Lady and Dylan raced into the room, awakening Sophia perched on the top shelf of her cat tree, as well as Mirabelle, who was prettily sleeping on the bottom shelf.

After the dogs ran through the room, around the circular floor plan that Caprice's animals loved, she suspected they'd detoured into her office where a few of Lady's toys lay strewn across the floor. Mirabelle hopped down off the cat tree, came over to the sofa, sat at Caprice's feet, and meowed at her.

"Do you want closer company?" Caprice asked as she waited for Roz to answer her question.

Mirabelle hopped up onto the sofa and padded over onto Caprice's lap. She settled in and purred.

Roz studied the beautiful Persian for a few moments. "Vince wants me to move in with him."

"Wow," Caprice said without stopping herself. "That's huge for him."

"And huge for me. Maybe it's too soon. I don't know what to do. I don't know what to tell him. I don't want to hurt him, either by rejecting his offer or by moving in and having it all not work out."

Hard questions that had to be answered. "Do you think you're over Ted?"

"How does anyone get over a situation like that? Some days I think I am, and some days I think I'm not."

"Do you believe on the days you're not that Vince will support you through it? Or will he just get impatient that you haven't moved on?"

"He hasn't been impatient so far."

"But you think that just might be romance's rosy glasses, or Vince not showing you his true self."

Roz took another gulp of wine. "Yes."

"There's only one way you're going to know Vince's true self, and that's if you're around him more. Not just for wine-tasting dates and movie dates and dinners out. But first thing in the morning and last thing at night, when he hasn't shaved and when he has, when you can't find something in your closet to wear even though your closet's full, when you have an argument with him and he leaves and you don't know what's going to happen next."

Roz raised glistening eyes to Caprice. "I want it to work."

"If you want it to work, then you have to give it a chance. If you shut down now, how will you ever know?"

"You think I should move in with him?"

"I think you need to talk to him about it more, and maybe compromise."

"How do you compromise on something like that?"

After a few sips of her own wine, Caprice responded. "I don't know how busy Vince is this time of year, or you either for that matter. But what if instead of moving in with him, the two of you went on a vacation for a week? I'm sure he could use one, and you probably could too. Just be with each other day and night. No, it's not real life. But you'd be in each other's company whether you're in a good mood or a bad mood, whether you're having fun or whether you're not."

Roz set down her glass and turned it in a circle as if she was nervous about all of it. "Do you think he'd go for it?"

"You won't know until you ask. At least you

wouldn't be saying no. You'd be taking a step forward."

Roz thought about it some more. "I don't want to board Dylan."

"Board? I'll take him. You don't have to board him. He's used to my house, and he's used to Lady. He's even getting used to having two cats around. It would be fine for a week."

Roz rubbed her hand across her temple. "All of this is making my head spin."

"That's probably the wine. You're a one-glass girl like me. You've had two. In fact, why don't you just stay the night?"

After her husband's murder, Roz had stayed with Caprice for a while. They gotten along great, and right now, Caprice could use the girlfriend company too.

"I don't want to put you out."

Caprice brushed her concerns away. "You're not."

Lady and Dylan trotted into the living room and sat down beside each other near the coffee table.

"It's better if I don't drive," Roz agreed. "That's the smart thing to do. And I'll think about your idea of a vacation. Bella might like the extra hours for a week if she can find a babysitter. It will be a matter of whether Vince can get away."

"Ask him."

"I'm seeing him tomorrow evening after you and I have our tennis match. I'll broach the subject then."

Caprice knew life could be about compromise, about taking baby steps one at a time. A jump into the ocean wasn't necessary when you could just jump into the little pond where you were sure you could swim. However, her relationship with Grant was more complicated than Roz's with Vince. Weren't their situations different?

Caprice poured herself another glass of wine and thought about her tennis match with Roz next to Bronson's court. She needed to form a strategy for her approach to him. That was much easier than thinking about Grant and his ex-wife having an intimate dinner together . . . or more.

Chapter Fifteen

Roz left the next morning, and Caprice missed her after she was gone. It was fun engaging in girl talk again with a "roommate."

Of course, Grant popped into her mind as a possible roommate, and she shooed the image away.

On her to-do list this morning was a stop at Rack O' Ribs. Later Nana would be pup-sitting while Caprice staged the Spanish house. She would definitely make it a Hacienda Haven, then Denise Langford could bring her other agents through the mansion for a tour. Later this afternoon, she'd meet Roz on the courts.

She wouldn't think about Grant all day.

Lady looked up at her and barked. Her cocker knew she was in denial.

As Caprice drove to Rack O' Ribs, she understood that restaurants weren't staffed only during their posted hours. The manager and kitchen staff had to prep, and they came into work long before the restaurant opened. She drove around the side with the drive-up window and parked on the other

side of the restaurant. Instead of going to the front
doors, which she knew would be locked, she went
around to the back. Lady had wanted to come
along, but Caprice promised her she wouldn't be
gone long and then she'd take her to visit Nana to
play with Valentine.

She was as fond of the animals that filled her life
as she was the people in it.

There was a buzzer on the back door of the
restaurant and Caprice pushed it. It was possible
the manager wasn't here.

A member of the waitstaff answered, his apron
messy with barbecue sauce streaks. "Can I help
you?" he asked impatiently. She read his name tag.
It said STAN JONES.

"I'd like to talk to the manager, Bertram Dennis.
Is he here?"

The young man glanced over his shoulder. He
couldn't have been more than twenty, and his im-
maturity showed when he answered, "I'll check if
he wants to see anyone."

Caprice held the door as he went back inside,
and she stepped in. Once inside, it would be easier
to get her answers. Once inside, it would be harder
for Bertram Dennis to ignore her.

But Bertram Dennis had apparently dealt with
whatever came up. He entered the hallway and saw
her standing there. "Can I help you?"

"I hope so." She held out her hand. "My name's
Caprice De Luca."

He cocked his head as if he was thinking about
her name, as if he might recognize it. But he wasn't
making any connections.

"You're Mr. Dennis?"

He nodded. "I am." He still looked puzzled as to why she was there. "Did you have a meal you weren't satisfied with at the restaurant? Something like that?"

"Oh, no. My sister and I were in a few weeks ago, and the ribs with that new barbecue sauce are wonderful."

He appeared pleased to hear that. "They've been good for business, that's for sure. Everybody must be spreading the word. Do you want to buy in bulk?"

She gave a small laugh. "No. That's not why I'm here. I'd like to talk to you about Drew Pierson."

At that, Mr. Dennis took a step back and frowned. "I don't think that's a good idea. Besides, why would I want to talk to *you* about him?"

"I'm friends with his grandmother, Rowena Pierson."

Mr. Dennis looked a little less hostile, but he still wasn't ready to cooperate. "I already talked to both detectives on the case. What do *you* have to do with it, besides being friends with his grandmother?"

"My sister and I found Drew."

Mr. Dennis's eyes opened in shock, then he checked over his shoulder. Noise poured from the kitchen area. He and Caprice both knew workers were milling about. He motioned to her to follow him. "Let's step in here."

They proceeded a few feet down the hall, and he opened an office door. It was a small office, messy too. Papers were strewn all over the desk. But Dennis didn't go behind the desk. He just closed the door and stood right beside it.

"Tell me again why I should talk to you."

"Because my sister is looking for answers. She worked with Drew for a while. She runs Catered Capers."

Dennis snapped his fingers. "The caterer who was fighting Drew for clients. Do the police think she had a reason to kill him?"

"They might," Caprice admitted honestly. "So I'm trying to stay one step ahead of them. Please tell me what you knew about Drew."

Dennis paced the office, then went around his desk and shuffled a few papers, from one side to the other. Afterward, he looked up at Caprice with a troubled expression. "I'll tell you what I told the police. Pierson was a scumbag in nice duds."

Caprice wasn't necessarily surprised by the admission, but she was a little surprised by the venom in Bertram Dennis's voice. "Can you give me a reason why you thought that?" If she had to push, she would. Because she had the feeling this man knew something . . . something important.

"So many reasons I probably can't count them all," he muttered. "But let's start with my daughter, Tabitha. Pierson acted as if he was interested in her. He took advantage of her. He used his charm on her so that he could present his barbecue sauce to me. Somehow he found out that I knew the CEO of Rack O' Ribs personally."

"Why do you think he used your daughter?"

"Because as soon as the contracts were signed, he dropped her. If it weren't for me, the CEO never would have heard of his barbecue sauce, let alone tasted it. I got him that deal because I thought he and Tabitha were serious."

The bitterness was so obvious that Caprice

wondered if there wasn't more to this story. "Did he bother your daughter after he dropped her?'

"No. He wouldn't even take her calls."

"Did he ask you for more favors? After all, you manage the local restaurant that was going to sell his barbecue sauce."

"I had to sell the sauce, and it had to do well or my ass was on the line. I threatened to tell the owner of the chain what a true jerk Pierson was, but Pierson blackmailed me."

"How's that possible?"

"Tabitha trusted him. She thought they had a future. She told him things she didn't tell anyone else. She told him things about *me*."

Caprice kept silent, not knowing if this man would tell her what those things were. When Dennis didn't go on, she prompted, "Personal things about you?"

He looked uncomfortable. "Do you really need to know this?"

"Anything I know about anyone's connection to Drew will help me . . . and my sister."

He ran his hand through his hair. "All right. The detectives already know and so does my wife. No secrets anymore. Tabitha found out I had an affair last year. She saw a text that came in on my phone. I didn't even know she knew, but Drew Pierson did. He threatened to tell my wife if I made any statements about him to the CEO of the chain. He had me. I made a mistake, and he knew about it, so I was going to sell his barbecue sauce if it killed me."

"And now?" Caprice asked.

"And now my daughter thinks I'm a cheater. My wife *knows* I'm a cheater, because Tabitha told her after Pierson was murdered. She was so upset about everything that it tumbled out. And Drew Pierson's barbecue sauce is a doggone success. There's irony in that, don't you think?"

There wasn't only irony in it, there was motive for murder in it. Tabitha, Bertram Dennis, and maybe even his wife could be placed on that suspect list. The suspects for Drew's murder were multiplying much too fast.

The tennis courts at the Country Squire Golf and Recreation Club were much different than the public courts Caprice and Nikki had played on. These courts were maintained with pristine white nets and janitorial care that rivaled any a maid would give inside a mansion. Caprice knew her way around the Golf and Recreation Club because she'd gone to dinners here, given workshops here, even played golf—very poorly she might add—with clients. But she'd never played tennis here.

Walking along a golf course on a beautiful day was preferable to running and sweating and tripping and exerting energy in the late-afternoon sun. But today she'd do that. Anything to get more answers to her questions. She'd wondered on the way here if she should just go visit Bronson's Happy Camper RV site. But if she did, he'd be on guard. If she did, he'd know his way around and she wouldn't. If she did, she couldn't have easily cut off conversation she might want to, or leave when questions got too sticky. No, this was the better venue and she should stop second-guessing herself.

Was Grant second-guessing himself now that

he'd brought Naomi to Kismet? Did she like the Purple Iris, the small town bed-and-breakfast? Did she feel Kismet could house her aspirations? Those questions led to the fact that Caprice was concerned Naomi would move here to be close to Grant. Should she text him that she was thinking about him?

With all of that racing around in her head, it was very easy to work off her frustration. Every time she imagined one of those questions she couldn't answer, she slammed that ball so hard, she won her point.

Roz was a little taken aback at how hard she tried. "When did you learn to play like this?"

"I'm just playing to get the most out of the game."

"Or demolish your opponent. This is just a friendly game, Caprice. I lob a ball to you. You lob one back to me, and we keep it going."

"I don't know if that's enough to attract Bronson's attention."

"Then find it another way."

Caprice and Roz were into another set when Bronson and a second man about his age came onto the court next to theirs. Caprice kept playing, not wanting to be obvious. This could be a very long exercise stretch if she wanted their meeting to seem casual.

She and Roz played. Bronson and his partner played. Finally, somehow they all managed to take a break around the same time.

Plucking a towel from a nearby bench, Caprice flung it around her neck and Roz did the same. Bronson and his partner were talking at a bench close by. When he looked away for a moment, their gazes connected. After a few seconds, she smiled and gave a little wave.

Bronson said something to his partner and came toward her. "Caprice, isn't it?"

"Yes, it is. And you're Bronson."

He laughed. "So we both have a good memory, except . . . I've never seen you playing tennis here before."

"Roz Winslow invites me to the Country Squire as her guest. I guess our court times have never matched before."

He didn't know this was her first court time.

He looked in Roz's direction as Roz spotted a friend on another court and crossed to speak to her. "Mrs. Winslow. She was widowed last year, right?" He snapped his fingers. "You helped solve that murder, and now she's dating your brother."

"You *are* up to date."

"Partly that. But Mrs. Winslow is a high-profile woman. She was before her husband was murdered, and she is now."

"I don't know if that's good or bad."

"People consider her a mover and shaker. Ted Winslow definitely was. She owns a shop in town, doesn't she?"

"She does. All About You."

Bronson gave a nod toward Roz again. "And she knows everybody under the sun. She has great public relations skills."

"That sounds as if you wouldn't mind dating her yourself," Caprice observed.

"I wouldn't. But I didn't want to move in too quickly. Then she started bringing your brother around. I don't horn in on another man's territory."

If he was being honest, she respected that. "Since we're being so honest"—she gave him a somewhat flirtatious smile—"I have a question for you."

"Go ahead. I'll answer it if I can, especially if it's about recreational vehicles."

Always the salesman, she thought. "No, not about campers. It's about Drew Pierson."

"What about Drew?"

"I know you were good friends, and I know you let him work out of your kitchen."

"I did. It was stupid of him to pay for another facility when I had that big kitchen that he could use."

"Did you ever talk about his cooking with him?"

Bronson considered her question. "He tested recipes on me, and I tasted them. He said I should get some benefit from his cooking in my kitchen."

"My sister says that Drew was an adequate cook but that he never created recipes, that he didn't have that talent. Did you notice if he created in the kitchen?"

Moving his towel back and forth across the back of his neck, Bronson shrugged. "When I watched Drew in the kitchen, he usually had a recipe to follow, one printed off the Internet, or something like that. Does that help?"

"I'm not sure. Nikki claims he stole one of her recipes and served it at the wedding expo. Someone else who knew him claimed he stole his recipe. That's why I wondered."

"I just knew Drew was a good cook, not where his inspiration came from. Though if you're talking about the barbecue sauce recipe, I know Mario Ruiz thinks Drew stole it from him. The two of them had a loud and serious argument a few days before

Drew was killed. I came home from work and found them practically at each other's throats. I didn't want my place torn apart, so I told Mario to leave or else I'd call the police."

"Do you think Drew *did* steal the recipe?"

"I don't know. Drew wouldn't talk about the fight afterward. He just muttered some comment about everybody was angry with him. Bertram Dennis was the other man who wanted a piece of his hide. Drew told me if Dennis came around, I should tell him I didn't know where Drew was."

"Would you have lied for him?"

Bronson didn't hesitate. "I would have lied if it meant keeping Drew from getting beaten up or hurt. Sure."

"Nikki believes that Drew was using her to get ahead. Do you think that's something Drew would do?"

Bronson sighed. "I hate to admit it, but Drew could be a real cad with women, dating them if he thought he could gain something from it. We were friends, but that didn't mean I approved of all of his tactics."

In spite of her concerns about who killed Drew, Caprice found herself liking Bronson. He could be lying to her, that was true. But he seemed honest about his friendship with Drew, and what he thought about it.

Roz came back on the court about the same time Bronson's partner stood at the bench and motioned to him.

Bronson gave Roz a wave, saying to Caprice, "If she ever splits up with your brother, let me know."

Then he smiled and jogged over to his friend, who was already on the court again.

When Roz came to meet Caprice at the bench, she asked, "Did you find out anything essential?"

"I'm not sure. He just confirmed a lot I already knew. Though he did tell me Mario and Drew had a fight a few days before Drew was killed—a serious fight. Mario neglected to tell me that."

"He doesn't want any suspicion coming down on him. Can you blame him?"

"No, but if the police talk to Bronson and find out, he'll be under suspicion anyway, maybe doubly so."

"Anything else?"

"Bronson could be interested in you."

"You're not serious."

"Very serious. If you and Vince ever break up, he told me I should let him know."

Roz glanced over at Bronson. "I never thought of him in that way. I mean, we see each other around here a lot, but he's never shown any interest."

"He was giving you time."

"I see," Roz said seriously. "That was kind of him."

Standing there together, they watched Bronson and his partner play. Anyone could tell Bronson was a consummate athlete. He handled himself, the ball, and the racquet to perfection.

"I certainly can understand why he's one of Kismet's most eligible bachelors," Caprice said.

"But I'm dating your brother, and I like it that way."

Caprice waved her racquet at the courts. "Have you had enough of this?"

"I have if you have." A sly glint came into Roz's

eyes. "How about an ice-cream sundae from Cherry on the Top after all this good exercise? I'm not meeting Vince until eight o'clock."

Caprice knew she shouldn't. She should eat a healthy meal and forget the ice cream and toppings. But Roz was her friend, and she needed a breather from worry and work. An ice-cream sundae and chatting with Roz again could be just the break she needed.

The following morning Caprice did a last examination of the hacienda that was so much more than a house. Real estate agents would be here in about fifteen minutes to take a walk-through. They'd be snapping photos and shooting their own video footage. This was an absolute gem, and Caprice was sure she and Juan had done a beautiful job of staging it. It wasn't trying to be something it wasn't. The house had an earthy energy that flowed throughout. Its magnificence would come through easily in the photos and on its video. If the open house tomorrow didn't sell it, the agents and the photos and Web sites would. She was sure of it.

The woven rugs Juan had found bore geometric designs in blue and orange and fuchsia, the same colors that dominated the tiles lining the staircase. As she climbed those stairs, she peered down over the railing into the living room. Juan had found sectionals in leather and wood in a rich shade of royal blue. The end tables were topped with intricate mosaics in rust and orange. Somehow the splash of colors in each room worked together to coordinate the whole house.

She'd reached the master suite with its dark wood floor and brass bed, with a headboard that reached halfway to the ceiling, when her phone buzzed. She stepped into the master bathroom with its marble sunken tub and stand-alone shower big enough for two and pulled out her phone.

She saw Bella was calling. "Hi, Bee, what's up?"

"We sold our house!"

"That's wonderful. Tell me about it."

"Two contracts came in at once, so we got full asking price."

"I'm so happy for you, Bee."

"I wanted to tell you because . . . I have a favor to ask."

"What kind of favor? Do you need me to sit in on the paperwork?"

"I don't know about that, but that's not the favor. I know you're busy, but I've been watching the stats on two houses that are online. One of them has been on sale for a year. Can you come look at them with me and Joe?"

Caprice checked her watch, estimating how long she'd be tied up here. "What time do you have in mind?"

"We're open to what works for you."

"How about five o'clock? That will give me all day here if I need it. I never know how long the real estate agents will take. Where do you want to meet?"

"My neighbor will be watching the kids, so why don't you just come over here."

"I'll be there at five."

"You're the best."

Caprice ended the call, smiling. Then she heard voices coming from downstairs. The house had a state-of-the-art alarm system, but she wasn't the only one who knew the code. Denise Langford knew it, and she was probably letting all of the other agents in. Caprice took a last look around the upstairs and then went down to meet them.

Two hours later, after hearing more oohs and aahs, and everything in between, Caprice told Denise, "I'm going outside to the patio. I want to make sure nothing got moved around so it's ready for tomorrow."

She'd raised the outdoor umbrellas that would lend a festive quality to the back patio. Guests who filled their plates with Nikki's food could go out there and sit too if they wanted. Fortunately, the weather was all clear and called for a sunny day tomorrow.

When Caprice emerged from the sliding glass doors off the dining room onto the covered terraced patio, she approved of Juan's concept of using outdoor furniture with brushed copper frames and colorful orange, blue, and rust cushions.

She'd walked the perimeter and was studying the rest of the yard when the back door from the kitchen opened and a man dressed in a gray uniform with TROY'S DELIVERY SERVICE stitched onto the pocket of his shirt stepped outside. His gray cap matched.

He held up a large bag. "Are you Miss De Luca?" he asked.

The man was probably in his early twenties with a thin mustache and brown eyes that looked more sheepish than anything. He said, "You look like the woman in the photo I was sent."

Caprice's skin started to crawl. "What photo?"

"This was a crazy order," the delivery man said,

setting the bag onto the frosted glass-topped table. "I have a courier service in York. I received an e-mail telling me I'd get a big bonus if I delivered a package to this address and to you. Your photo was included in the e-mail. I think it had been in the newspaper. That was so I'd know exactly who to give this bag to."

Chills ran up and down her spine now. "So you don't know who placed the order?"

"Nope. I was just instructed that this bag would be sitting on the ledge outside of Rack O' Ribs. I should pick it up and deliver it. No questions asked. Five hundred dollars for my trouble."

"You didn't think that was odd?"

"Sure, I thought it was odd. But money is money. My wife's pregnant. We need it."

She could certainly understand that. But still. . . . She studied the tall white bag and didn't know if she wanted to know what was in it.

He motioned to the bag. "Aren't you going to open it? It felt kind of hot underneath when I picked it up."

Hot. Oh great. Maybe she should get the hose or the fire department or the police department.

But the delivery man said, "It feels like one of those boxes like Rack O' Ribs gives you when you go through the drive-thru."

She approached the table warily. The white bag was folded down at the top, and she opened it slowly. When she peeked inside she did see the Rack O' Ribs box. What the heck?

She tore the bag wide open around the container and studied it carefully. It didn't look threatening. Not at all. It even smelled good. It smelled like barbecued ribs. She slipped open the flap that closed the container.

Inside there was indeed a rack of ribs. But that wasn't all. There was a waxy paper with grease pencil lettering on it. It was attached to the ribs with a paring knife. The note read, *Stop asking questions or this is what will happen to you.*

Caprice must have given a little squeak because the delivery man looked at her and said, "Are you going to faint?"

But she didn't faint. She pulled out her phone and speed-dialed Detective Carstead.

Chapter Sixteen

A half hour later, Caprice and the delivery man stood on the patio with Detective Carstead as the detective listened intently to what had happened.

"And the bag was just sitting on the ledge by Rack O' Ribs?" Detective Carstead asked.

Troy Weyland answered quickly, as if he wanted to make sure the detective knew he wasn't the perpetrator. "Those were my instructions. Pick up the bag sitting outside the door on the brick ledge at Rack O' Ribs. I wasn't supposed to look inside or anything—just pick it up and deliver it here."

"And this is your business, courier service, so to speak?"

"Yes, I have two trucks. A friend and I went into business together about a year ago. We mostly deliver legal documents, like from lawyer to lawyer, and that kind of thing. But we're a courier service. We don't ask questions. We just do our job. The more deliveries we make, the more money we make. This seemed to be a simple one. I thought it was a birthday gift or something."

"Some gift," Caprice muttered, staring down at the rack of ribs with the knife protruding from it. Detective Carstead had brought a tech along with him, and now he nodded to him.

"Bag it all up and record it. We'll have it analyzed for fingerprints."

"This isn't going to affect my open house is it?" Caprice asked the detective.

He looked angry for a minute. "You're worried about the open house rather than your life?"

"They're not in the same category," she snapped, then was sorry she had. "Look, Detective, there's nothing I can do about this. Apparently someone knew I was going to be here. That wasn't any secret. It's the day before an open house. I have a lot to get ready. I've spent valuable work time on this, and I don't want it messed up because some idiot is trying to scare me."

"You think that's all it is? Scare tactics? What if it's more? What if it's a prelude? What have you been doing, Miss De Luca, to cause this?"

With a sigh, she told him about her conversation with Bertram Dennis, and then about "running into" Bronson on the tennis court.

To her relief, Carstead didn't ask about how she'd come to be playing tennis on a court next to Bronson's.

He said, "We knew about Bertram Dennis's daughter. We'll follow up again with him and with her about the package." He shook his head. "I'm not sure how you get the information we do."

"I want to clear Nikki from your persons-of-interest list."

He scowled, gave her a narrowed-eyed look, and

then maintained, "We have to consider anyone who had contact with the victim."

"But my sister tops your list?"

"I'm not going to say." He turned to Troy. "I have your information. I'll give you a call if we need to go over this again. Thanks for letting me examine your phone and retrieve the number where the call came from."

"It's probably a burner phone," Caprice muttered.

This time the detective gave her a look of respect. "We'll check into it, but you're probably right."

The tech had taken charge of the bag. He'd used some kind of electronic device and fingerprinted the delivery man so they could distinguish his fingerprints from others. The police already had Caprice's on file with AFIS—the Automated Fingerprint Identification System.

The detective nodded to Weyland. "You can go. I'll be in touch if I need anything else."

The tech went into the house at the same time, and that left Caprice with Detective Carstead. He'd come through the inside of the house, and now he gazed over the vast yard, with its butterfly bushes, hydrangea, and uniform flower beds planted with pink geraniums.

Although Caprice expected Detective Carstead to give her more warnings, he didn't. Instead, he said, "I can't quite imagine living like this. Can you?"

"You mean the largesse of it?"

"Yeah. It's almost too big to contemplate. A house with enough rooms to get lost in, and probably so many bathrooms no one would ever use them all." His arm swept over the landscape. "This kind of yard where a dog or a kid would be out of sight in a minute."

That was interesting. It sounded as if Detective Carstead dreamed of a house with a yard where he could have a family, including a dog and a kid.

She asked, "Do you have a yard now?"

He gave her a look that said he didn't know if he should answer or not. But then he did. "Not my own. I rent an apartment on the first floor of an old house. I cut the grass for the landlord once a week, but that's about it."

"I know real estate agents," she teased, "if you're ever looking for a house to call your own."

He actually gave her a smile. "I guess you do." He stared at her a few moments, shifted on his feet, and then asked, "Is your sister involved with anyone?"

Thinking about his question, studying his almost embarrassed-looking expression, she asked, "Is that a question for the investigation, or is it personal?"

"It's personal," he admitted.

Without causing them further awkwardness, she answered, "No, she's not, but she's very picky."

Detective Carstead's eyes gleamed with what Caprice thought was amusement as he nodded. "Good to know." Then his warning came again, but it was a little different from those he'd given her before. "Watch yourself, Miss De Luca. Remember that talking to the wrong person could be as dangerous as chasing a getaway car down a high-traffic highway."

"I understand, Detective, I do, and I promise, I'll keep you in my loop."

He shook his head. "Your persistence is admirable. I just don't want it to be regrettable."

On that note, he left her standing on the beautiful patio, thinking about what he'd said.

Caprice wasn't telling anybody close to her about the Rack O' Ribs threat. She didn't want her family worrying about her. She would take care and not go anywhere alone . . . at least not for the next few days. She was meeting Bella to look at the houses, and then she'd go home to her pets inside of her alarm system. She'd keep her phone near her hand so she could dial Detective Carstead if she needed to. Tomorrow was the open house, where scads of people would be all around her. Nobody would be able to get near her. For today and tomorrow, at least, she would stop asking questions. However, at some point, everything would come to a head. It always did. If the murderer had his eye on her, she'd want it off of her.

But for now, she'd help Bella and Joe decide whether they should buy a house.

At five-thirty, Caprice rode with Bella and Joe in their red van to the first house on their list. The real estate agent was there when they arrived. The neighborhood, maybe about ten years old, was located near the shopping center on the east end of town.

As they entered the house, Caprice knew it was considered a high rancher. That meant inside the foyer, steps led down to a family room and basement area. Another set of steps led up to the first floor, which consisted of the living room, dining area, and four bedrooms. That was the main aspect of a new house that Joe and Bella were looking for—a room for the baby that could be a guest room later, a room for Timmy, a room for Megan, and a suite for themselves.

The bedroom area in this house stretched over the garage, and Caprice thought about that garage being unheated in the winter and the cold floors. They went upstairs first without Bella and Joe making many comments. They would have to install new carpet in the living room and dining area. When they toured downstairs, they saw that the family room was large and spacious, but there was only a small basement area for storage. And, of course, the whole place would have to be redecorated to Bella and Joe's taste.

After they'd scoped the yard, which was mostly grass with no shrubs, they all gathered on the front walk. Their real estate agent, Kayla Langtree, who was in her late thirties, wore her hair in a blunt, straight cut, neck length. Her large green eyes were her best feature.

She was only five foot three, and Joe seemed to tower over her as he asked, "Will they come down in price?"

"Every deal is about negotiation now," Kayla said. "But this house has been on the market for a year, and they've cut the price three times. So I don't know if you can get them to go lower."

"The question is," Caprice interjected, "Do you like the house?" She studied Bella, not Joe.

"It's all right," Bella said, not with much enthusiasm.

"It has four bedrooms," Joe pointed out. "That's what we need. Even without the price going lower, it's in our range."

"I don't know if that's a good-enough reason to

buy a house that you're going to live in the rest of your lives," Caprice advised them. "Bella, you're not saying much." That wasn't like her sister at all.

Finally, a conclusion burst out of Bella. "It doesn't have any character."

Joe looked puzzled. "What do you mean, *character*? We can decorate it however we want. You can even paint the walls your favorite color instead of the green I like. We need to find *something*, Bella."

Although Bella and Joe's marriage was back on track, they still had their disagreements and their personality quirks. Joe obviously didn't understand what her sister was talking about.

"Can you explain to Joe what you're looking for?" Caprice asked Bella.

"I'll know when I find it," she said, crossing her arms over her chest. "It's just something—" She waved her hand in the air. "The house where I grew up has character. It has a red-tiled roof and casement windows and plaster walls. It has a multitiered yard and a little balcony."

"Your parents' house would be way out of our price range," Joe grumbled.

"Caprice's house has character too," Bella protested. "It has that arched front door that you don't see anymore, and that little copper overhang. It has a fireplace and a cute back porch."

"Caprice's house wouldn't be big enough for us," Joe pointed out, still not quite getting the message.

Caprice put her hand on Bella's arm. "Joe, what I think she's looking for is a house with unique qualities. This isn't like buying a car with a check-list. It's more like finding a house that had some love in it, even if that was just in the choice of a Quoizel ceiling lamp.

Joe shook his head. "How about we go look at the second house." He apparently had learned to accept Bella's thinking without arguing with it. That was smart.

As Joe drove them to the second destination, Caprice noticed they were headed toward her parents' neighborhood. Maybe they were just going to drive through that area.

"This house is near Mom and Dad's?"

"About a block away," Joe said, with a straight face, not letting his feelings on the subject show.

Bella glanced over her shoulder at Caprice and just gave a shrug. "In the listing it seemed to have what we need. It's a much older house, probably a hundred years old. But it has four bedrooms and a renovated kitchen. The picture on the Internet shows some large spruces on either side of it, so that could be why we haven't noticed it and why I don't remember it."

When Joe pulled up to the curb in front of the house, Caprice remembered it. She'd once ridden her bike up and down these streets and often passed it. It was tucked between the spruces, which had grown larger over the years. There was a myrtle-covered bank in the front, and eight steps led up to the full front porch where a wooden swing was attached on the left side. A cane rocker and a small table sat nearby it. Caprice guessed if she peeked in the large plate-glass window there, she'd see into the living room.

After they climbed the steps, Joe said, "Someone's

going to have to paint these porch railings at least
every other year."

"I like the white with the pale yellow siding, don't
you?" Bella asked, ignoring his paint remark.

He gave her a shrug.

The door was an old-fashioned one with side-
lights on either side. The white storm door was
decorated with a black emblem of a carriage with
a horse.

Once inside the foyer, Joe stared down at the
parquet floor. "Is this practical with kids?"

Kayla said, "It has a polyurethane finish."

Blue and brown tweed carpet covered the steps,
which led to a landing, then turned left to the upstairs. Caprice could see the kitchen straight ahead.
To her left, wooden pillars looked as if they supported the living room. The woodwork over and
around the doors and the archway were a deep rich
golden brown and appeared to have been taken
care of over the years.

Bella ran her hand down one pillar. "Isn't this
beautiful? And look at those French doors."

French doors led from the living room into what
could either be a dining room or a family room.
Bookshelves in a beautiful birch lined the wall
straight ahead in that room.

"A lot of care has gone into this house," Bella
said. She turned to Kayla. "Why are they selling?"

"An older couple lives here. They're moving into
one of those retirement villages. You know—one
floor, wheelchair accessible. The steps are becoming a problem for them. But they raised their family
here, and as you can tell, the house has been renovated through the years and well taken care of."

In the kitchen, Caprice glanced around and couldn't find any fault. There was a unique corner sink with a counter that stretched across the room. The dishwasher was housed on one side of it, but on the other side were four stools for anyone to sit and snack or have a light meal. There was a large-enough area behind that for a dining room table and a hutch. A four-foot-square plate-glass window looked out over the backyard.

Kayla motioned to the left. "That's the downstairs powder room." She opened a second door beyond it. "This leads to the utility room and the pantry."

"What's the basement like?" Joe asked.

"Basic. Cement floor. Furnace."

"And what about a garage?"

"There's a wooden structure in the back that the couple had sided when they sided the house. It can house two cars."

"But you have to walk the length of the yard to get to it," Joe murmured.

"Good exercise," Bella maintained, and Caprice understood with just one look at her sister that she'd fallen in love with the house.

"We'd have to redo the basement for a family room," Joe said.

"Or," Bella proposed, "we could just use that middle room for a family room and the TV. The kids would be right here with us. We don't need a formal dining room. A table in the kitchen's dining area can seat six or eight, and we have the counter too where we could always put the kids."

Kayla smiled. "You haven't seen the upstairs yet. Granted, there's only one big bathroom for all of you, but there's a screened-in balcony off of the back bedroom. It was once a porch, but now it's closed in and weatherproofed. There's room for three or four lawn chairs, maybe a chaise. It's sort of a little sunroom."

"Oh, let's go look," Bella said enthusiastically. She followed the real estate agent to the stairs.

"She likes this place," Joe said with surprise in his voice.

"It has character," Caprice said calmly. "How do you feel about being so close to Mom and Dad's house?"

"I'm fine with it," he assured her. "I don't know what we would have done without them over the past year. I never thought I'd say it, but I'm grateful for all of you, even you."

She and Joe had had their head butts, but underneath it all, he was a good guy.

"If this is what she wants, we'll see if we can negotiate a good price. I can live with the garage," he decided.

She laughed. "And if you need help decorating, you know my number."

Chapter Seventeen

The Monday morning breakfast meeting of the Kismet Chamber of Commerce at the Purple Iris Bed-and-Breakfast seemed to be attended by more members than usual. Because summer allowed for more freedom? Or because the Purple Iris with its beautiful restaurant wasn't only a tourist destination but also a popular place for residents of Kismet and York to gather?

The bed-and-breakfast had a quaintness about it, from its stained glass windows with iris motif to its vintage wood trim. The restaurant, a recent addition by owner Holly Swope, had already garnered great reviews. The Chamber of Commerce had managed to reserve it for this morning's meeting. Holly had offered to serve her guests breakfast in their rooms to accommodate the Chamber patrons. Naomi, Grant's ex, could be having breakfast in her room right now. The nine guest rooms were usually occupied throughout the summer because the bed-and-breakfast was at a convenient location between York, Gettysburg, and Lancaster. Lots of sights to see in the area, from the Amish country, to the battlefield, to the historic buildings in downtown York.

When Caprice entered the dining area with its lilac-colored drapes, yellow-and-purple pin-striped wallpaper, and framed iris prints, Holly—all dressed in purple—greeted her. "I'm glad you could come," Holly said, her blue eyes sparkling.

The evening Caprice and Seth Randolph had enjoyed dinner here, the owner of the B&B had reminded her that the Chamber of Commerce breakfast was a way to network and that new projects were afoot. When Caprice thought about Seth, she didn't regret her decision to end her romantic relationship, if not her friendship, with him. But they hadn't been in contact since the night she'd chosen Grant. She hoped sometime in the future they would be again, no matter what happened with Grant and Naomi. Grant's ex should be leaving soon. Had he made a decision yet?

Her attendance at this morning's breakfast was just another way for her to put that out of her mind. Besides, she wondered if Jeanie Boswell might be here, or another business owner who might have had dealings with Drew.

Holly ran her hand through her short black hair. "You're early. Have a seat at any table. Service will start soon."

Members of the Chamber were scattered around the room at the round tables, over which hung white enamel and crystal chandeliers. Caprice scanned each table until her eyes fell on someone she knew. Kiki, Rowena's friend, was seated at a table all by herself. She'd been reading a pamphlet, but when she raised her head, she spotted Caprice. She waved and Caprice crossed to her.

"Have a seat," Kiki said, motioning to the one beside her. "Unless you're meeting someone else here."

"My friend Roz will probably attend. Maybe we could save her a seat?"

"Of course we can. Are you talking about Roz Winslow who owns All About You?"

"I am."

"I often frequent her shop. She doesn't just carry those short dresses with bare midriffs for twenty-somethings but classy clothes I can wear too."

"She tries to appeal to all ages and all sizes."

"Rowena told me you're still looking into Drew's background. You heard about the break-in at her house?" Kiki wanted to know.

"I did. I can't believe she went after the burglar with her cane. She is one gutsy woman."

Kiki harrumphed, "Or foolish. I told her she should be staying with me until this whole situation is taken care of, until the police catch the murderer. She insists no one's going to drive her out of her home. I suppose that's a good thing because that means even Jeanie can't do that."

"Is she trying to?"

"She brought an antique dealer to the reception after Drew's funeral. I was furious when I found out."

"How did Rowena feel about it?"

"Maybe she's survived by taking everything in stride, or maybe she just accepts Jeanie as she is. But she didn't seem overly upset by it. Jeanie's trying to convince her to move into a retirement center, but Rowena won't hear of it. She even told

Jeanie she appreciated having the antique dealer come in to appraise some of her belongings. To tell you the truth, I think that got Jeanie's goat."

Caprice had to smile until she reminded herself that Jeanie could very well have murdered Drew. "Do you know if Jeanie's coming to this meeting?"

"I doubt it. She really keeps to herself and doesn't mingle much. She never has. Quite the opposite of her brother."

"So she was a loner as a teenager?"

"Yes, she was. On the other hand, she could fly off the handle quite easily. In that way, she was different from Drew. Jeanie was fifteen when she pushed a girl down a flight of stairs because the girl said something mean. I advised Rowena then she should send Jeanie to counseling. But Rowena didn't want a stigma attached to Jeanie's name. She did make appointments for her, though, with the guidance counselor at the high school, and that seemed to help."

"Sometimes all teenagers need is an objective listening ear."

"I suppose. I have a feeling she resented Rowena because she missed her parents so deeply. Rowena was the surrogate she didn't want to deal with."

"That's a shame."

"Drew was always closer to Rowena, and maybe Jeanie resented that too."

"Maybe she just wanted someone of her own to love her."

"Possibly. That's why her marriage was a flop."

"She's made Posies into a success, though," Caprice offered.

"Yes, she has, and kudos to her for that. She did

well in business school. She has an associates degree. When she used her inheritance to buy Posies, Rowena was concerned. But she's done well with it, except for one problem. She has trouble keeping employees. I don't know if that's because of her temper or because she's very particular. However, she does do beautiful work with flowers."

Did Jeanie just have an artistic temperament? Had she become a smart businesswoman, or was she an unstable loner who was capable of committing murder? Caprice didn't feel she could be that blunt and ask Kiki that particular question.

Nevertheless, she could probe a little deeper. "So you believe Drew and Jeanie were very different personalities?"

"Oh yes. Drew could charm the skirt off of you if he put his mind to it. He had charisma and he knew it. I knew him much better than Jeanie. He'd talk to me when Rowena and I got together. If we played cards, he might even sit in on a hand. If we cooked, he joined us. He came into the bookstore often too." Kiki frowned and looked sad. "We had our last falling out over that."

"You had a falling out with Drew?"

"Since he returned to Kismet, he'd come into the store and page through cookbooks. However, he didn't just page through them. He used his phone to snap photos of recipes. I couldn't allow that. It's not fair to the cookbook author. Rowena's my friend, and I didn't want to cause a real fuss, so I warned Drew not to do it. After the warning, I caught him doing it anyway. He always tried to get his own way, no matter what."

And when Drew was thwarted, he apparently

made enemies. Now that she had Kiki talking, she wondered if the woman would confide in her about Rowena's recipes. "I have a question for you, and I'll understand if you can't answer. When I found Drew, the Tiffany floor lamp had been overturned and was lying on the floor. I saw a piece of paper sticking out. Can you tell me if Rowena's recipes were hidden in there?"

Kiki didn't say a word, but her expression said it all. At first she showed surprise and then a shuttered look that said she was hiding something.

Caprice patted her hand. "It's okay. I haven't asked Rowena yet, but I'm going to. I feel her recipes could be an important part of the puzzle—of solving who killed Drew."

The dining room was filling up now with more Chamber members arriving and seating themselves at the tables. Caprice caught sight of Bronson Chronister, who entered with two men. One of them, Warren Shaeffer, was the president of the Chamber of Commerce. Caprice didn't know the second man.

Caprice said, "I heard Bronson might run for Chamber of Commerce president. He's with Warren."

Kiki targeted her gaze toward the door. "He's not only with Warren, he's with Ira Rogers."

Caprice thought she knew most of the Chamber members. After all, they received a list with every newsletter, and she could identify most of the names. "Who's Ira Rogers?"

"He is a fund-raising guru."

"Does the Chamber intend to have a fund-raiser for a special project?"

"That's possible. But I suspect Bronson brought him along as a guest for another reason. You know my bookstore is a haven for gossip. Residents come in and I overhear lots of conversations. Some I'm not supposed to hear—women leaving their husbands and the reasons why, businesses failing because of poor management, some of the doings in the police department even."

Caprice could bet Kiki kept her ear tuned in to all of those conversations. She'd formed little reading nooks where her bookstore patrons could be as comfortable as guests as they paged through the latest novels or magazines.

"So what other reason might Ira have for being here?"

"There's scuttlebutt that Bronson's throwing his hat in the ring for a seat in the state house. I've also heard he has his eye on Congress after that. With his family money behind him, fund-raising at grassroots level on up, and his own success, he has the wherewithal to rise in the political scene. You mark my words. State house. Senator or governor. President."

Wow. Caprice hadn't thought that far ahead for Bronson. But why not? "I imagine he'd interview well and look good on a TV screen too."

Kiki laughed. "That's what it's all about these days, isn't it?"

Caprice hoped if Bronson was elected, he would be elected for more than his good looks and facile interview skills.

With her attention focused on Bronson, she didn't see Roz come in, but her friend hurried over to the table and asked, "Did you save a seat for me?"

Kiki motioned to the seat on the other side of her. "With you two smart women here to have a confab, I imagine we could think up projects on our own that would benefit this Chamber of Commerce. Let's give them ideas to bring more tourists to this town."

Roz laughed. "I'm game."

Caprice said, "I'm in too."

The three of them had much to talk about over breakfast, and Caprice had a lot to think about concerning Jeanie Boswell and her brother, who might have been her rival not only for Rowena's affection but also for her inheritance.

When Caprice returned from the breakfast, she realized the meal and the meeting hadn't taken as long as she'd expected. Parking at the curb instead of in her driveway, she decided to take a short detour over to Dulcina's house to see how she was doing with the cat, and to find out how Rod and his girls had enjoyed the concert. Lady would be okay for another fifteen minutes.

She knew she probably worried about her furry crew more than most, but they were like her kids. Though she had to admit, she wanted children, as well as fur babies.

Caprice crossed the street and went to Dulcina's door. She pressed the bell. If Dulcina was busy, she wouldn't stay.

When the door opened, Dulcina's headphones lay around her neck.

"If you're working, I don't have to come in," Caprice assured her. "I just wanted to see how you and Halo were getting along, and if the concert made any inroads to relationships with Rod's girls."

"I do have a bunch of records to transcribe this morning, but come on in. I want you to see what I fixed up for Halo."

No mention of Rod. Hmmm.

After they transversed the living room and entered the kitchen, Dulcina motioned under the cubicle where a stool could sit at a built-in desk. Halo was nestled into receiving blankets in the storage bin, sound asleep.

"She likes this one best," Dulcina pointed out. "I put another bed in a darker corner of the sunroom. She uses them both, so maybe she knows what they're for. It's as if she's nesting. Sometimes she'll get in, go around in a circle, and paw the receiving blanket before she sits down."

The receiving blanket was patterned with cute little yellow ducks waddling across it. Caprice crouched down beside Halo. Although the cat had looked as if she were sound asleep, her ears twitched and she gazed up at Caprice.

Caprice said, "You're going to be a mom. I guess you're getting ready. Are you eating a whole lot?"

"I've been feeding her about every four hours and she gobbles it down. I give her crunchies in between. She's such a sweet cat. I don't know how she ended up out there on her own."

"She could have gotten lost and not been able to find her way back. Then if she was injured and hurt, she might have wandered even farther. Or someone could have put her out because they couldn't pay for the cat food. It's hard to know. But she does seem like a real sweetie. We can hope she knows how to mother."

"I'll help her," Dulcina said with certainty.

"I won't hold you up," Caprice said. "How did the girls enjoy the concert?"

When Dulcina hesitated, Caprice knew there were probably problems.

"Leslie wasn't impressed. She said she didn't connect with Ace's music. But during the concert, I saw her foot tapping along. I even caught her snapping her fingers at one point. She wants to seem so removed, and I don't know if I'll be able to reach her."

"And his younger daughter?"

"Vanna was into it. She even asked her dad if she could download Ace's music after they were back here. They stopped in for a few minutes because Vanna wanted to see Halo. That was the only hopeful sign of the evening. Leslie even asked me questions about the pregnancy and how long it would be until the kittens were born. I told them after the kittens were old enough, they could come over and play with them because I'm sure they'll have energy to burn. So maybe kittens can make a difference when a rock concert didn't. It was sure nice to have the evening out, to sit next to Rod and just hold hands. For a change, he didn't seem to mind doing that in front of his daughters."

"So there's progress."

"Yes, there's progress. How about your investigation?"

"I feel like I'm advancing in baby steps. At the Chamber of Commerce breakfast this morning, I learned a few things about Drew and his sister.

But also about one of Drew's friends, Bronson Chronister."

"There was talk on one of the local shows about him running for office," Dulcina offered.

"I guess the rumors are true. There's scuttlebutt he might run for a seat in the state house with an eye on more."

"He's easy on the eyes."

Caprice laughed. "On that note, I think I'll leave you to your work. Lady misses spending time with you."

"And I miss her. Maybe you could bring her over and let her meet Halo."

"We can talk about that more later."

She offered her hand to Halo, and the cat rubbed her cheek against Caprice's palm. Already she could see a difference in the feline. She was beginning to trust humans, and that was a big step. Dulcina's kindness had done that.

Caprice left Dulcina's, walked across the street, and fished her key for the front door out of her purse. Once inside she pressed in the alarm code to disengage the system.

Lady came running. Mirabelle was stretched out on the fuchsia oversized chair, while Sophia sat atop the afghan on the back of the sofa. Two sets of golden eyes studied her while Lady danced around her feet. Caprice had picked up the mail from her porch mailbox on the way in. She didn't pay much attention to it, because her first concern was letting Lady outside. Still she gave Lady the hand motion for "sit." After a bit of tail wagging, sit Lady did.

Caprice praised her and petted her, and then

patted her hip and said, "Come on. After you do
your thing, maybe we can play a little fetch."

In the kitchen, she deposited her purse on the
counter but kept the letters in her hand as she let
Lady outside and followed her onto the porch. Lady
wasted no time running into the yard. Caprice remembered the days when she ran along with her to
give her the "go potty" command. But now Lady
didn't need that.

The day could turn into a sweltering one, and
she might have to turn on her air-conditioning.
The zinnias were starting to bud. The snapdragons
she'd planted in bunches were colorful against the
reblooming lilacs. She took in a deep breath of
the summery air, closed her eyes, and appreciated
the scents of the season.

Sitting on the glider on the porch, she turned to
the letters in her hand. There were bills, of course.
There were always bills along with ads for products
she'd never use. A letter-sized envelope caught her
eye. It was one of those envelopes with the blue
stripes so that you couldn't see what was inside. No
one wrote letters these days. They sent e-mails. So
she couldn't imagine whom it was from. There was
no return address.

That should have been her first warning.

But she was watching Lady and appreciating the
day and thinking about meeting Roz and Vince at
Cherry on the Top for ice cream. Roz had suggested
it at breakfast. Vince and Roz would give her fresh
eyes on everything she'd learned about her investigation.

She wasn't surprised by the white piece of paper

she pulled out of the envelope. It was folded in thirds. But when she opened it, the printing alerted her she might not like what it was going to say.

She didn't.

The printed letters more reminiscent of a child's writing than an adult's, even a little jagged, read, *If you value that pretty dog and your life, stop asking questions.*

As explicit as the knife in the rack of ribs, there was only one thing to do, of course. She speed-dialed Detective Carstead.

Cherry on the Top was like a step back to the fifties when ice-cream sundaes could be the best part of anybody's week. Caprice often tried to convince herself that the dairy concoction with walnuts on top could be a balanced meal. Tonight she'd skipped supper to have the sundae sitting before her, a scoop of vanilla with strawberry glaze, and a scoop of vanilla with chocolate fudge sauce. Whipped cream topped it, and walnuts were sprinkled over the whole thing.

She sat across the Formica-topped table from Vince and Roz. Up until now, they'd kept the conversation light. The way Vince and Roz interacted, the way he laughed at her jokes and she fondly brushed his arm, told Caprice they were definitely a couple. But how serious a couple?

Vince took a spoonful of his sundae, a CMP, and licked the spoon. Then he eyed Caprice. "Roz mentioned to me that she told you I asked her to move in with me."

"She did."

Caprice wasn't about to reveal any confidences or what Roz had told her in private.

Vince seemed to realize that. "Are you going to convince her she should?"

That surprised Caprice a little. Vince didn't usually ask favors of her, especially not this kind.

"Then I guess you haven't made a decision," she said to Roz.

"No, I haven't. You know where I'm coming from, and so does Vince."

Instead of convincing Roz of anything, Caprice addressed her brother. "Don't push."

With a sigh he leaned back in his chair and crossed his arms over his chest. "You're supposed to convince her, not give me advice."

"Since when did I ever do what I was supposed to do?"

His lips twitched up in amusement. "Maybe when you were about five."

"You two will work it out," she said. "Just be patient with each other."

"We're thinking about planning that vacation you suggested. It could be a smart idea," Vince responded.

"I have them now and then," Caprice teased.

Yet she wasn't in a teasing mood. She was worried. She couldn't hide much from her good friend or her family, so she decided to tell them about the letter. "I had a meeting with Detective Carstead this afternoon."

Now Vince was on alert. "What about?"

Deciding to confide in her brother and Roz, she

explained about the rack of ribs threat and the letter. "When I called Detective Carstead initially, he told me not to touch it more than I had to and to slip it into a Ziploc bag. So that's what I did. He came by to collect it."

"And?" Vince asked.

"I saw those doubts in his eyes. I asked him if he thought I sent it to myself to get Nikki off the hook."

"He wouldn't think that," Roz protested.

"I believe he did for about a minute. But then he admitted from what he knows about me, he doesn't believe I would do that. Of course, he wouldn't share any information about the investigation, but he did tell me they have positive leads they're following. At least that's something, coming from him."

"So now what? Is he going to send a patrol car by your house every once in a while?"

"He said he'd inform the patrol officers to be on the lookout, but they don't have the manpower to do that. He knows I have a good alarm system and I'll be careful. I'll be especially careful with my pets. If anyone comes near them, I'll use more than what I learned in that self-defense class on them."

Roz and Vince exchanged a look that said they believed she would.

"I can't just sit by. I can take care of myself, but anybody who threatens Lady is a real pervert and I'm going to find out who that is."

"And just how are you going to do that?" Vince asked.

"I'm still thinking about it."

"Who are your suspects?" Vince wanted to know.

She went down the list from Jeanie Boswell with her motives, to Mario Ruiz and his, to the relationships Drew had with Larry Penya and Bronson Chronister, and Bronson's aspirations to run for political office. She didn't know how they all played together, but they might.

After Caprice finished, Roz looked pensive. "I keep thinking about that Tiffany lamp. Sometimes the shades are attached to the base. It's not that easy to just lift it up and use it as a weapon. What if that shade was removed from the lamp beforehand . . . before the murder? What if it was just sitting on the table?"

That took Caprice's mind in a different direction. Certainly the murderer didn't remove the lampshade from the base before he hit Drew. The scene seemed more like an impulsive situation where maybe the murderer hadn't even intended to strike.

Caprice realized if she learned the answer to why the shade was off the lamp, she might possibly know who the murderer was.

There was only one thing to do in the morning. Visit Rowena again.

Chapter Eighteen

The summer breeze blew in the kitchen window of Rowena's house the following morning. Caprice had brought Lady along today, and Rowena seemed to enjoy interacting with her. While Caprice sat at the kitchen table, Lady lounging with one of her toys at her feet, Rowena served pineapple pomegranate tea in a cherished rose-patterned porcelain teapot.

Caprice accepted the cup offered her. This time, she'd brought along biscotti *she'd* made.

Rowena took a bite from a cookie. "You say they're not like your nana's. And they aren't quite. But they're very good. I love the lemon icing."

"She must have magic in her hands when she rolls them," Caprice offered.

"I appreciate your visit today," Rowena admitted. She nodded to the cocker spaniel. "And Lady's. Kiki is going to be at the bookstore until eight o'clock tonight. So I enjoy the company. But I know you probably have more questions about Drew, don't you?"

"Having tea with you isn't just about Drew," Caprice assured her. "After his murder is solved, we're going to have that grand tea party with Nana. And I'll still visit. I promise."

Rowena nodded as if she believed Caprice and bent to pet Lady again. As always, Lady enjoyed the attention. "I have a whole collection of teapots and teacups that we can use when you come over. We'll try every flavor of tea there is to try. Kiki's not a tea drinker. She likes coffee. But nothing is more relaxing or comforting than a well-steeped cup of tea."

After Caprice finished her cookie, she sipped at her tea from a cup of delicate fine china. She understood that Rowena treasured some of these belongings she'd had for decades. That brought her back to the subject of her Tiffany lamps. "I'd like to ask you about your Tiffany lamps again."

"Ask away."

"As far as you know, the shade was not off the small lamp before you left that day?"

"That's right. Everything in the room was as it should be."

"Do you know any reason why it would have been taken apart? That the shade would have been taken off the base?"

Rowena appeared troubled. "I really have no idea. Unless, of course, Drew did it." She studied her hands, then her teacup. Finally, she turned her gaze on the floor lamp in the living room. "I do have my recipes hidden in the floor lamp. That channel inside is perfect. Yes, the lamp's heavy. But I can easily tilt it against the arm of the sofa and take recipes in or out . . . if I want to. But I never want to. I put them in there because I know them by heart. I don't need them to bake or to cook."

"As far as you know, had Drew ever seen you take the recipes in or out of the floor lamp?"

"No. Because I just don't. I don't know how he could have known they were in there."

"How long have you done this?"

"Since that episode of my card club member trying to steal them from me."

"How old was Drew?"

"That was shortly after he came to live with me. He might have been eleven."

"Is it possible that over the years he heard you talking about those recipes being hidden in the floor lamp? Possibly to Kiki?"

"I suppose that's possible."

Caprice continued with that train of thought. "Maybe he suspected you kept recipes hidden in the table lamp, too. Maybe he checked every once in a while to see if you had inserted any."

"I suppose that's likely. Do you think he was look-ing for the recipes in the lamp when he let the murderer in?"

"If whoever came to the door was someone he knew, maybe he just left the lamp apart while he answered the door. There's no way of knowing, but it's as likely a theory as any."

Rowena suddenly snapped her fingers. "You know what? I found Drew's yearbook for his senior year. Would you like to see it?"

"I would."

Rowena crossed to a stand of cookbooks on the counter and pulled a tall volume from the wooden holder. "After I found this, I just put it here so I could get my fingers on it easily. Kiki looked through it. I haven't. I remember too well what Drew and his friends looked like back then." She handed the book to Caprice.

Caprice began paging through the volume. There were the usual shots—the football team and the cheerleaders. She found a photo of Drew and Larry and Bronson, standing at what looked like a lab table. The picture must have been taken during a science class. She commented about it to Rowena.

"Larry was the one interested in science," Rowena explained. "I remember I bought Drew a chemistry kit one year. The three of them were in the basement using it. Suddenly they ran upstairs and told me I had to open all the windows. I don't know what they had done, but I think Larry was the instigator of that one. Now and then I found him helping Drew with his math. I think if Larry could have gone to college, he would have done well. But his family didn't have the money. And I don't think his achievements showed up well enough on paper to earn him scholarships."

Paging through the rest of the yearbook, Caprice found Drew's photo in the lineup of the senior graduates. She studied his face. Larry's photo was right before his.

As she turned each page, she thought about her own high school reunion that was soon coming up. For her, the past fifteen years hadn't changed the way she looked at the world that much. She might be more confident about what she did and how she did it, but her basic values were still the same. What her parents and teachers had taught her was ingrained and had become part of her moral code.

As in most yearbooks, at the end of the volume, pages had been saved for autographs. She studied the signatures Drew had collected, which were mostly short comments—*You did it! Congratulations, you passed. What's next, bro?* But then she passed her finger over one that was a little longer. Larry had written, *Hey Drew—Never forget we've got a pact. All for one and one for all. Larry.*

Just what kind of pact had this trio made? Something general, like they'd always be friends? Or had that pact been about something more particular?

She considered both Bronson and Larry. Bronson's manner was too facile to give anything away. He considered carefully what he said and who he said it to. But from her conversation with Larry Penya, she had a feeling he might be more open.

"Do you have any idea where I can find Larry?" she asked Rowena. "You mentioned he separated from his wife and moved out. I left a message at that number, but she hasn't called me back or given Larry the message to call me."

"From what I understand, Linda is bitter about the marriage he couldn't give her. She stayed in the house, and she's a single mom trying to make payments on her own. You might want to give her another call or just try to see if you can snag her in person."

"Do you know where she works?"

"She works at that daycare center over near the mall—Little Tykes."

"Then she should be home in the evening. I'll

try to visit her tonight. Her attitude would probably be even more closed if I tried to visit her at work."

"You're right about that," Rowena agreed. "Though it might not be much better if she's trying to take care of a four-year-old and get supper at the same time."

"I'll have to take my chances."

Caprice remembered the threat that had been made against Lady. She wouldn't let anything happen to her dog, her friends, or herself. The best way to keep harm from happening was to figure out who killed Drew and to do it quickly.

The house Larry Penya had moved out of was basically a box shape with a carport attached to one side. As Caprice had driven up to the curb, she'd spotted a shed in the back. The yard wasn't very big, so that outbuilding was close to the house. Still, there was a small swing set and a Big Wheel bike crisscrossed in front of it.

As she walked to the front stoop, she had no expectations. Linda Penya might slam the door in her face. She hoped she could prevent that.

When she pressed the bell, she didn't hear a corresponding ding inside. Not working maybe?

Opening the screen door, she knocked.

From inside, she heard "Just a minute" in an impatient voice. That didn't sound like a good start.

The woman who opened the door looked frustrated. Her ash-blond hair was gathered in a messy topknot. Strands escaped around her face.

She didn't even wait for Caprice to open her mouth. "If you're selling something, I don't want any. I have a four-year-old in the kitchen who's in the middle of supper."

She turned and was about to close the door when Caprice stopped her. "Wait. This is important. I want to talk to you about Drew Pierson and your husband."

That froze the woman in her tracks. She turned around slowly. "Who are you?"

"I'm Caprice De Luca. My sister worked with Drew. I know Drew and Larry and Bronson were good friends. I'd like to speak to Larry. Do you know where he is?"

The woman crossed her arms over her chest, thought about it a moment, and then opened the screen door. "Come on in. I have to get back to Joey or he'll have food all over the kitchen."

As Caprice stepped into the small living room, she could see at once that the house was in disorder with Joey's stuff thrown here and there and toys scattered across the floor. But it looked clean. Not only that, but Larry or his wife had framed their little boy's drawings and hung them on the wall. There were pictures, too, of when Joey was an infant and later photos taken in the backyard. This appeared to be a house that had once held love.

Linda didn't stop in the living room but went straight into the kitchen, where a towheaded four-year-old in a T-shirt and jeans was digging into what looked like a bowl of SpaghettiOs. He had sauce all over his mouth and his little fingers, and he'd picked up one of the tiny meatballs and was holding it in his hand.

Linda shook her head, went over to him, and

advised, "Put the meatball in your mouth, then I'll wash your hands."

Joey's hazel eyes twinkled as he did as she'd asked and then grinned at her.

"Gotta love the cuteness," she murmured.

Caprice knew what she meant. Megan and Timmy could get away with a lot too with a smile like that.

She said to Caprice, "Larry doesn't live here anymore."

"Drew's grandmother told me that. She said you were separated?"

"For about six months now. Larry lost his job, and then he tried to set up his own handyman business, fixing people's appliances and things you can't get repaired anymore. He's good at that." She motioned out back. "He has his workshop out there. He always went there to smoke. He still stops in to use it now and then. But sometimes he doesn't even let me know he's out there. Probably when he's been drinking. That's one of the reasons I asked him to move out."

Caprice wondered if Larry could have a Tiffany lamp base in his shop somewhere. Nothing ventured, nothing gained. "Can I take a look at the workshop?" she asked.

Linda looked perplexed. "Why would you want to do that?"

"I'm just curious to see how big his enterprise was. I heard Bronson helped him out." A little fib now and then to get information didn't hurt.

Looking embarrassed, Linda admitted, "Bronson gave us money to tide us over—so our electricity wouldn't get shut off and we could pay our mortgage. But he didn't help with the shop as far as I know. Larry already had tools, a workbench, things like that. But advertising is a problem. I think Bronson lent him money to do an ad in the paper, but that didn't bring in many people. I think he's looking into setting up a social media page. But he really doesn't know anything about all of that."

"I saw Larry at the gym," Caprice said, wondering where he got the money for the membership. It wasn't cheap. If they were having financial difficulties, wouldn't he drop that first?

"That was also a gift from Bronson last Christmas. He thought it might help Larry's mood if he kept up physical activity. Bronson's been a good friend. We owe him so much. Life just got too overwhelming for both of us. We argued all the time. Jocy was getting upset. It just seemed better if Larry moved out for a while. Do you really want to see the shop?"

"If you don't mind."

"I don't mind. It's never locked."

Linda went to one of the cupboards and pulled out a pack of cookies. She unfastened the package, took out five of them, and placed them on the table in front of Joey. She said to him, "You can have these with your milk. I'll be right back."

The back door was already open to let in the hot breeze. As she led Caprice outside, she said, "I know I should be giving him carrot sticks instead of cookies, but those cookies were on special and I got them really cheap. Everything for me is about money these days. I hate it."

Caprice felt sorry for Linda, who seemed to be in the middle of a hurricane with everything around her spinning out of control. What if it fell apart even further? What if Larry had killed Drew? For what reason? Caprice had no idea.

It was only about ten steps to the shed. It looked as if it had been hand-built by either Larry or a previous owner. She said as much.

"It was here when we moved in," Linda said. "It was one of the reasons Larry liked this place."

She threw open the wooden door, and a wave of heat and stale smoke accosted Caprice. There were two windows, and they were open. But the small building seemed to draw the heat into itself. She spotted a fan sitting on the workbench and realized that Larry probably kept that going during the summer. On one side of the building, shelves were filled with small appliances—mixers and blenders. She thought she spotted two XBoxes. A canister-style vacuum cleaner with its attached hose was sprawled across on the floor. The workbench held the usual tools—chisels, pliers, a utility knife, and even a small hammer. Rows of jars with different types of screws and nails lined the back of the workbench against the wall. A roll of appliance cord leaned against two rolls of duct tape.

On quick inspection, she didn't notice a Tiffany lamp base anywhere. But then it would be foolish to keep that here, wouldn't it?

"I'm checking into Drew's background," she told Linda. "I'm trying to discover if he had any enemies that nobody knew about. Did Larry ever talk about Drew? What he was doing now? Or maybe the old days when they were drag racing in high school?"

"Drag racing?" Linda asked. "I never knew about that. Larry had it rough growing up, so he never talks about that very much. I knew he and Bronson

and Drew were friends since then but not much
else. Larry and Bronson drove down to D.C. when
Drew worked there. And when Drew came home
they'd meet for drinks."

"So Larry never mentioned a pact that he and
Drew and Bronson might have had in high school?"

"A pact? No. They did act like blood brothers,
though, when they were around each other . . . the
joking, arm punching, sports stuff."

"You said Bronson helped out Larry. Did Drew
know about that?"

"Sure. I don't think they kept anything from
each other. And Bronson was helping Drew too. He
let him open his business from his kitchen. Granted
he has a huge house and he isn't there much, but
still . . ."

"So Drew and Larry got along fine?"

"As far as I knew. Sometimes I thought Drew
looked down his nose at Larry. You know, like he
was going places and Larry wasn't, especially after
he sold that barbecue sauce recipe. From what
Larry said, the last time he phoned, Drew wouldn't
stop bragging. Larry was down on his luck, and it
was like Drew kept throwing it in his face . . . all that
success. I'm sure that annoyed Larry some, but as I
said, they were like brothers."

Like brothers. There was only one way Caprice
could get a real beat on this. She had to talk to
Larry. "Can you tell me where Larry's staying? He
might know some detail that could lead to Drew's
murderer."

"He stayed at Bronson's for a while, but I don't
think Bronson liked him hanging around when he
was drinking so much. So I think Bronson sent him

to the cabin that belonged to his dad. Larry always liked fishing, being in the woods. I think Bronson figured it would help."

"Are you in touch with Larry?"

"I haven't been for a couple of weeks. We couldn't afford cell phones anymore, so we don't have those, and that cabin doesn't have a landline. When Larry calls, he does it from a convenience store. Bronson told me if I needed to get in touch with Larry, he'd go get him. But I haven't needed to. I'm just trying to make life work for me and Joey now."

Caprice could call Bronson to find out where his dad's cabin was located. But what if Bronson, or Larry, had killed Drew? What if one knew the other had done it?

No, she didn't want to raise Bronson's suspicions. She didn't want to think he'd sent her the note . . . or the ribs. On the other hand, she didn't think Larry in his mental state right now would devise that plan either. That was just a gut feeling. She'd gone with gut feelings before. If only Detective Carstead would share what he knew. But she knew he wouldn't. If she talked to Larry and figured anything out, *she'd* go to the detective. Again.

In the meantime she knew someone who could find out the directions or the address of Bronson's dad's cabin. Reporter Marianne Brisbane had helped her before. She had access to all kinds of databases and public records. Caprice was on a mission now, and she wouldn't stop until she had some answers.

She studied Linda. "You know, don't you, that there's a food pantry connected to the soup kitchen. They even have fresh produce this time of year.

Gardeners who have extras bring it in. By August there will be tomatoes and cucumbers and zucchini."

"I haven't wanted to go that route," Linda confessed with pride in her voice.

"You're going through a tough time, and Joey deserves the best you can give him, doesn't he? Even if you have to accept a little help from others." Caprice took out one of her business cards and handed it to Linda.

When Linda looked at it, she laughed. "A home stager? That's the last thing I need right now."

"I'm not handing it out for professional reasons. My home number's on there if you want to know more about the Kismet Food Pantry or Everybody's Kitchen."

Linda glanced down at the card again, then at Caprice. "I don't have any family. Larry lost his mom, and his dad has his own problems with alcohol, so he's no help. I don't like to keep taking from Bronson either."

"There's a social worker who comes into Everybody's Kitchen. She tries to hook people up with the programs they need. She's usually there from four to five while volunteers are preparing dinner. Just think about it, okay?"

Linda nodded. "Okay." Then she headed toward her house and her son.

Caprice hoped she'd accept help to get her life back on track.

Chapter Nineteen

All the house needed, Caprice surmised the following day, was a rotating strobe light in the octagonal-shaped room. It was a silly notion, but it seemed fitting.

Denise Langford, the broker handling the Nautical Intertude house, had called her this morning and told her she had a couple who wanted to look at the property late this afternoon. Kim and David were moving from Delaware to Pennsylvania to be closer to her family who lived in York. They'd love to be near the Chesapeake Bay, but that was just a little too far away from her parents. However, this house in Kismet would give them the nautical feel that they'd like, yet put them in a good location. Both husband and wife were self-employed. He was a video game developer and she was a web designer, so they could work from anywhere. And from what they'd seen of this house online, they thought it might be perfect for them.

And Denise was eager for the sale.

Caprice wasn't sure why they needed her here, but she supposed she'd find out.

Denise was already at the house with the couple when Caprice arrived. She was sure she was on time. She set her phone on vibrate so any calls coming in wouldn't disturb the meeting. She found the front door, with its porthole window, unlocked.

After she pushed it open, she stepped inside onto beautiful teak floors. She'd used the colors of the waterfront to decorate—from furniture to wall hangings. This was an eastern seaboard retreat, splashed with yellows, blues, whites, and reds. The downstairs, or main level, was basically one large open space that encompassed the great room, dining area, and kitchen. There was a study and, although it was still open to the other rooms, it was tucked into an alcove to provide privacy. The first floor also boasted, of course, the lighthouse room with its two-and-a-half-story ceiling. The upstairs level held the master suite, in addition to three other bedrooms. An outdoor balcony ran across the second floor and met the widow's walk, which circled the lighthouse room.

As an additional incentive for this couple, the basement level, which was a walk-in from the back with French doors and several plate-glass windows, housed a large bedroom suite, kitchenette, and sitting area.

Caprice heard voices as they echoed from the up-stairs down the circular curved staircase to the downstairs. She heard Denise say, "I understand you both want a home office."

"We do," a male voice answered. "Kim likes to be closed up and quiet when she works. I, on the other hand, like activity. That first-floor den would be perfect for me. She could use the lighthouse."

A woman's voice responded, "I love the lighthouse. I'm thinking that eventually my parents will move in here with us. That suite downstairs could be perfect for them. But my mother likes floral tones. She wouldn't go for the Cape Cod atmosphere we like. We'd have to redecorate."

As Denise descended the last few steps, she spotted Caprice. "Caprice! I'm so glad you're here. This is Kim and David Wilkins. They like the house a lot. But Kim has some concerns about decorating—in the bedrooms, the lighthouse room, and the lower level. I told her you're an expert at that."

Caprice stepped forward and extended her hand. "It's good to meet you." She shook both Kim's and David's extended hands.

Kim was scanning her outfit and grinning. Caprice had worn coral clamdiggers, a Bohemian-styled bell-sleeved coral-and-green top, and her sneakers with peace signs.

"I love your outfit," Kim said.

"Thank you." Caprice was pleased somebody appreciated her wardrobe. "What are your concerns about decorating? You don't want the nautical theme throughout?"

"David and I like it, but as I was telling Denise, I anticipate my parents eventually moving into the basement. Though it's really not a basement with that outside entrance and all the out-of-ground windows. That's what makes it perfect. There's lots of light down there."

"And heated floors, too," Caprice said.

"Really?" David asked. "Denise didn't mention

that. Even more perfect. And just imagine the sunsets from that balcony upstairs. We have friends in New York City who would want to come here just for the view."

"I can decorate however you'd like," Caprice assured them.

"We checked out your website online when we saw that you'd staged the house. One of your credits was that you decorated for Ace Richland. Is that true?"

"Yes, it is. I redid a room for his daughter and did his pool area."

"And you staged the house that Ace bought too, Denise told us," Kim added.

"I did. His was a wild kingdom theme."

Kim laughed. "I think my mom would like something sedate—florals in peach and green and maybe cherry furniture? She has a four-poster bed she'll probably want to move in here."

"You have to convince them that moving in here with us is the right thing to do," David said to his wife.

"That might take a year or two . . . or maybe three. But once they see this house, I'm sure they'll love it too. They'll have room to roam and not have upkeep. We can drive them to doctors' appointments if need be. Especially when Dad has his knee surgery, he might be able to recuperate here, which will get them used to the idea."

"Tell Miss De Luca about the changes you want in the lighthouse room," David reminded his wife.

"I'd like my office decorated all in blues. It's my favorite color—from turquoise to aqua to baby blue. Do you think you could make that work?"

"I can make anything work," Caprice assured her with a smile. "I have a few catalogs in the van. Would you like to see them? Sample books too—for wallpaper and material for upholstery fabric or drapes."

"That sounds wonderful. Maybe we can take a look out back while you get them."

"I'll meet you back here." Caprice spun on her heels and headed out the door.

This sounded like an imminent sale. It would be great for Denise's pocket and good for Caprice's reputation. She liked this couple a lot. They were positive and upbeat and seemed to have a handle on their lives. Denise had confided that David was a multimillionaire because of the video games he'd developed. But they didn't have an arrogant attitude that some wealthy people adopted. She liked that. She also liked that they were thinking about caring for Kim's parents.

She was in the back of her van stacking sample books when her cell phone vibrated in her pocket. She might have let it go to voice mail, but she was hoping Grant would call. Soon. Hadn't Naomi had enough of Kismet and sightseeing yet?

Maybe Naomi wasn't going to leave. Maybe Grant wouldn't call. Maybe—

Cutting off that thought, she also realized she hadn't heard from Marianne, who was supposed to get back to her with an address for Bronson's dad's cabin.

When she checked her phone's screen, she saw Marianne was the caller. Disappointment stabbed at her, but she ignored it and answered. "Hi, Marianne. Could you find it?"

"I did. It really wouldn't do me much good to just give you the address. It's a rural P.O. box near Wellsville."

Wellsville was located about fifteen minutes from Kismet.

"I have explicit directions. I e-mailed them to you," Marianne said.

"Thank you. You don't know how much I appreciate this. I owe you one."

"Yes, you do. Remember, I get first scoop if you find out anything juicy. Or if you solve this murder. You're going to soon be a celebrity."

"Bite your tongue."

Marianne laughed. "So what are you going to do?"

It took Caprice only a few seconds to think about it. "I'm talking to a couple now about buying and decorating a house, and as soon as I'm done here, I'm going to follow your directions. I want to talk to Larry Penya sooner rather than later."

It was later than Caprice would have liked when she finished up at the Nautical Interlude house. The couple had loads of questions and had pored over her sample books. Caprice knew Denise was chomping at the bit to settle the sale, to actually hold earnest money in her hand. This was all part of the process. Kim and David had to see themselves in the house . . . and enjoy the adventure of it. So Caprice had patiently aided them in finding exactly what they wanted.

After they all said good-bye and Kim and David headed off with Denise to her office to begin the paperwork for buying the property, Caprice headed

home to give her animals attention—and supper.
Eager to drive to the Wellsville area, she grabbed a
container of broccoli salad and ate it outside while
Lady ran and played.

Between bites, Caprice said to her, "I wish I could
take you along. But I can't. And Dulcina has a new
guest who isn't used to you yet. Maybe . . ." She took
her phone from her pocket and dialed her mom.
After her mother answered, she asked, "Are you
busy tonight?"

"Need a listening ear?" her mom asked.

"No, I need a pupsitter. I was away most of the afternoon, and I have an errand I need to run tonight.
I really don't want to leave Lady alone again."

"Sure. Bring her on over."

Twenty minutes later, Lady happily soaked up
Fran's attention as Caprice told her parents where
she was headed and outlined the directions to
her dad.

Her father said, "I know that area. It's near
Pinchot State Park. Lots of woods. Creeks. Beautiful farmland too. You should be okay if you follow
those directions."

She should be okay. Of course she should. She
was just going to question one of Drew's friends.

Dusk was falling as Caprice found the gravel lane
Marianne had detailed and turned her van onto it.
The narrow road wound around a few curves and
then stopped abruptly before a wooded area. No
one had told her she'd be hiking tonight.

Once she exited her van, she spied a three-foot-
wide path that led through the stand of maples and

sycamores. It wasn't long before the cabin came into view. Even though it was rustic, it was a hidden gem because no one would suspect it was here. It was a square with a slanted roof. She suspected the floor plan would show a loft and an open ceiling. The screened-in porch ran along the front and side of the cabin.

As she approached it, the silence of the woods was broken by male voices. A pickup truck zigzagged along the far side of the cabin, and she realized that either there was another winding entrance that ran around the back or she'd missed a turnoff that circled around the trees.

Who was here with Larry?

Glad she'd worn sneakers that made little noise on the gravel, she stood at the corner of the screened-in porch and unabashedly listened.

"Give me plane fare and a stake, and I'll just disappear. Linda doesn't care if I'm gone."

That was Larry's voice. His words sounded slurred, as if he'd been drinking. "I don't have anything to offer Joey," he added morosely. "Nothing's holding me here."

If he was running, did that mean he'd killed Drew?

Then she heard another male voice. "You can't just leave. We have to stand up to Fairchild together. I don't understand why he called this meeting now."

Fairchild? Louis Fairchild, the men's high school shop teacher? Caprice recognized the second voice too—it belonged to Bronson Chronister.

"Exactly what did Fairchild say?" Larry asked shakily.

"He said he wanted to talk over old times." Bronson sounded agitated, his tone rising and falling as if he was pacing. "You know what that means. I can't have that accident brought up now."

"*You* weren't even in the car!" Larry shot back. "Drew and I ran him down."

"*Drew* ran him down. You were about as drunk as you are now. I wasn't in the car, but I knew about it after the fact. The whole mess could ruin my career in politics."

"We have something worse to think about," Larry whined.

"What would that be?" Bronson sounded genuinely perplexed.

"Drew's murder."

"I didn't have anything to do with that. Neither did you."

All was silent a few seconds until Bronson asked, "*Did* you?"

"Not me," Larry protested. "But I did see Drew that night and I didn't tell the police. I'd fixed the cord on that light that he said was so expensive. Apparently Drew was messing with it and the cord gave way. It's old. But he didn't want his grandmother to know. After Rowena left for the day with her friend, I picked it up and took it to my workshop to repair it."

"Did Linda see you had it?" Bronson sounded appalled.

"She wasn't home. She takes Joey to the playground on Sundays."

"What did you do with it after you fixed it?"

"Drew called me when he was through at that expo. I took it back to the house. But . . ." He hesitated, then went on. "But Fairchild came to the door. He said he wanted to talk to Drew privately. So I left. But I stopped outside to smoke and . . . I heard them arguing. That's when I headed out."

"And you didn't tell the police?"

"If I ratted out Fairchild to the police, I knew he'd tell them about me and Drew and the accident."

"If you hadn't spilled the beans to him when you were drunk back then—"

Suddenly the hairs on the back of Caprice's neck prickled. It was as if a cold wind had blown through the summer night. Before she could react, take a breath, or turn around, she felt something poke the middle of her back. Something hard. Something like the barrel of a gun.

She recognized the voice when Louis Fairchild shouted to the two men inside. "You've confessed everything in front of a witness. What do you think we should do with her?"

After a silent moment, Bronson and Larry both rushed out of the porch and down the front steps. They saw Caprice and Fairchild behind her.

"What are you doing here?" Bronson asked her.

She could hardly find her voice, but she finally did. "I came to talk to Larry. I never expected to run into . . . all three of you."

All three of them had committed crimes. But it seemed Louis Fairchild had killed Drew.

Why else would Fairchild have pretended he

hadn't had any contact with Bronson, Larry, and Drew for years? Why else would he have a gun pointed at her?

Now was no time for cowardice. She needed to get them to turn on each other so she could slip her phone out of her pocket and dial Detective Carstead.

Fairchild's gun wasn't tight against her now. That didn't mean he couldn't kill her in an instant, but this might give her a little leeway. It sounded as if Larry and Drew and Bronson had been caught up in something as teenagers and they hadn't known how to get out of it.

Her gaze went from Bronson to Larry, making a point. Then she said, "You trusted Mr. Fairchild back in high school, didn't you? After all, he was your teacher. But he wouldn't be holding a gun on me if he can be trusted."

Bronson shook his head. "I didn't trust him. Larry did. But he said he'd always keep the secret."

Larry's eyes were glazed, but his words were clear when he said in a low voice, "I've never been able to forget the sound of the car hitting that old man. Never."

And that's why he drank.

"I knew what had happened before Larry told me," Fairchild muttered. "All those years ago, they thought I didn't notice Drew's dented bumper and the piece of material caught on it. I knew about their drag racing. When I heard about the hit-and-run accident, I put two and two together. But by then a friend of Drew's had fixed his bumper and the car was cleaned up. I found Larry drunk on the bleachers one night and he spilled it all. A secret is a handy thing to have in your back pocket . . . especially when you want to retire."

Caprice understood that the only reason Fairchild was talking was because he was going to kill her. What would Bronson and Larry do? Let him?

She was panicking inside but she had to keep her wits about her. She could get out of this somehow. She could. She should have texted Grant that she was thinking of him. She didn't want him to think she'd died hurt and angry.

She wasn't going to die.

"You were going to blackmail Drew, weren't you?" Caprice asked in order to keep Fairchild talking as her hand slipped to her pocket. She hadn't brought her mace gun. Stupid, stupid, stupid.

"Drew was making it big, and I wanted some of that," Fairchild said.

Caprice nodded to Bronson. "Why not blackmail *him*? He had the money."

"He wasn't in the car that night. Larry and Drew were. But I called him out here tonight because now that he has politics on his mind, he can grease my palm to keep me quiet. Enough of this chitchat. You've got to go, girl. Apparently my threats didn't work with you. The woods are dark and deep. Let's move it."

But before Fairchild could poke her with the gun again, she caught the appalled expression on Bronson's face when he realized that Fairchild had intended to blackmail *him* and that he intended to kill *her*.

With an angry shout, Bronson rushed Fairchild. When he did, the gun went off!

Both men staggered, and Caprice didn't know if either of them had been hit.

Suddenly Fairchild pushed away from Bronson. As he did, she saw Bronson clutch his shoulder. Fairchild stooped to retrieve the gun that must have fallen out of his hand when Bronson grabbed him.

Caprice didn't need any advice on what to do next. She ran for the woods, yelling at Larry to use Bronson's phone to call 9-1-1. She grabbed hold of her phone as she ran and pressed the number to speed-dial Carstead. After tripping over a tree root, she caught herself, hung onto the trunk, and rounded another tree.

When Carstead answered her call, she didn't give him a chance to speak. She rat-a-tat-tatted her location—Elliot Chronister's cabin near Wellsville. Then she added, "Louis Fairchild killed Drew. I think he shot Bronson. Need paramedics. Get here." Then she pocketed her cell phone so she could run faster.

Fairchild was in shape, but she was younger. Maybe she could fool him and circle around . . . or climb a tree. As she scurried through the brush, she heard a loud grunt and swearing behind her. Maybe Fairchild had fallen over a tree root. She could only hope. She ran faster, increasing the distance between them.

Her cell phone vibrated in her pocket. Carstead wanting her to keep the line open? That would be the smart thing to do. But as she pulled out her phone and saw its glow in the dimming light, she realized the caller was Grant!

He sure picked a dandy time to call. She was torn, but she knew she had to answer. This was the first he'd contacted her since Naomi's visit. Grant and his call were as important as her life.

Breathless, she asked in a low voice, "Can I call you back?"

But Grant knew her moods and her voice. "What's wrong?"

They didn't keep secrets between them. She whispered, "Hold on a minute," and ducked behind a thick tree truck.

But Grant wasn't holding on. "Where are you?"

She heard brush cracking, branches moving. If she talked to Grant, Fairchild would hear her. She whispered, "I'll text."

Moving farther into the woods and the night, she curled herself behind a sycamore so Fairchild couldn't see the glow from her phone and quickly texted, Murderer chasing me at Elliot Chronister's cabin. Dad has directions. I called Carstead.

Pocketing the phone, she moved a little farther through the trees, then decided the best thing for her to do was to climb one. Fortunately Vince had taught her well. In fact, he'd taught her lots of skills that could save her life as well as any self-defense course. She jumped at the lowest branch, caught it with her arms, then used her sneakered feet to scramble up the tree. It was practically dark now, with no moon lighting the woods.

She didn't know how long she was in that tree. It seemed like centuries. How much distance had she put between herself and Fairchild? Had he gone off in another direction?

She waited and waited and waited, afraid to make a move. Maybe she should climb down and run again. But which way? Toward the cabin? Into the woods? She could run right into him.

Minute after minute slowly ticked by. Then suddenly she spotted a beam of light and suspected it was the flashlight app on Fairchild's cell phone. Wasn't technology a wonder? All she could do was say Hail Marys and hope.

Fairchild was obviously trying to be quiet, but she could hear his shuffles through the brush, his low grunt when a branch grazed him or a bramble caught his jeans.

Her body was rigid and stiff. Finally she decided she'd better breathe. She took a few shallow breaths. He was using that flashlight beam in circles but not shining it up into the trees. Maybe he was too afraid he'd trip again. After all, maybe he wasn't as nimble as she was. The light inched closer to *her* tree. She didn't move. She didn't breathe. She didn't even flinch.

"I'm going to find you," he called out to the general area. "You know I will. You might as well come out."

She wondered if he underestimated all women. Maybe that's why he never married. Or maybe women always discovered his mean streak, because he obviously had one.

He stopped, probably to listen. When he didn't hear anything, he moved on. Now he kept quiet, maybe thinking he could sneak up on her wherever she was hiding. But the woods *were* dark and deep, and soon he was farther into them. Now she could scramble down and run back to the cabin . . . maybe even reach her van.

The wail of sirens broke the stillness of the night.

The sound was faint at first but grew louder with
each second. Thank goodness for GPSs and cell
phone towers. Thank goodness for detectives who
knew how to find addresses. Thank goodness for
Hail Marys and brothers who didn't mind her tag-
ging along. And self-defense courses.

The siren sounds were almost deafening now in
the hushed night. Not caring about scratched and
cut hands or brush and brambles, she scurried
down the tree, lit up her own phone's flashlight
app, and ran as fast as she could back toward the
cabin.

Before she emerged from the trees, she could
hear officers shouting to each other. She heard
them spreading out through the woods. As she
reached the cabin, she spotted Bronson and Larry
sitting on the porch steps, Carstead looming over
them.

"I'm here," she called as she waved and approached them. She could see Bronson holding his
arm across his chest, blood staining his shirt sleeve.

But before she reached Carstead, another man
came running from the makeshift road. A man who
was tall with black hair and broad shoulders—the
man she loved.

Grant rushed to Caprice and took her into his
arms. "Are you all right? What are you doing out
here? I don't know whether to shake you or kiss you."

She didn't wait for him to decide. *She* kissed him.

He wouldn't be here if he didn't love her. He
wouldn't be here if he'd made a different choice.

After Grant pulled away, he said, "Everything's
going to be all right. I promise. We can talk later."

Just then, two patrol officers dragged Louis

Fairchild from the edge of the woods. He was handcuffed and looked as if he wanted to murder someone again. They none too gently pushed him toward the patrol car.

Finally Detective Carstead approached Caprice. He gave her a look that said he'd never understand her. He muttered, "Maybe I should put you on the Kismet P.D.'s payroll. Can you meet me at the station and fill me in on exactly what happened?"

"I'd be glad to," she answered agreeably. She wasn't shaking now that Grant was holding on to her so tightly. He'd promised everything would be all right . . . and she *did* trust him.

As Carstead walked away, Grant said, "He likes you."

She heard that hint of jealousy in Grant's voice again, and it made her heart sing. Turning to him, remembering Nana's advice to jump without a net when she knew what she wanted, she gazed into his eyes and assured him, "But I like *you*. You're the only man I want to consider a future with. That is, if you want a future with me."

"We have a lot to talk about," Grant assured her, pulling her close again. "Naomi went back to Oklahoma. This week put resentment and recriminations to rest. We revived good memories of Sally. But my life with Naomi is in the past. After you and I finish at the police station, I want to talk to you about what comes next for us."

That was a conversation she couldn't wait to have.

Epilogue

Ten Days Later

The cafeteria at Kismet High School had been transformed for the night. The committee developing the reunion wanted to make the night affordable for as many classmates as they could, so they'd decided to have the reunion at the school. It was a sweltering July night, but no one seemed to mind as they stepped into the air-conditioning and the music that poured from the speakers the DJ had set up in the lobby adjacent to the cafeteria.

On Grant's arm, Caprice was glad she'd dressed up. She'd found a fifties-style lacy crinoline dress in off-white with an embroidered flower pattern. Donned in its capped sleeves, sweetheart neck, and tight waist, along with teal strappy pumps and a teal and cream purse, she felt good.

When Grant looked at her, she felt pretty.

They'd been spending as many hours together as they could. She could tell his time with Naomi had settled things in his mind. He'd shared some of the conversations he'd had with his ex-wife. He'd also shared some of his grief at losing his daughter. She knew that would always be with him. But she accepted that, just as she accepted him. And he seemed to accept her just the way she was, even when he was angrier than an irate bull that she'd put herself in danger again, inadvertently or not.

They sat at one of the tables in the cafeteria beside Roz and Vince. Other members of the reunion committee were seated across the table.

Vince waved to the centerpieces. "They're looking good." He turned to Roz. "I hear you helped with those."

"I did. I've always liked arranging flowers. Jeanie Boswell gave us a discount on them, as well as the vases."

Since the apprehension of Drew's murderer, Caprice had learned more about Jeanie and the way she often hid her emotions behind indifference and anger. That hadn't made her a guilty sister, just a grieving one.

"We've finally decided we're going to take a vacation together," Roz told her in a low voice. Her friend sounded excited . . . and happy.

"Where?" Caprice asked.

Vince answered, "The Finger Lakes in New York State. We'll have a whole week together—day and night."

Roz blushed.

Grant leaned close to Caprice. She caught a whiff of his woodsy cologne that was one of her favorite scents these days. He looked so handsome tonight in a charcoal suit with a blue tie and pale blue shirt.

But then she thought he looked handsome no matter what he wore.

He murmured near her ear, "Did I tell you how beautiful you look tonight?"

She smiled. "In spite of the fact that I was up all last night watching Halo deliver her kittens?" The tortoiseshell had given birth to three—a dark tortoiseshell, a gray-striped tabby, and a lighter tortoiseshell—all still to be named. Watching them being born and settling in to nurse had been an awesome experience.

Grant's voice went a little lower. "Do you remember the night we delivered Shasta's pups?"

"Of course I do. I'll never forget it."

Grant took her hand and asked, "Would you like to dance?"

"I definitely would."

They stood and excused themselves.

Roz winked. Vince gave them a thumbs-up, and Caprice didn't even feel embarrassed.

Before they reached the lobby, where couples were dancing, Helen Parcelli, whom Caprice had run into at the Raspberry Festival, approached them. "Hi. I've been wanting to talk to you, but I didn't want to interrupt at your table. I want the real scoop on what happened at Elliot Chronister's cabin."

Helen wasn't the first person to ask Caprice, and she answered by rote. "Marianne Brisbane reported what happened in the article in the *Kismet Crier*."

Narrowing her eyes, Helen prodded, "Come on now. Fill in the details for me."

Caprice looked at Grant, and he gave a shrug.

Caprice studied Helen. "What do you know?"

"Everything I've been reading online. Larry and Drew were involved in an accident in high school and didn't report it. Bronson made a public apology concerning his knowledge of it. I think he hopes if he comes clean about everything, maybe he still can have some kind of career in politics. After all, he wasn't in the car when it happened. What exactly are the charges against all of them?"

Those were points of public record, so Caprice answered easily. "Larry was charged with conspiracy to commit homicide by motor vehicle and obstruction of justice."

"Don't forget breaking and entering at Rowena's when he tried to find Drew's yearbook," Grant interjected. "An inscription in the yearbook could have been damming if it came to light. A prosecuting DA could have used it to his advantage."

"I heard Bronson is paying for a good lawyer for Larry," Helen said. "Maybe he'll get a minimum sentence."

"That's what they're hoping," Grant agreed. "Bronson was charged with obstruction of justice but will probably be sentenced to probation or community service. I doubt if a political career is in the cards for him anymore."

"I can't believe Louis Fairchild murdered Drew. Exactly why did he do it?" Helen asked.

Caprice knew Fairchild was having the book thrown at him—homicide, attempted homicide, and obstruction of justice. The prosecutor also tacked on a charge of terroristic threats for scaring her out of her wits with the knife and note on the rack of ribs and the letter in the mail.

"When Louis Fairchild wanted to retire," Caprice

explained, "he had a problem. He'd blown most of his 401K on gambling debts, and social security wouldn't fund the retirement he wanted. He knew Larry, Drew, and Bronson had each other's backs, and he decided to cash in on their secret. He couldn't blackmail Bronson—this was before Bronson's political ambition—because Bronson only *knew* about the hit-and-run. He hadn't been in the car. But after Drew hit the big time with his barbeque sauce, Fairchild thought he could squeeze money from him."

"So Fairchild confessed?"

"He did," Caprice responded. "The whole story came out when the police questioned him, because he was so angry . . . at me, at Bronson, at Drew, at Larry. Apparently Drew had been snooping for recipes in Rowena's Tiffany lamps. When the cord broke on the table lamp, Larry fixed it and returned the lamp. After Fairchild showed up at Drew's, Larry left. But he stood outside to smoke and heard raised voices. He didn't stay because he didn't want to get involved in whatever was brewing. Fairchild said that when he tried to blackmail Drew, Drew just laughed at him. They argued. Drew turned away, and Fairchild picked up the lamp base that Larry had returned, conked Drew with it, and took it with him. On his rush to leave, he knocked over the other Tiffany lamp. The police found the base of the lamp stashed in a closet at his residence."

"The irony of it," Grant added, "was that if he'd just stolen the lamps, he'd have had a windfall of sorts."

"I'd heard they were Tiffany," Helen said. "I

wonder if Drew's grandmother is going to keep them."

"She's selling them," Caprice revealed. "They're going up for auction."

"I knew you could tell me more than was in that newspaper article."

Another classmate waved to Helen from across the room. She waved back. "I'd better get going," she said. "You two have a nice time tonight."

After she moved away, Grant wrapped his arm around Caprice's waist and led her to the dance floor. A ballad had begun playing. As he took her hand in his and guided her to the music, she knew murder and mayhem were behind her for now.

"What are you thinking about?" Grant asked her as they danced.

She answered honestly. "You."

He pulled her closer and rested his chin on top of her head.

Smiling, she squeezed his hand and sighed. She was right where she wanted to be . . . close to his heart.

Original Recipes

Caprice's Easy Beef Bourguignon

- 6 bacon slices, plus 3 tablespoons of the
  drippings
- 2 ½ pounds stewing cubes
- 2 cups flour
- 1½ teaspoons salt
- ½ teaspoon pepper

Coat a 5-quart slow cooker with no-stick spray.

Fry bacon, then remove it from the drippings. When
it is cool, crumble it and set it aside in the refrigerator. Save 3 tablespoons of the drippings.

Dry beef cubes as much as possible with food-
friendly paper towels. Combine flour, 1½ teaspoons
salt, and ½ teaspoon pepper in a Ziploc bag. Drop
in a few stewing cubes at a time to coat them, then
place the coated cubes in the slow cooker.

- 1 cup chopped onion
- 1 cup peeled and sliced carrots
- 1 cup chopped celery
- 1 clove grated garlic

⅛ teaspoon marjoram
1 teaspoon salt
½ teaspoon pepper
3 cups beef broth (use Swanson for no MSG)
1½ cups white burgundy wine (red burgundy
    discolors the mixture)
4 or 5 red pepper flakes

Add onion, carrots, celery, garlic, marjoram, 1 teaspoon salt, ½ teaspoon pepper, and the red pepper flakes to the beef cubes in the slow cooker.

Pour broth over the mixture, then add the three tablespoons of bacon drippings and the wine. Cover and cook on low for 5 hours or until beef cubes are tender. Stir every two hours for a smooth gravy base without flour lumps.

I serve over 1 pound of wide egg noodles and top each portion with crumbled bacon.

Serves six to eight.

Bella's Lima Bean Casserole

2 16-ounce bags frozen lima beans, *thawed*
8 slices fried, crumbled bacon
¾ cup chopped fresh onion
¾ teaspoon salt
½ teaspoon pepper
¼ cup melted butter
½ cup water

8 ounces finely grated cheddar cheese
6 tablespoons Italian bread crumbs

Preheat oven to 400 degrees.

Combine thawed lima beans, crumbled bacon, onion, salt, pepper, butter, water, and grated cheese. Turn into a two-quart casserole sprayed with no-stick cooking spray.

Bake covered at 400 degrees for 45 minutes. Remove cover and sprinkle with bread crumbs. Bake an additional 10 to 15 minutes or until bread crumbs are browned and beans are tender.

Serves six to eight.

Nikki's Carrot Surprise Cake

Cake
   1½ cups flour
   2 teaspoons baking powder
   1 teaspoon baking soda
   1 teaspoon salt
   1½ teaspoons cinnamon
   1 teaspoon orange zest
   1½ cups sugar
   1 cup vegetable oil
   3 eggs
   1½ cups shredded carrots
   ½ cup crushed pineapple, drained
   ½ cup chopped walnuts
   1 cup flaked coconut

Cream Cheese Frosting
   ½ cup softened butter
   1 8-ounce package softened cream cheese
   1 teaspoon vanilla
   ½ teaspoon orange zest
   1 pound confectioner's sugar

Preheat oven to 350 degrees.

Grease and flour 9 by 13-inch cake pan.

Cake

Stir together the flour, baking powder, baking soda, salt, cinnamon, and orange zest in a large mixer bowl. Add sugar, oil, and eggs. Beat on medium speed for about 1 minute until well mixed. Fold in carrots, pineapple, walnuts, and coconut until completely blended.

Pour mixture into the greased and floured cake pan. Bake at 350 degrees for 35 minutes or until toothpick comes out clean. Let cake cool completely before frosting.

Cream Cheese Frosting

Beat softened butter with softened cream cheese until smooth. Add vanilla and orange zest. Blend in confectioner's sugar and beat until smooth and spreadable. Frost the cake and refrigerate until you are ready to serve it.

Please turn the page for an exciting sneak peek of
Karen Rose Smith's next
Caprice De Luca Home Staging Mystery

SHADES OF WRATH

coming in December 2016 wherever
print and e-books are sold!

Chapter One

The mansion that stood before Caprice De Luca was a bit run-down but still magnificent. As an early September breeze tossed her long, dark-brown hair as well as the leaves around her feet, Caprice remembered that the Tudor revival had hit America during the 1920s and 30s when this edifice had been built. It was a monstrous home, yet charming too because of the steeply pitched roof with prominent cross gables. Those gables were embellished with half-timbering against stucco walls. Decorative chimney pots topped the thick brick chimney.

End-of-the-day light flickered against the tall windows arranged in groups of three. Each had diamond-shaped panes that reflected the sunlight. As a home stager, Caprice considered how light shone into a room. However, she wouldn't be looking at this house to stage it to sell. She'd be planning how to furnish and decorate it.

Caprice ascended the front steps, passing under the arched portico that supported a room above it.

She couldn't wait to see the inside. Wendy Newcomb had said she'd be waiting for her.

This estate had been donated to Sunrise Tomorrow, a cause that had been a passion of Wendy Newcomb's since she'd established a foundation for the women's shelter in Kismet about a decade ago. She ate and slept her work, advocating for and caring for women who were victims of domestic violence. Caprice was here today to take a look at the mansion and propose ideas for decorating it so that it was suitable for a housing facility for women who were in need of transitional care. She was going to make their rooms feel like places they'd want to spend time.

The heavy wood-paneled door stood slightly open. Before Caprice understood what was happening, a yellow tabby cat ran up the steps and slipped inside. Did the Wyatt estate have a resident feline? Caprice pushed the door open wider, but it took an effort. Maybe the hinges were just warped . . . or maybe that door was meant to be a barricade. Instantly, she was in awe of the Carrera marble floor in the grand foyer and the spacious living room before her. She'd started across the foyer when she heard angry voices near the wide, curved stairway that led to the second floor. Since the mansion was practically empty, except for sawhorses, ladders, and building supplies, she could hear some of what was being said across the room. There was no sign of the cat. Where had he disappeared to?

A man's voice rose. "Where is she?" he demanded.

Caprice recognized Wendy's voice, lower than his. She couldn't catch every word. From what she knew of Wendy, the director of Sunrise Tomorrow was trying to remain calm and serene in the face of an angry male.

Whatever explanation Wendy gave didn't seem to satisfy the man, and now Caprice recognized his voice too. It belonged to Warren Shaeffer, CEO of Kismet's Millennium Printing and the president of the town's Chamber of Commerce. He didn't fly off the handle easily. Stoic was usually his middle name. Apparently not today.

Moving closer to the stairway, Caprice saw Warren point his finger at Wendy. "You have no right to interfere."

Unsure exactly what to do, Caprice continued to approach them. She could see Wendy was red-faced. Oblivious to a third party, she poked Warren in the chest and determined in a clipped voice, "I don't need to tell you anything. You'd better leave before I call the police. I don't think you'd want the general public to know that you can't hold your temper."

Suddenly Shaeffer shifted on his feet and spotted Caprice. He seemed to take a breath, rein in his anger, intentionally relax his shoulders, and act as if this interchange with Wendy was no big deal.

Caprice was almost at Wendy's side now as he made a nonchalantly composed remark that she didn't expect.

"I'll look forward to seeing both of you at the next Chamber of Commerce meeting." With a forced smile at Caprice, he hurried to the front door and exited the house.

Wendy looked so relieved as he left. She pasted on a smile just as forced as his had been and pretended as if her conversation with him hadn't affected her at all. "That was an unexpected meeting," she apologized. "Come on, let me show you around. The workmen have left for the day."

It was obvious Wendy didn't want to talk about the encounter that had just happened. But as she walked beside Caprice and led her up the stairs, Caprice could see the woman's hands were shaking a little. A result of stress . . . her position . . . the legacy of the Wyatt estate? Or because of Warren Shaeffer?

Caprice had never seen him lose his temper. As head of the Chamber of Commerce, she had watched him remain cool over many a heated discussion. However, those discussions hadn't been personal. Today's discussion with Wendy had sounded *very* personal.

The stairs led to a second-floor hallway. As they reached the second-floor landing, Caprice could see a balustrade that stretched from one side of the hall to the other. It overlooked the spacious foyer.

She could smell the dust in the air, spotted sawhorses down the hall and drop cloths in the first bedroom. Roller window shades, perhaps collected from the upstairs rooms, lay in a stack near the balustrade. Sitting next to the pile of shades was the yellow tabby, blinking at her with jewel-like green eyes.

Caprice started toward the wooden railing, intending to get closer to the cat.

Wendy caught her arm. "Oh no! Don't go near that. The balusters aren't stable. I told the contractor he should put a warning sawhorse there or something, but he hasn't. I'll remind him again tomorrow."

Caprice glanced down at the pile of shades, with

their scalloped edge and fringes and wooden bar across the front for lowering and raising the window covering. They were yellowed and looked as old as the house. Then she again studied the feline.

"Are you friendly?" she asked him.

As if in answer, he stretched and came to her, rubbing against her retro plaid slacks with an insert side pleat that ran from knee to ankle. Retro fashion was one of her passions. Cats and dogs were another. She crouched down and offered him her hand. He butted his head against it.

"He's very friendly," Wendy said. "I found him curled up in one of the bedrooms upstairs when nights began turning colder. I've been here almost every day to check on something so I feed him wet food then leave a bowl of dry in the bedroom upstairs. I think he slips in through a broken basement window when the door isn't open. He doesn't seem to mind the workers who are in and out."

The tabby purred as Caprice petted him. Then suddenly he left her, crossing to sit once more beside the pile of window shades.

Wendy motioned to the rest of the upstairs and began walking. Caprice glanced over her shoulder at the tabby who seemed quite contented where he was.

As they walked down the hall, she asked Wendy, "Is most of the work here cosmetic, or are there structural issues?"

"Fortunately, inside the house most of the work is cosmetic—steaming off wallpaper, patch plastering, painting, modernizing a few of the bathrooms. We also have to add a new roof. I don't want any problems in the next few years with leakage. But all in all, the mansion is in amazingly good shape. Houses were built to last in the 1920s. This one had a grand past with good upkeep until the last dozen years or so. When Leona got sick, everything seemed to be a burden, even lifting the phone to call a plumber."

Leona Wyatt had faced a battle with cancer. Scuttlebutt had it she thought she'd won after her first bout with it. But ten years later it had come roaring back and had taken her.

"She had children, didn't she? Couldn't they help her?"

A look passed over Wendy's face that Caprice couldn't quite decipher. But then Caprice learned its meaning—disgust. Wendy said, "Her son and daughter didn't pay much attention to her, even when she was sick. They were no help at all."

Caprice wondered if that was why Leona Wyatt had left her son and daughter money in trust yet left the mansion and the rest of her money to Sunrise Tomorrow. She'd heard the Wyatt siblings were squabbling over the fact they felt they should have received the legacy left to the Sunrise Tomorrow Foundation. However, there had been a stipulation in Leona's will that if they contested it, they would receive nothing. The Wyatt estate had been through probate and settled without incident. Apparently, the brother and sister hadn't wanted to take the chance of contesting the will and losing.

Caprice followed Wendy from room to room, snapping photos on her phone, loving a peek into the house that had to be filled with memories of days gone by. They chatted about goings-on in Kismet as they walked. When they finished on the second floor, they descended the back stairs into the kitchen area where a grand brick fireplace stretched from floor to ceiling in the sitting area. A butler's pantry and maid's suite were located behind the kitchen. Caprice noted the utility room was almost as large as her living room.

Wendy explained, "I want to uphold the original grandeur of the house, yet I want it to be homey too. Does that make sense?"

"Perfect sense. You said this would be a transitional facility. Just what does that mean?"

An old-time deacon's bench still sat in one corner of the kitchen. Wendy motioned to it, and they both took a seat there.

"Most of the women who come to Sunrise Tomorrow need a port in a storm for a couple of nights until they find shelter with a friend or a family member," Wendy explained. "Once they've left their immediate situation, obtained a PFA—Protect From Abuse order—most are involved in programs such as counseling and job training."

She shifted a bit on the bench. "But some women need a haven for longer than a few nights. Before the Wyatt legacy came through, I'd encouraged the board of the Foundation to consider buying some sort of apartment building to house women in those circumstances. Now the Wyatt estate will be perfect for that. Clients can stay a month or two or three, do job training on site, pick up skills they need, as well as self-confidence and independence. Our main facility will be what it still is—an emergency haven with services for follow-up. But this place? This place can be so much more. I'm so excited about it, Caprice, because we can help so many more women."

Caprice waited a beat, but then asked, "Do you want to talk about what happened earlier . . . when I first arrived?"

Wendy stared into the empty fireplace, soot-stained from years of use. "I can't talk about most of it, you know that. Although I'm not a therapist, the work I do is confidential. It has to be."

Wendy said that last with such vehemence, Caprice studied the woman's face. There were lines around her eyes and around her mouth. Her nose looked as if it might have been broken. Strands of gray salted her medium brown hair. Caprice didn't know Wendy's story. Nobody did, as far as she knew. And that was a feat to keep background a secret in a town the size of Kismet. On the other hand, Wendy's present-day life seemed to be an open book. She lived with her significant other, Sebastian Thompson, and his two sons. But her past was a blank slate on the gossip mill.

"I know you have to keep confidences," Caprice agreed. "But that discussion I walked in on concerned you too, didn't it?"

After hesitating, Wendy admitted, "It did. And I'll confess Warren Shaeffer scares me. He has one of those Jekyll-Hyde personalities. Only those closest to him see the Mr. Hyde side."

No, Wendy couldn't break any confidences, but what she was implying was that Warren's wife had probably sought services at the shelter. His question, *Where is she?* could mean that Wendy had helped his wife relocate somewhere else, at least for now.

Obviously wanting this discussion to be over, Wendy stood. "Let me show you the rest of the house. I have a meeting in half an hour, but we can finish touring the inside anyway. You can explore the grounds when you come to actually do the decorating. I'm going to trust you with the furnishings for most of it. I think you understand what I want. But after you turn your proposal in, I'd like to discuss updating our original quarters. Do you have time to fit that into your schedule too?"

Furnishing and decorating the Wyatt estate and updating the original Sunrise Tomorrow facility could bring in substantial income. She'd fit it into her schedule somehow.

"I'd be glad to talk about updating. When would you like to do that?"

"Why don't we keep that less formal? Why don't you come to dinner on Saturday with me and Sebastian and the boys?"

Caprice didn't know how long Wendy had been living with Sebastian Thompson and his sons, but it sounded as if they'd formed a family.

"I'd like that. Where do you live?"

"We live in the Poplar Grove Co-housing Development. Do you know where that is?"

Although Caprice wasn't exactly sure what co-housing meant, she'd passed the Poplar Grove development on occasion. It was located east of town.

"I've never visited the development itself, but I've gotten a glimpse of it when I visited Ace Richland's estate."

"That's right, you helped him out of a sticky situation not so long ago."

Last spring, Ace—a rock star legend—had found

himself a suspect in a murder investigation, and Caprice had indeed helped clear his name. Treating that lightly, however, she responded, "Ace and I have gotten to know each other since he bought the house I staged."

"He's on tour now, isn't he?"

"He's zigzagging across the country. He returns every couple of weeks to spend time with his daughter."

"The way it should be," Wendy said. "Sebastian complains he wants to spend time with his boys, but they don't want to spend time with him anymore. You have to take advantage of bonding time while you can."

"I'd like to find out more about co-housing."

"Basically, it's cooperative living. We're not self-sustaining like many co-housing communities, but we help out each other when we can. I'm sure Sebastian can tell you all about it. He's the one who developed the mission statement."

"I look forward to it," Caprice said.

As Wendy walked Caprice out of the kitchen into a smaller dining room, and then a much larger one, Caprice began envisioning the colors she would use to warm up the house as well as the groupings of furniture she'd select that would invite conversation. This project could easily consume her.

She smiled to herself. It was exactly the kind of project she liked best.

Caprice would have loved to have taken her dog, Lady, along to the Wyatt estate, but she hadn't known what she'd find there. She also hadn't known whether Wendy liked dogs. So she'd asked her neighbor Dulcina if she'd watch Lady while she took care of business. Now as she climbed the steps onto Dulcina's porch, she couldn't help thinking about Warren Shaeffer and his anger toward Wendy . . . and Wendy's obvious fear.

However, when Dulcina opened the door, Caprice forgot about her experience at the Wyatt estate. Not only had Dulcina come to greet her at the door, but Halo, the pregnant tortoiseshell stray cat she'd adopted in July, wound around Dulcina's legs while her seven-week-old tortie kitten, Miss Paddington, as well as Caprice's cocker, Lady, chased through the living room.

Caprice couldn't help but laugh. "How do you get any work done?"

"They were all napping until about fifteen minutes ago. Then Paddy decided she wanted crunchies and the gang all woke up."

Mason and Tia, Halo's other two kittens, now came racing into the living room too. Halo was a silver-haired tortie with tabby-like stripes and golden spots of coloring. Her firstborn was Miss Paddington, who had a unique split color face—tan and gold on one side and dark brown on the other. Her body was likewise defined. Mason, a gray-striped Tabby with a white chest, was the boy in the bunch, and as rowdy as could be. Tia, third-born, had fur that displayed striking tortoiseshell colors and lots of white. A princess, she usually held herself above the fray. But not this evening. They were all joining in.

Caprice stepped inside, careful to watch the screen door close so no fur babies escaped.

"Coffee?" Dulcina asked.

"Sure. I have time."

The kittens and Lady continued their chase, but Halo followed Caprice into the kitchen. She was becoming quite attached to humans. No one knew her whole story. Caprice's uncle Dom had found her when he was pet-sitting for a client. Caprice had captured her and taken her to her veterinarian who surmised Halo had been in an accident. She had a slight limp, and he suspected a broken bone had healed. Dulcina had decided to take in Halo, even though she'd been pregnant. The birth of the kittens had been a joy to watch and experience. They were seven weeks old now, and Caprice had some good news for Dulcina.

As Dulcina brewed two mugs of coffee in her single-cup brewer, Caprice asked, "So do you think Tia and Mason are ready for their forever homes?"

"If I can find good ones," Dulcina answered, sounding worried. "A couple of people have asked me about them, but I just didn't feel they were right. Not real cat lovers, know what I mean? I almost feel like I have to do background checks and home studies."

Caprice laughed. "They've been your babies, as well as Halo's, since they were born. Of course you're invested in their welfare. But I might have a solution."

"You know two cat lovers?"

"I know one cat lover, and wouldn't it be good to keep Mason and Tia together?"

"It would! Who do you have in mind?"

"My uncle Dom. He's living in his own place now, and he'd like to adopt the kittens. He does book-work at home for a few clients, and when he pet-sits, the two of them could keep each other company."

"Doesn't he house-sit too? What would happen during those times?"

"He's already thought of that. I told him I'd bring them to my place."

"Wouldn't that be a riot with your two cats and Lady? I suppose I could bring them back here too."

"I know he'd love Tia and Mason and care for them as if they were his kids. But it's your decision to make. Don't feel pressured because I suggested it."

"Before I make any decision, he should meet them. I'd like to see him interact with them. Do you think he'd come over for a visit?"

"I'm sure of it."

Dulcina and her uncle had met in the summer when they'd all attended an Ace Richland concert together. In fact, Dulcina had been dating then. But she'd broken up with Rod.

One of the mugs had finished brewing, and Dulcina set it in front of Caprice at the table. "Pumpkin spice."

Caprice took a whiff and smiled. "Perfect for this time of year."

As Dulcina watched her mug of coffee brew, Caprice asked, "How are you doing?"

"Thank goodness I have the kittens," she said as the three balls of fur ran into the kitchen and tum-bled over the cat bed Dulcina had tucked under the desk area of the counter. "Between work and them, I don't think about much."

"Have you talked to Rod since your breakup?"

"No. There's no point. His girls were having a hard time accepting me dating their dad, and he was doing nothing to make the transition easier. Yes, they come first. But if I was going to interact with them, and we would eventually try to make a family, he needed to include me in their family life. He wasn't doing that. He wouldn't even discuss it."

"The concert didn't help as it should have."

"No, it didn't. His older daughter, Leslie, had her mind closed to Ace's music even before we attended the concert. I think Vanna and I could have become friends, but Rod prevented us from trying. Even when they came over to visit the kittens, he wouldn't let Vanna stay a little bit longer even though she wanted to. He could have left her here while he took Leslie to her activity, but he wouldn't do it. That was the final straw for me. I understand his wife walked out on him, and he has trouble trusting women. But with that huge issue between us, we couldn't form a real relationship."

"Were you ready for one?"

"I thought I was. But my marriage to Johnny was unforgettably right. I'm just afraid I'll never have my expectations met again. How are you and Grant doing? I know you had a rough patch this summer when he saw his ex-wife."

"He needed to do that." Caprice was sure of it now, even though at the time she hadn't been. "He and Naomi lost a child. That's something both of them will deal with for the rest of their lives. He's been sharing more with me about what they talked about and what he felt, and we're becoming closer every day. I love him, Dulcina. I'm all in."

She'd known Grant Weatherford, her brother's

law partner, since he and her brother were college roommates. Divorce and tragedy had brought Grant to Kismet to find a new life and join her brother in his practice. She and Grant had had their ups and downs, but he was now the love of her life.

Dulcina nodded. "That's the way it should be if your relationship is going to last."

Mason chased Tia over to Caprice's chair, and then he climbed up her pant leg and ended up on her knee, looking up at her.

"You're just too adorable and you know it," Caprice told him.

He meowed at her, a squeaky little meow that he was growing into.

Dulcina just shook her head. "They make me laugh and they fill me with joy. Just call me or text me when your uncle wants to visit. You know me. I'm flexible."

Caprice liked to think she was too. "I'll check with Uncle Dom and see when he's free. I know he's anxious to make his new place a home."

For some reason, Caprice's mind wandered once more to the Wyatt estate. Had that mansion ever really been a home? Her objective would be to turn it into one for women who sorely needed a place of warmth and stability.

On Thursday morning, Caprice stood at the door to Sunrise Tomorrow, the original facility. Wendy had received her proposal and had a few questions that she wanted to talk over in person. Caprice said her name through the intercom and waved at the camera. She recognized the security camera setup as one that accompanied her own alarm system. The shelter had to be careful about whom they let through its door. Caprice did too when she was involved with solving a murder. Not so long ago, danger had come calling.

Wendy opened the door herself, wearing a smile. "Come on in. We can talk in my office."

The original facility for Sunrise Tomorrow was very different from what Wendy wanted to accomplish at the Wyatt estate. This building had once been an assisted living facility that had gone bankrupt. Wendy had rounded up a group of investors and taken on the challenge of turning it into a shelter with rooms where women could spend the night. An office area had been utilized for day-to-day administration. As she walked through a small reception area and around a large desk where a receptionist sat to monitor not only who came in and out but what was going on inside too, Caprice could see that the inside of the shelter could use a little polishing. The furniture was looking shabby. But she wasn't here to talk about that today.

She suddenly stopped as she spotted a woman who came from a back hall and walked through the reception area to the other wing. Caprice recognized her. Alicia Donnehy . . . and she was carrying a stack of what looked like just-washed laundry.

As if her high school classmate could feel Caprice's eyes on her, Alicia stopped and glanced over her shoulder. She didn't wave or say hello. A shuttered look came across her face, and she turned toward the direction where she'd been headed and continued walking.

Alicia had been on the committee with Caprice to plan their high school reunion in July. What was she doing here? She was carrying laundry. Did that mean she was a volunteer? If so, why?

Caprice's curiosity had gotten her into a lot of trouble . . . from childhood to the present day. She'd always asked questions that had baffled her teachers, stumped her priest, and amused her parents. Now the implications behind seeing Alicia here were serious.

Caprice hurried to catch up with Wendy and noticed a woman rifling through Wendy's file cabinet. She turned when Caprice and Wendy stepped inside.

Wendy said, "Lizbeth, this is Caprice De Luca. Caprice, this is Lizbeth Diviney. She's my second in command and can answer questions when I'm not around. She's going to be the director of the new facility once it's up and running."

Lizbeth was a redhead with a pixie hair style. She was only five foot two and as slender as Caprice would like to be. In a quick movement, Lizbeth pulled a folder and shut the file drawer. Then she shook Caprice's hand. "It's great to meet you. I've heard good things about your work."

She waved the folder at Wendy. "I'll get right on this." In the next moment, she was gone from the office.

"She's high energy," Wendy said with a smile and motioned Caprice to a chair.

Wendy's desk held stacks of papers, but otherwise the space looked feminine with its flowered chairs and pin-striped wallpaper. She didn't waste any time. "Your proposal makes a lot of sense to me, and I agree with ninety percent of it. The other ten percent has to do with the grand salon at the mansion and your bunk bed idea for two of the rooms upstairs. I'm thinking of having a partition divide the grand salon into two rooms. Two workshops could be conducted at the same time that way."

"No problem there," Caprice agreed. "Do you want them decorated the same way or do you want two different designs?"

"Even though I have the money with the legacy, I'm not going to splurge. Let's keep them both uniform. That's more economical, isn't it?"

"Yes, it is. And the reason you don't want the bunk beds?"

"I don't want these rooms to have a prison-cell feel. Bunk beds could suggest that, don't you think?"

"I proposed the bunk beds because it would give residents more room for a sitting area or double desks. Those rooms upstairs are anything but small or cell-like, and of course the decorating would make all the difference. Light airy draperies and coordinating bedspreads would never give a jail atmosphere. But again, that's up to you."

"Let me think about it."

Wendy had pulled a list in front of her along with Caprice's proposal that she'd printed out. They went over several more items.

Wendy was an easy client to work with because she seemed to take Caprice's suggestions, and Caprice had no problem compromising to give Wendy exactly what she wanted.

"I suppose you'll have volunteers working at the transitional facility too," Caprice said finally.

"We count on our volunteers," Wendy agreed. "And the women who've been helped by us want to give back."

"Are your volunteers all women who've needed to take refuge in the shelter?"

Wendy didn't hesitate to answer. "They usually are. The truth is, most people don't want to get involved, not with anything that has to do with domestic violence and protective orders."

"I can see that."

She again thought about Alicia and wondered if her best friend, Roz, knew Alicia better than she did. Roz had been on the reunion committee too.

Wendy glanced up at the clock hanging on the wallpapered wall. "I have another meeting in fifteen minutes. I think we've covered everything."

Caprice rose to go.

Wendy snapped her fingers. "I forgot to tell you that you're most welcome to bring Grant Weatherford to dinner on Saturday. Rumor has it that the two of you are dating."

"We are," Caprice answered. "I'll ask him and see if he'd like to come along. He might be interested in the co-housing concept too and enjoy talking to Sebastian."

Wendy's phone rang. She held up her finger to Caprice and picked it up.

Caprice waited.

Even three feet from the phone, she could hear an angry voice on the other end, and it sounded male. Wendy seemed to take a bolstering breath and then she slammed down the receiver without saying a word.

"Trouble?" Caprice asked.

"Trouble we often get here."

"An angry husband?"

Wendy just nodded. Then she said, "That's one of the reasons why a state-of-the-art alarm system as well as security cameras are a must for the new facility, no matter what the cost. I'd like to have a few inside too, in the public areas. Do you think you can come up with inventive ways to disguise them?"

"My family insists I can be very inventive."

Wendy gave Caprice a weak smile. "It's coming together, Caprice—all of it. I'm determined to keep these women safe from anyone who intends to do them harm."

Wendy's vehemence came from more than a desire to do good, Caprice suspected. Maybe someday soon she'd find out what had driven Wendy into this life's work.